PRAI[

"As he demonstrated
paced, winning style,
fans of Carl Hiaasen or Elmore Leonard."

—*Library Journal*

SILENT APPROACH

*Jim,
I hope you enjoy
the story*

Bobby

OTHER TITLES BY BOBBY COLE

The Rented Mule

The Jack Crosby Series

The Dummy Line

Moon Underfoot

Old Money

SILENT APPROACH

BOBBY COLE

THOMAS & MERCER

This is a work of fiction. Names, characters, organizations, places, events, and incidents are either products of the author's imagination or are used fictitiously. Any resemblance to actual persons, living or dead, or actual events is purely coincidental.

Text copyright © 2017 by William Robert Cole
All rights reserved.

No part of this book may be reproduced, or stored in a retrieval system, or transmitted in any form or by any means, electronic, mechanical, photocopying, recording, or otherwise, without express written permission of the publisher.

Published by Thomas & Mercer, Seattle

www.apub.com

Amazon, the Amazon logo, and Thomas & Mercer are trademarks of Amazon.com, Inc., or its affiliates.

ISBN-13: 9781477818312
ISBN-10: 1477818316

Cover design by Cyanotype Book Architects

Printed in the United States of America

For my sweet daughter, Jessi, whose adventuresome soul loves to be still and read.

Chapter 1

Except for pulling a baseball cap down over his eyes to shield his face from the security cameras, the man simply acted like what he was: someone visiting a friend in the hospital.

He'd thought through his lunch-break activities carefully. He noticed his hand was shaking as he reached out to press the elevator button. The first floor of the Baptist Memorial Hospital in Columbus, Mississippi, was busy, but the third floor, where his intended victim lay in a bed, was as quiet as he'd hoped it would be. He'd timed his visit around the lunch hour, hoping the staff would be limited. He also knew the patient's wife left at noon every day to help out at the diner they owned.

Though the man had committed a few minor crimes, he'd never killed anyone before. Now he was about to murder an old friend. Only an hour earlier he'd been ordering truck parts for the mechanics shop where he was gainfully employed.

His friend, a partner in a long-ago theft, had been stricken with dementia and had taken to bragging about their heist to anyone who would listen. The secret that had been bottled up inside both of them for thirty years was now pouring out of his old partner with no regard for—or understanding of—the consequences. His friend couldn't remember his own daughter's name, but he could recall the events of that night with extraordinary clarity.

The way the man saw it, he didn't have any choice. Sooner or later his old pal would say something to someone who would start asking questions and connecting the dots. Hopefully, he hadn't already run his mouth to the wrong person.

Thirty years ago they'd both been young working-class men looking to make a big hit and quietly change their lives. Though not foolish enough to rob a bank or smart enough to embezzle money, they'd had an idea that lured them across the line and into the criminal world. When they added up the pros and cons and weighed the risks, their final analysis had come down in favor of committing the crime. The men felt like they'd been given a gift.

Their loudmouthed neighbor had talked all the time about the value of the Native American artifacts at the Jones Archeological Museum in Moundville, Alabama, where he served as part-time curator. He'd claimed they were worth a small fortune and unknowingly had described the security of the place in enough detail that the two men had realized there was none. For two months they'd drunk beer, played poker with the man, and listened to him describe everything.

According to their poker buddy, the museum's main visitors were occasional busloads of sixth-grade students on field trips. The three hundred or so acres of property where the museum was located were very rural and bordered the Black Warrior River, which provided the perfect late-night entry point. The archeological site held twenty-six ceremonial mounds, including a huge pyramid-shaped one that was almost sixty feet high. More important, inside the small building were hundreds of irreplaceable artifacts that could be sold on the black market for cash. They knew there were collectors of Native American artifacts who would pay, but they would have to be careful. Sell to the wrong person—someone who would eventually have to show it off—and it could get them caught. They knew how to steal the artifacts, and they would determine how to sell them later.

They hatched a plan that began with stealing a key from their passed-out-drunk friend one night and having a duplicate made. Then a few nights later they stole as many artifacts as they could in one haul. They'd planned to make a second trip that same night, but a flat tire on their borrowed van had slowed them down.

It was just as well. Selling the artifacts for anything close to what they'd wanted to get for them had proven a lot tougher than they'd thought. As the years had dragged on, they'd been forced to shuffle the remaining pieces from one hiding place to another to avoid detection. Now they'd been living with their crime without profiting from it for thirty years while they'd raised families and become upstanding members of the community.

The man in the baseball cap couldn't let their secret get out.

Taking care that no one saw him walk into the hospital room, he was pleased to find his old partner was asleep. The television was playing a rerun of *The Price Is Right*, and the remote speaker lay next to his friend's ear. He looked just like he always had, but the man had witnessed his increasingly talkative friend's mental deterioration during previous visits to his home. Now he was battling pneumonia in the hospital, where educated people could listen to him—specifically his doctor, who was a collector of artifacts himself.

Turning a valve to stop the flow of the IV running into his friend's arm, he then pulled a drug-filled syringe from his coat pocket, forced its contents into the port below the saline bag, and stepped away, leaving no evidence behind.

He thought about waking the victim but decided against it.

Standing at the foot of the bed, he took a moment to experience what he hoped was his first and last murder.

Later that day when a nurse checked the IV and turned it back on, the drugs would flood his friend's system, triggering complete muscle paralysis, and he would suffocate without being able to talk. He was nearly sixty-five years old, overweight, and a candidate for a stroke. No one would suspect a thing. And best of all, a standard toxicology report—if the authorities bothered to run one—wouldn't catch the drug.

Without a twinge of guilt, the man opened the room's door and vanished down the hallway.

Chapter 2

John Allen Harper gritted his teeth and exhaled deeply, punctuating his frustration as he settled the office phone onto its base after disappointing his wife yet again. He had no idea just how upsetting this day would turn out to be.

Staring at the enthusiastic accountant who sat across the table from him shuffling reams of papers, John Allen wondered when his life had careened off course. Precisely when had work become more important than family? When had business meetings become easier to remember than family events? Rubbing his forehead, he fought to understand how managing his time had become such a challenge, and he was suddenly pissed at Frank Riley, the branch accountant who was now stealing this valuable commodity.

As he watched Frank fan the pages of the spreadsheet, indicating how much more they had to go over, John Allen exhaled again and cursed silently. This was the third time in less than two weeks that he was in danger of missing a birthing class. Today it was a Lamaze class; last week, a birthing video that he wished he'd never seen. Somewhere in the mix he had completely missed a meeting to pick out paint for the nursery and, worse, a checkup with the doctor. His wife had cried after the missed doctor's appointment, and the last thing he wanted was to hurt Sadie. He was happily married and excited about the baby. He just couldn't get his workload lightened. Sadie understood both his responsibilities at work and his motivation for working—which, ironically, was family—but he knew her patience was wearing thin. He hoped she truly understood. Every Monday morning she would remind him of the weekly birth-preparation activities, hoping he'd be in attendance, but his absences were, if anything, becoming more frequent. She was the rock in his life, and he hated to disappoint her.

John Allen looked at his watch, knowing he had saved himself about fifteen minutes during their phone call by arranging to meet her at the hospital for the class instead of picking her up at home. But then his eyes fell onto the stack of spreadsheet pages, and he knew that small amount of time wasn't going to come close to helping.

"Frank," he said, "I need to call this a day. I forgot I had something important this afternoon."

Frank Riley was recently divorced and waiting patiently for eHarmony to put him back in the game. In the meantime he always put work first, logging an amazing number of hours in his quest for John Allen's job. Armed with another excuse for poor branch performance, the determined bean counter feigned frustration and gathered up an armload of printouts before waddling down the hall to his cubicle.

John Allen couldn't care less about Frank's issues. Relieved to get away from the boredom of analyzing his branch's own numbers, he began preparing for his exit.

He was tired of everything, especially of accounting discussions where every word had to be considered before spoken. He did much better when he could say whatever came to mind without first passing it through an "accurate answer" filter. He promised himself that tomorrow, reinvigorated by sleep and caffeine, he would answer the accountant's questions. Dragging the mouse as he'd done a million times, he clicked "Quit," and the mind-numbing spreadsheet magically disappeared somewhere onto his hard drive.

Coat and briefcase in hand, John Allen wasn't surprised to see he was the last one in the office except for Frank, who always worked late. It was 5:02 p.m., and in just two brief minutes the other nine employees in the accounting office had deserted the building with extreme efficiency. He locked the back door and started for the parking lot, then after taking a few steps went back and double-checked. His head was so full of deadlines, often the simplest tasks went undone or completely slipped his mind.

The Jeep TJ's engine cranked over, and for a few seconds John Allen relaxed in the seat. Then he shifted into drive and headed off to learn how to help his wife birth their son. He doubted he could provide anything other than moral support, but he wanted to do all he could. Sadie wanted an epidural to prevent pain, and he hoped the doctors and nurses would do all the heavy lifting.

It was spring, and college baseball was in full force. He had the radio tuned to a local sports call-in show, and he listened to the announcers previewing that night's matchup between Mississippi State and a nonconference opponent. He wished he were headed to Starkville to watch the game from the infamous Left Field Lounge instead of learning what to expect in the delivery room, then reminded himself that he would soon have to put tailgate parties behind him to be a dad.

◆ ◆ ◆

Sadie Harper had waited until the last minute to leave, hoping her husband would arrive on time and that they could travel as a family.

She always gave him every chance to participate. She knew he wanted to, but that he also had responsibilities at work that required him to be there, as his bosses seemed to reward manager workaholics based on hours spent behind a desk and not just on productivity. At least that's how John Allen had explained it to her.

She was proud of him. He was the regional manager for a national accounting firm. He spent all his days surrounded by numbers and number crunchers and, according to John Allen, had come to hate every minute of it. The saving grace of his job was that he had three states' worth of offices to manage, which allowed him to travel and to escape the prison of his desk. She knew he slipped his fishing gear into his travel bags, and she always acted as if she didn't notice. The quick fishing trips before and after work helped him keep his sanity, and she figured he could be slipping away and doing much worse things. Last month he'd caught a four-pound smallmouth bass in Tennessee and was still gloating about it.

John Allen's salary was more than that of most men his age in Columbus, Mississippi, and until recently she had devoted most of her energies to helping spend it. They had a nice house on the north side of town that probably cost more than they could afford. Basically, their life was good. Once Sadie found out she was expecting, though, she quickly became more interested in building a family nest than acquiring assets. Where not long ago she would have pined for a new television, now Sadie found herself researching car seats with the zealousness of a consumer-review magazine.

Like her husband, Sadie felt stress, but hers was different from John Allen's. She now felt the strain of molding a family together along with the accustomed pressures of teaching special-needs students at a local public elementary school. Unlike John Allen, though, Sadie mostly felt energized rather than oppressed by her life's intensifying challenges. She'd always been that way. Recently named Educator of the Year in her region, she'd excelled at teaching from the start. Sadie was also a fitness freak and always made sure John Allen ate healthy when she was around. She played tennis, ran half marathons, and tried diligently to encourage John Allen to join her in self-improvement activities. He promised he would one day soon, when he had the time.

A quick glance at her car's digital clock caused Sadie to accelerate, pressing her way through traffic instead of just flowing with it. Forced into Plan B after John Allen's call asking to meet at the hospital, she'd known she'd have to hurry to arrive at the class on time. They were always late, and today would be no exception.

◆ ◆ ◆

John Allen drove north on US Route 45 from his office in downtown Columbus. *Sadie should almost be there,* he thought as he stopped at a red light.

Traffic was heavy for the small town, and worried that he might be late, he'd stomped on the gas to pass cars and change lanes all across town as he'd hurried to the class. As luck would have it, though, it seemed like he'd gotten caught at every red light along the way.

Glancing across a busy intersection, he was surprised to see Sadie in her white Tahoe, waiting in the turn lane. He recognized her Ole Miss tag and smiled. They were a mixed couple: he pulled for Mississippi State, and she rooted for Ole Miss. It only caused issues a few times a year when the schools collided in athletic events.

John Allen waved, but he could see she was busy looking in her rearview mirror. For a moment he wondered what she was looking at, then he saw it as it passed an eighteen-wheeler and revealed itself. A fire truck was approaching Sadie rapidly, its lights flashing. Turning his radio down, John Allen could hear the siren.

With the multilane intersection jammed with late-afternoon traffic, the fire truck had few options. Cracking his window, John Allen could hear the roar of its diesel engine under the whine of the siren as it pulled the heavy load of the truck and its gear. Adding to the cacophony, the fire truck's driver began blowing his air horn as he braked to a stop behind Sadie's bumper. What in the hell did he expect her to do—just shoot on through the four-way intersection against the light?

John Allen was watching the drama unfold, mesmerized, when he suddenly noticed Sadie glancing around and awkwardly easing her vehicle forward.

"No, Sadie!" he screamed. "Stop! *Stop!*"

From his front-row seat, John Allen saw that the cars flowing through the intersection weren't acting as if they saw the fire truck or understood its urgency. Blowing his horn, John Allen screamed pointlessly at his wife.

The fire truck's air horn blared again, and Sadie, clearly confused and scared, punched her gas pedal to give the fire truck her lane.

John Allen watched the scene play out in front of him in what seemed like slow motion: the fire truck beginning to navigate the traffic, its air horns blaring; Sadie staring in her rearview mirror as she accelerated into her turn against the red light. He could only watch in horror as she pulled right in front of a fully loaded log truck trying to beat the yellow light.

The surprised driver slammed on his brakes, smoking its tires seconds before the impact. He carried a heavy load of hardwood trees and had absolutely nowhere to go. Everyone watching could see him yell and brace for impact.

Sadie had nowhere to go, either. Seeing the log truck bearing down on her and realizing she had no control over what was about to happen, John Allen watched as she hunkered down in the car. His mind pictured her closing her eyes and placing her arms over her belly to protect their unborn baby.

The impact caved in Sadie's Tahoe like it was made of thin aluminum. Logs hurled into the cab of the truck and into the street like matches spilling from a dropped box.

The fire captain immediately radioed in the accident, and his men were off the truck almost instantaneously, attempting to rescue any vehicle occupants.

The impact of the accident was later reported in the newspaper to have been more violent than anything anybody had ever witnessed. With no other reference point available to them, witness after witness had compared the horror to a scene from a Hollywood movie.

John Allen Harper had witnessed it all.

Chapter 3

John Allen went back to work sooner than he probably should have, but he didn't see any alternative. Even though he hated his job more than ever, it got him out of bed each day and took his mind off the accident for short stretches of time.

Lawyers chased him mercilessly, trying to get him to sue the logging company for negligence and wrongful death. When they learned that the ambulance had been delayed, they swarmed around him again. He emphatically said no. He didn't blame the log truck or the ambulance, and he never blamed the fire department. John Allen blamed himself. He should have been there for Sadie. He should have left work in time to pick her up at home. Now he wanted no part in profiting from his family's death.

◆ ◆ ◆

Two months after John Allen buried his wife, he sold their house along with most of their furniture and possessions. The house had become a constant source of pain. Everywhere he looked, he saw his wife or heard her voice. There was the den they'd repainted together and the nursery she'd worked so hard to make perfect. He just couldn't stay there any longer—everything reminded him of Sadie. Even the daylilies outside made his heart ache each time one bloomed. She'd loved her daylilies.

With the money from the sale of everything, he purchased forty acres just outside of Columbus, Mississippi. The property included an old barn that John Allen had a contractor buddy convert into modern living quarters. From the road it looked like a dilapidated outbuilding, but inside his man cave he had everything he needed.

He loved the anonymity of the place. He knew it would rarely earn a second look from someone driving by.

Behind the barn was a five-acre pond that John Allen hoped one day to enjoy properly. Before the accident, his main hobby had been bass fishing, and he hoped he would eventually get back into it. Being out on the water had always calmed his nerves, but each time he looked at his old boat and fishing rods he thought of how Sadie had enjoyed going with him, reading books while he'd fished or listening to stories of his childhood that had made her laugh. He'd loved hearing her laugh. When he did hook a decent-size largemouth, she'd been quick to assist and net the fish. John Allen had called her his "net girl," and they'd spent many Saturday afternoons in his little aluminum fishing boat, enjoying the peacefulness of the water and the Mississippi sunshine.

◆ ◆ ◆

A month shy of the one-year anniversary of his wife's death, John Allen mentioned to someone at the accounting firm that he was considering resigning from his position. The corporate office got wind of it and talked him into taking a few months off instead, getting a fresh perspective, then coming back to work. They wanted him to stay, since he was one of their most talented branch managers. Their key clients trusted him, and trust was a highly prized trait in accountants.

The first few weeks, John Allen stayed locked in his barn, nearly going crazy. The Sunday-school class fed him for about ten days. Then when the ladies noticed he was barely eating, they stopped feeding him but continued to pray for him. For the next two weeks he rarely went home—just visited the grave during the day and stayed at a local hotel at night. He was lost and searching for answers he couldn't find.

The next month John Allen loaded up his Jeep and started driving. Sadie had always wanted to visit Savannah, Georgia, and John Allen decided he would do it. He narrated the whole experience to her just like she was there. It pained him that he'd never taken time off work and indulged his wife in a short vacation to this or any of the other cities she'd wanted to see. Sadie would have loved Savannah, the charm of its houses, and the food.

John Allen had so many regrets. They were eating him alive.

◆ ◆ ◆

He was standing on a bridge in Savannah when he received the phone call that took him down a new career path. It was a member of the Mississippi Choctaw Nation, calling to offer him a job that he hadn't even known existed.

For years he'd worked with the Choctaws, managing the books for their lucrative casino and other ventures. He was familiar with them, and they were certainly comfortable with him. It had taken years to earn their trust, but now, out of the blue they were offering John Allen a job as a cultural liaison whose main function was to gather, purchase, and reclaim artifacts that had originally belonged to them.

The Choctaws considered all the artifacts, especially bones, to hold immense spiritual value, and with the success of their casino they had the financial means to purchase the artifacts back from the collectors who'd stolen them, come by them in some other shady fashion, or simply picked them up in their grandparents' gardens.

John Allen was interested in the job mainly because it was something different and would get him out of the office routine. But he'd always been fascinated with artifacts and knew there were many collections scattered all over the South. Because the job entailed occasionally carrying large sums of cash in a briefcase, its holder required the complete trust of higher-ups in the Choctaw Nation. They understood there was a slimy underworld of artifact diggers and traders who were in it only for the money. Cash was the easiest way to gain acceptance in this subculture and get what the tribe wanted. By virtue of his years of service to them, John Allen had unknowingly put himself forward as a candidate for the position. They knew he could be trusted with the money and could handle himself in negotiations. In a strange way, the tragic loss of his wife had sealed the deal for them, his widower status somehow burnishing his already unimpeachable qualifications. They'd decided he was the man who could be trusted to discreetly retrieve their sacred artifacts—and had decided to wait until he had his feet under him to tell him that the last agent the Choctaw Nation had hired had been missing for a little bit more than two years.

Standing on a Savannah bridge watching the boat traffic, John Allen realized his life meant little, and that while auditing the books of millionaires paid well, the work could never be fulfilling to him. He didn't care whether he ever looked at another spreadsheet or explained another tax loophole to another rich asshole trying to beat the system.

John Allen needed more.

It was then and there that he decided to become an agent for the Mississippi Band of Choctaw Indians and see where the adventure would take him. For the first time since the accident, John Allen Harper felt a sense of purpose.

Chapter 4

The sun glistened off the frosted leaves of the waist-high foxtail grass as the dog worked the cover ahead for the glorious scent of bobwhite quail. It was thirty-two degrees in Mississippi, though the blue sky was a sure promise it would warm up fast.

Jim Hudson walked with a twenty-gauge shotgun tucked into the crook of his left arm, carefully pointed away from his hunting companion and their guide in a fruitless attempt to set a good example for his boss, whose gun barrel was all over the place. Maybe the guide would say something to him.

Other than that, it was a beautiful winter morning, full of the anticipation that only hunters know. *It sure beats a day in the office,* Jim thought. He had no idea he was going to die today.

His boss, Winston Walker, loved to hunt quail because he thought that's what wealthy men did. It was part of a never-ending act he put on to fit in with the local elite. On rare occasions, he invited Jim along on his weekly trips. The hunting lodge had provided a guide and a dog, and the two men had planned a morning hunt that would also give them a chance to talk business. Afterward they would enjoy a lunch of smothered quail, cheese grits, and black-eyed peas, along with cathead biscuits. The lunch was Jim's favorite part.

They had already bagged a few birds, and the smell of gunpowder clung to Jim's hunting vest and jacket. As expected, Winston was already bragging about his shooting skills. Winston Walker was a pompous ass who took a great deal of patience to be around. Only those who wanted something from him could tolerate him for very long. He had to be the best at everything, he always had to be in charge, and everything had to go his way. Winston had money, but not the kind of money he acted as if he possessed. Jim suspected that Winston was mortgaged up to his eyeballs, and probably with several different banks. Jim was a good Christian whose goal was to save his boss's soul. It hadn't taken long for him to realize what a long-term plan this would have to be.

As the dog worked the wild plum thickets, Jim tried repeatedly to discuss their failing magazine-publishing business and how they could save it, but Winston either flat out ignored him or barely answered, acting as if nothing was wrong that he couldn't fix. A master of sleight-of-hand business deals, he could pitch naive advertisers and sign them up for six issues before they even realized they'd committed. He planned to make use of the magazine's inevitable downtime to fleece unsuspecting advertisers until the magazine's ship was righted. Jim didn't like the plan, and as a result, they'd endured many relationship-stressing arguments.

"We gotta point," Winston said with excitement as he drew Jim's attention to the motionless dog up ahead.

While the guide encouraged his dog to remain steady, Winston directed Jim to cover their left while he took any birds that flushed to their right.

As they moved into position in anticipation of the flush, Jim noted that the guide was keeping a careful eye on their alignment. Jim was glad to have him around to encourage safety. He told himself to watch out for the dog. The last thing he wanted to do was accidentally shoot her as she chased a low-flying bird. He glanced at Winston and wondered whether he was even thinking about the dog. He knew Winston was a threat to shoot at anything.

During the covey flush, Winston knocked down a pair of birds, and Jim managed to kill a single. As the dog happily retrieved the birds, Winston made sounds of frustration as he looked through the pockets of his vest.

"I'm running out of shells!" he called out, holding up his last two. "I must have dropped some somewhere."

"You can have some of mine," Jim called back.

"You're shooting a twenty. I'm shooting a twelve-gauge," Winston explained in a tone that made Jim feel like a dumbass.

The guide took the last bird from his dog's mouth and offered a solution. "I'll cut through the pines there, grab a box of shells from the Jeep, and meet you at that big oak tree down there," he said, pointing ahead. "Y'all take Willow and keep hunting. There should be a few singles between here and there. You got enough shells for that?"

"Yeah, thanks."

Jim watched the guide hustle off in the direction of the Jeep, then turned to follow the dog. If he couldn't get Winston to talk business, at least he would enjoy the morning's sights, sounds, and smells. He glanced at his watch in spite of himself. His wife would be driving their kids to school about now, and she would be stressed until they exited the car in a screaming, mad rush. Somebody would inevitably forget something.

With the guide gone, Jim remembered a promise he'd made to the other ad salesmen.

"Winston," he said, "we need to pay the sales guys their commissions soon, or they're all going to jump ship." Ads were the lifeblood of a magazine business, but keeping the guys who sold them happy was an ongoing battle. Winston treated them all like shit, and Jim spent way too much time calming everyone down.

Ignoring Jim's comment, Winston dropped two shells into his over-and-under and snapped it shut. "There should be some birds in the cover up ahead. Let's get 'em."

Jim fell in behind Winston with a sigh while the dog quickly worked the open area ahead of them and moved on to more promising cover.

They'd walked about seventy-five yards in silence when Winston pointed at the dog, who'd locked up with her nose in the direction of a knot of brush. As they watched, she picked her left paw up slowly and formed a tripod position—a classic point.

"The birds are going to want to fly to the right, so get into position," Winston told Jim.

Jim approached the right side of the dog, expecting Winston to approach on the left. Noticing Willow wanting to ease forward, Jim coaxed her just like the guide always did. "Steady, girl. Steady now."

"Don't worry about her," Winston barked from behind. "You're always worried about the wrong things. You just concentrate on the birds."

Jim slowed down and searched the ground ahead for hiding quail. Nothing could blend into its surroundings better than a hen quail. Just as he stepped into some thick knee-high grass, two birds exploded and rocketed away. Jim shouldered his gun, but before he could pull the trigger on the flushing quail, a shot rang out.

Jim Hudson, thirty-four years of age, married with two children, collapsed lifelessly to the ground.

Winston Walker, standing only ten feet behind him, clicked his shotgun open and sent one spent shell leaping out.

He knew no one was watching, but still he looked around him. The only witness was a bird dog and a giant water oak tree. Neither would talk.

"Problem solved," he muttered to himself.

Chapter 5

The investigation of the accident went just as Winston Walker had expected it would. A local sheriff and his crew, along with the county game warden, tried to piece together what had happened. There were lots of questions and forms that needed to be filled out. Winston sat in the small hunting lodge, sipped coffee, and tried to act as if he were upset.

◆ ◆ ◆

It wouldn't surprise anyone that Winston Walker's ex-wife was suing him for back alimony and claimed he had undervalued the business at the time of the split. Some even suspected he was actually letting it run into the ground so he wouldn't have to pay her any more.

They had met after high school and had dated for three years. She was a bartender at a local tavern and got Winston his drinks for free. Once they were married, he'd conned her mother into giving him the start-up cash—that he'd never paid back—to fund his first enterprise. She'd taken the money from her deceased husband's 401(k) based on Winston's promise to double it before returning it to her. Greedy herself, she'd wanted to believe it could happen. It took his ex a few years to figure out what Winston was up to and to get out of the relationship. Fortunately there had been no kids involved.

Winston was kicked out of high school in the tenth grade. The only class he'd been passing at the time was one on the history of Mississippi. He'd excelled in the precolonization time period because of his interest in Native American cultures. The only break he'd received in life had been when an uncle who was serving in the military had agreed to pay for his continuing education at the Marion Military Institute in Southwest Alabama. Winston had lasted only one year, and it was rumored that his attendance played a role in the institute's decision to drop its high school program to concentrate only on college-level courses. Winston went on to earn his GED from a detention program near Hattiesburg, Mississippi.

His parents were never able to control Winston. He sold anything they had of value, and he stole whatever was in their wallets. He ran with a rough crowd but always admired the lifestyle of the wealthy and tried to emulate it, determined to fit in. He wanted the rewards of hard work but just lacked the ability to do it the right way. Winston was all about taking shortcuts and didn't care whom he hurt along the way.

At a time when most people his age were graduating from college and heading off into the world to start a career, Winston was perfecting the art of dialing back the odometers on used cars that he sold on craigslist. He later sold aluminum siding on television infomercials in southern Mississippi until he stopped paying the TV stations and they cut him off. He then ran a telemarketing scam that sold fake I SUPPORT THE STATE TROOPERS window decals for fifty-dollar donations. After that peaked and fizzled, he went to work for a gardening magazine selling ads. He hated gardening. But he excelled at selling ads and quickly learned how to talk people into spending money. He had a pitch that promised to change their lives.

Within three years the aging magazine owner became sick. With no one in his family to take over the business, he made a deal to sell it to Winston based on future earnings. When the old man mysteriously fell down his back steps, hitting his head and dying, Winston took the magazine and its future earnings as well.

Within two years he'd launched two more magazine titles—one about living off the grid, the other about NASCAR. But he didn't care about the subject matter, only the advertising base. Winston recruited a derelict team of six guys and two females to sell ads employing various high-pressure techniques. The office was a telemarketing boiler-room operation that spawned far more bad ideas than good, but Winston was making more money than he'd ever seen.

While the advertising boom was happening, Winston made a presentation to an executive of a major national garden-fertilizer brand. The meeting did not go well. Three days later the man died of a massive stroke, and Winston forged his signature on contracts and held the brand hostage to honor them. After several rounds of legal haggling, both parties agreed to honor half the contracts, and Winston netted $300,000 for his company. He became a legend around the office; the sales team saw the way he made money and strove to emulate his tactics.

But lately, with the birth of digital magazines, the publishing industry was changing faster than Winston could foresee, and even on his best day he wasn't capable of anticipating what he needed to do. Their sales had been tanking for two years, and they hadn't made money in the last twelve months. Winston had been scamming everyone, including the banks, to keep the doors open.

When he'd purchased—or, more accurately, stolen—the publishing business, the overhead had been low. The offices had been situated behind a check-cashing business downtown, and the building owner had been happy to have a tenant who just kept the place up and prevented it from deteriorating any further. All transactions had been handled over the phone, and an ad agency in Atlanta or Dallas had no idea what the insides of the Winston Walker Publishing Company looked like, nor would they ever see it. The address sounded good, and their letterhead looked impressive.

Friends were in short supply for Winston. The only people he was around daily were those he paid or promised to pay. Some he knew he had to pay every week, and others he strung out as long as he could. He rarely paid anyone exactly what he owed—he always promised more was coming. When money was tight, Winston would bring drugs to the guys and just leave them in the break room. This pacified them for a few days and even made them more energetic on the telemarketing sales calls. Cocaine helped them stay past 5:00 p.m. and make late-afternoon phone calls to the West Coast.

◆ ◆ ◆

Jim Hudson had been the one solid citizen Winston had ever hired. He'd needed Jim to be his "face man" to the employees and to the world. Jim was affable, and most everyone had liked and trusted him at first, which was a good qualification for what Winston had in mind for him. And Jim had had his own issues that he was working through: he'd stolen more than $100,000 from a bank where he was the branch manager and served two years in prison, losing his wife in the process. Upon his release he'd remarried, started a family, and worked at getting his life back on track—no easy task, it had turned out, as his past made it difficult to find a job he wanted.

For the first year he worked for Winston, he'd enjoyed managing the sales force and making sales himself. He'd found it to be a challenge. But in his quest to turn his life around, he and his wife had found religion and rarely missed a chance to go to church. Jim had decided it was up to him to reform Winston and dedicated himself to that task with great energy, purposely spoiling several good scams that Winston couldn't in the least afford to have spoiled. Winston had screamed and threatened physical violence, but Jim had just smiled and explained why it wasn't right. Winston had grown weary of the sermons Jim delivered daily and the way he was always trying to change him. Just that quick, Jim had gone from being an asset to being a liability, and Winston had begun preparing for life without Jim Hudson. He put a key executive insurance policy into place and condemned the man to death upon signing the document. Winston Walker Publishing could afford only $40,000 worth of insurance, but Winston figured Jim owed him at least that much.

While Jim had been good at managing the magazine sales force, he'd never wanted any part of the Native American artifact business. Winston, though, had been involved in digging and stealing artifacts almost all his adult life. Whenever things were going bad financially, he'd always revert back to making some bucks in the artifact black market. Try as he might to stay clear of it, Jim had known Winston was still stealing a lot of artifacts. He and three others had come back one day with a van full of what had appeared to Jim to be museum-quality pieces. There was no way Winston had the money to purchase these legally, and when Jim had asked, Winston had just smiled. Jim had scoured the Internet for any news of a theft and had never seen anything except a mention of a robbery in 1980 at a museum in Moundville, Alabama. That had been a long time ago, though, which had only puzzled him more. Jim had reluctantly helped unload the boxes, which Winston had bragged were valued at more than a million dollars. They put them in a metal storage unit that cost sixty bucks a month and had a ten-dollar padlock on the door.

Jim had asked a lot of questions, so many that he'd triggered a fit of rage during which Winston had slammed him against a wall and had told him to keep both his questions and his biblical opinions to himself. This encounter had been more intense than the ones Jim had shared with his wife as he'd encouraged her to join him in praying for Winston's soul. He'd decided to keep it to himself, as hearing it would only disturb her. He'd considered it his own burden.

Chapter 6

The first few months of John Allen's new job were a breeze. He spent most of his time meeting high-level members of the tribe and listening as each explained in their own very passionate way their desire to have as many true Choctaw artifacts as possible back in the tribe's possession. The fact that these artifacts—arrowheads, spear points, beads, pots, and various ceremonial pieces—had been gathered by all manner of people for the last 150 years and stored in buckets and shoe boxes in garages bothered the tribal members greatly.

The few collections that were treated with respect and with regard to their history didn't seem to bother them as much as John Allen had figured they might. However, the looters who dug in ceremonial mounds and graves created much aggravation. These thieves were robbing the tribe of spiritual pieces, and they were doing it with amazing efficiency. John Allen learned that they studied topography maps to identify areas where Indians would have likely built villages, such as on high, level ground in close proximity to freshwater, like a creek or a river. These midnight vandals would probe every inch of the soil with long rods until they heard a familiar *dink*, then start digging. All this occurred under tarps so as not to be seen by anyone passing by. Each dig brought new treasures to the surface that would be sold, gone forever. There seemed to be no locations that were off-limits. The looters were brazen and would dig in burial mounds along the edge of the Natchez Trace, as well as on national parkland known to have held Native American settlements.

Local law enforcement typically wouldn't do much. They had their hands full with the normal, everyday robberies, drug offenses, and other crimes plaguing police and sheriff departments. Occasionally an officer with a personal interest in artifacts would pressure the locals, but usually so that he himself could loot the same areas. All these activities constituted serious crimes against the Indian Nations, and they were committed with regularity all over North America—but especially in the Deep South.

John Allen also learned that many of the diggers were in fact meth heads who worked for a boss who would pay them in cash or drugs. The meth gave them energy to dig all night, and the artifacts created a steady supply of cash for more drugs.

The Choctaw Nation hired a retired SWAT team trainer to give John Allen a weeklong crash course in personal defense. He was given a Browning Hi Power 9 mm pistol and taught how to use it. It was during these training exercises that John Allen was finally told that the man he was replacing had never returned. His employers feared he'd uncovered somebody determined to protect his enterprise. Instead of being troubled by this revelation, John Allen was intrigued in a way. The recent loss of his own wife made him think about the woman and kids who'd lost their husband and father. Loss was something he understood, and now that he had no immediate family, there was no one at home who would worry about him.

The tribal leader who'd seen the potential in John Allen recognized the growing determination, not fear, in his eyes as she told him the story. She was pleased. John Allen would be their man, and he would be given more resources and training than they'd given their last agent. They wouldn't make the same mistake twice.

The Choctaw Nation now fully recognized the evil types of criminals attracted to their artifacts, people who were denizens of a murky underworld seldom seen but the tribe now knew existed. In most southern cities, there were normal-looking men—church deacons, county clerks, lawyers, doctors, and businessmen—who were quietly snapping up artifacts. Some did it out of a reverence for regional history, but most did it for a quick, tax-free buck. These men conducted their business in the woods at night and were capable of anything. The Choctaw Nation's representative had to be prepared. On the reservation he was a special agent of the tribe, with full authority to arrest. Outside the reservation's limited boundaries, however, where he would spend most of his time, he wouldn't have any jurisdiction. So he would have to network with local law enforcement and watch his back.

◆ ◆ ◆

John Allen found numerous small collections and was able to purchase most of them. He overpaid, but that's what he'd been instructed to do. There were many owners of country stores who had secret collections, and supposedly they would trade cigarettes and beer for arrowheads. They were the low-hanging fruit John Allen went after first. It was rare that he stopped at a rural store and didn't get a lead on someone who had artifacts. But sometimes the people wouldn't talk to him at all—they didn't want anyone to know they had a collection. John Allen tried to understand their motivation. They all seemed to fear something, but what?

The Choctaw tribe had decided they wanted John Allen to have the appearance of a high roller with plenty of cash. They felt this image would open doors into the darker underworld that was motivated by money, so they gave him a black Porsche 911 for a company car. At first he thought it was silly, but after driving it a few days, he appreciated the fine workmanship of the Germans. And it did open a lot of eyes wherever he stopped.

John Allen had lightly investigated the disappearance of his predecessor. His name was Wyatt Hub, and he had a wife and two kids. The Choctaw Nation had kept the paychecks coming for his family. The local and federal authorities had all run out of leads. They had their suspicions, but nothing could be proven. They knew that Wyatt had gotten wind of a collection in the Meridian, Mississippi, area and had been trying to gain the owner's trust. But there the trail had ended. Wyatt hadn't known any names, or if he had, he hadn't recorded them or told anyone.

John Allen was aware that Wyatt could have fallen prey to someone ruthless and that his own investigation could bring him to a similar end. Each time he thought about it, he swallowed and touched the pistol concealed on his hip. But mainly, he wanted to know what had happened to Wyatt because he felt the man's wife deserved closure. John Allen understood about missing someone.

Chapter 7

The Kemper County sheriff's department didn't see many hunting accidents. The two hunting-related incidents in the last five years had both involved hunters falling out of tree stands. Statistics show that the sport of hunting is actually safer than golfing, but when you're around firearms, accidents can happen. And when they do, the consequences can be grave. The worst part is that they oftentimes involve family members.

Kemper County had a few murders each year, but they were usually easily solved. They most often occurred at late-night beer joints and were crimes of passion committed in front of witnesses. These crimes almost always solved themselves once everybody started talking.

The game warden questioned Winston in great detail. He wished the sheriff's men hadn't moved the body but understood they were trying to help the deceased. He wanted to know the angles of the shooters' positions, and by the end of his questioning, he could visualize what had happened. In the excitement of the moment, Winston had swung on a bird, and Jim Hudson had ended up in the way.

The Kemper County sheriff spent more time in the field looking at the scene than his deputies, who'd concentrated on interviewing Winston. But in the end, the sheriff unearthed nothing that could prove the shooting was anything but an unfortunate accident. Personally, he didn't like Winston Walker—he just didn't get a good feeling from him. But he also knew that didn't mean the guy had committed a crime.

The sheriff had known the hunting guide for more than twenty years and trusted what he had to say. He was a struggling soybean farmer who was just trying to make ends meet. He guided bird hunts each fall and winter to supplement his income. It was honest, hard work.

The hunting lodge was a refurbished antebellum Greek Revival mansion. The leather-skinned guide sat on its front porch with his head in his hands, looking more shook up than the shooter. He'd told the sheriff he dreaded having to explain the events to the owner, who was away on a trip to New Orleans. A man had died today while he was in charge. This could have a big impact on the lodge and also his personal income. The guide had a son in college, and the tuition was probably draining him. There might be a lawsuit even though both hunters had signed releases. Several times he told the sheriff he blamed himself for leaving them unsupervised. The moment he'd left and wasn't there to personally make certain each man was in position, the tragedy had occurred. The sheriff found the timing interesting and mentally filed it away.

The body was taken by ambulance to a local funeral home that also doubled as the county morgue. An autopsy would be performed. Though the cause of death was obvious, the sheriff wanted to know whether the man had been drinking or using drugs. He'd insisted Winston take a Breathalyzer test, which he'd passed.

Now it was the sheriff's duty to properly and professionally get word of what had happened to the next of kin. Since Jim Hudson had lived several counties away in Meridian, he would notify the sheriff there, and someone would deliver the news in person. That was much better than explaining a tragedy over the phone.

◆ ◆ ◆

Three months after Jim Hudson's death, his widow, Jill, still wasn't satisfied with any answers she'd received. None of it made sense, and she didn't trust Winston Walker at all. She knew that Jim and Winston had been at odds and that their publishing business had been losing serious money. Jim had confided in her about some of the scams Winston had wanted to run on unsuspecting advertisers, and she knew Jim had pushed back hard, objecting to the cons. She was certain her husband had been murdered, and she set out to prove it.

Jill Hudson made an appointment with the Federal Bureau of Investigation in Jackson, Mississippi. The two special agents she met with listened as she poured her heart out, and when she'd finished telling her story, they looked at each other with interest. They were familiar with Winston Walker and, after consulting privately, decided to tell her what they knew. It seems they'd received numerous complaints alleging interstate fraud by Walker and his publishing company. They'd been considering opening an investigation, and now, fueled by the idea that he may have murdered one of his employees, they would definitely proceed.

Chapter 8

On a Saturday morning in September, approximately eight months prior to the previous events, John Allen drove down State Route 25 to Jackson, Mississippi, to attend an old-fashioned gun show. Similar gun shows occurred all over the country on weekends at small convention centers, American Legion halls, and Shriner temples. Such events offered someone like John Allen a wealth of opportunities to connect with red-blooded local males who had an interest in firearms, knives, and maybe arrowheads.

It was a beautiful fall morning, and the air was crisp. The roadsides were covered in the last remnants of the summer's wildflowers, drying in the sun before the Mississippi Department of Transportation mowed them down. The leaves on the trees were just starting to turn, and John Allen passed carloads of football fans headed to Starkville and Oxford to watch their favorite college teams play.

As expected, the gun-show venue's parking lot was crowded with four-wheel-drive vehicles ranging from expensive Land Rovers to worn-out, jacked-up Ford or Chevy pickups. John Allen's Porsche certainly stood out as he slid into a narrow spot near the front door.

Inside, the show's attendees were more diverse than their automobile choices. There were two guys in hospital scrubs who looked like doctors who'd slipped out between hospital rounds. They were buying ammunition as if they knew an invasion was imminent. John Allen watched a man a little older than he was with his son, who appeared to be about seven or eight years old. They were looking at a 0.22 rifle, and the father took great care to show his son how to hold the gun. It didn't fit him, but that didn't seem to bother either of them. The young boy listened intently as his father explained everything. The scene stabbed at John Allen's heart, bringing to mind his own unborn son.

On the third aisle next to a guy selling beef jerky was a small booth with a sign saying **WE BUY ARROWHEADS AND ARTIFACTS**. Sitting on a folding table were two wooden-framed glass boxes holding about forty neatly arranged arrowheads and spearheads. John Allen studied the artifacts as the ratty-looking young man in the booth studied his phone.

"Where were these found?" John Allen asked.

"They all came from East Mississippi," the young guy said, his eyes rolling up at John Allen.

"It's a great collection. Did you find them all?" He noticed the guy's stick-on name tag read "Billy."

"Some friends of mine did," Billy replied, finally looking all the way up at him.

"These for sale? That's a nice Kirk point."

"Like the sign says, we *buy* artifacts," Billy said with some disdain, as if he'd answered that question a million times already.

"Everything's for sale sooner or later," John Allen said, holding Billy's eye. "I just prefer sooner than later."

Billy stood up and gave John Allen the once-over. "Who are you?"

"I'm nobody. Just a guy who loves Indian rocks."

"You the law? These are surface finds. It's not illegal to buy and sell these, you know."

"Relax, dude, I'm not the law," John Allen assured him with a laugh. He wasn't lying; technically, he wasn't the police. He didn't want Billy, but he figured the young man was attached to a bigger organization.

"We play by the rules."

"I'm sure you do," John Allen said as he admired some really old Clovis-style points. "These heads in this case, they're probably worth about twelve hundred bucks if someone paid you full retail, but I'm willing to offer you fifteen hundred cash. Right now."

John Allen felt Billy sizing him up.

"They ain't for sale."

John Allen shook his head, truly disappointed. "That's too bad."

"Those points are too nice to sell," Billy added.

John Allen looked Billy in the eyes. "What I really want is skulls and certain bones. You know where a guy could buy some?"

Billy's eyes had widened. Indian skulls went for big money. Not everybody wanted one, but those who did paid well for the opportunity. "That's illegal," he said, looking around to see whether anyone else was watching. "I told you, we don't do no illegal shit."

John Allen rubbed his nose and bent over to pick a business card off Billy's table. It had a cell-phone number on it that could prove to be useful.

"Do you know anyone who might? I'd pay top dollar," John Allen said, then added, "And I'll pay a finder's fee."

Judging by Billy's old jeans and Walmart T-shirt, whoever he was working for wasn't paying him much. "No," he said, "but if you'll leave me your name and number, if I run across something I'll call you."

John Allen smiled. He pulled a business card out that only had his name and cell-phone number printed on it and handed it to Billy.

The show wasn't a big one, maybe four or five aisles of guns, knives, beef jerky, and ammo. "Are there any more artifact collectors with booths here?"

"Nah, man, just me."

"Do you get many folks bringing in artifacts to sell?"

"You'd be surprised. After they see our sign and remember their grandparents have a shoe box full of points collecting dust, they come back. Occasionally some country folks will have a five-gallon bucketful."

John Allen nodded in equal amounts of surprise and understanding. "Well, if you ever want to sell anything, as I say, I pay top dollar."

Billy watched John Allen walk off, then discreetly took a picture of his profile as he stopped at the next table. Ignoring two young kids asking him questions about his arrowheads, Billy watched him walk out the front door.

Through the windows he watched John Allen climb into a shiny black Porsche, and his interest in the stranger suddenly increased. Billy saw dollar signs in his head.

◆ ◆ ◆

After the gun show, John Allen decided to visit his parents since he was already in Jackson.

They still lived in the same house John Allen had grown up in. His father was a respected orthodontist who put braces on all the wealthy kids' teeth. His mother spent her days making sure her family was at all the right places to be socially accepted. John Allen and his younger sister both attended Jackson Prep School, then he went on to Mississippi State and studied accounting while she stayed in Jackson to attend Millsaps College.

He found his mother listening to NPR and eating a pimento-cheese sandwich on the sunporch. She'd been planting her fall flowers while his dad played golf with his buddies.

"I wish you would play golf with your father sometime," she said once he'd settled in with her.

"I just haven't felt up to it lately."

"You should, though. He's worried about you. We've all been worried about you."

"I'm okay, Mom."

"Have you thought about dating anyone? You know you have to move on with your life."

"No, Mom."

"I'm just worried about you being alone and changing jobs."

"I'm happy, Mom."

His mother smiled. That's all she wanted for him, happiness. "You need to tell me what you want for Christmas or you're gonna get underwear and T-shirts again."

"Christmas is three months away, Mom."

"Which means I may see you two more times before then if I'm lucky, and if I don't start now I'll never get a list from you."

John Allen's mother was a list-maker. She loved checking off items. In fact, a list had gotten him in big trouble with her as a very young boy. When asked one year, he'd gladly provided her with an "Xmas" list. When his mother had seen that he'd left "Christ" out of "Christmas," she'd lectured him for an hour. He never made that mistake again.

"I'll make you a short list. A *Christmas* list."

She looked him up and down. "I can tell you're eating better. I'm glad to see that."

John Allen smiled. "I'm fine, Mom."

"Come on, dear. I'll make you a sandwich," she said with a mother's smile. She was always happy for the chance to take care of him.

As he followed her into the kitchen, he thought about dating again. The very idea of it was still a little shocking to him. Following the one-year anniversary of Sadie's death, a few of his friends had begun trying to fix him up with their single friends, but he'd resisted vigorously. Sadie had been his sweetheart since his last years of college, and they'd had a strong love, the only true love he'd ever known. He honestly couldn't imagine loving someone else, or even wanting to. His friends were keeping at it, and although he appreciated their efforts and knew they meant well, the issue was uncomfortable for him. To avoid it, he'd stopped going to church and the places he regularly saw old friends. He'd unplugged himself from everything that reminded him of Sadie and immersed himself in his new job.

Chapter 9

After a couple of months of quietly investigating Winston Walker, the FBI special agents were at a dead end. They were positive that Winston was a world-class creep and up to no good, but catching him at it was something else again.

Much of their information came from the Kemper County sheriff's office, which had suspected something odd about Jim Hudson's death but hadn't been able to prove anything. The sheriff also didn't have the manpower to stay on the case. As more crimes occurred, his small staff was just spread too thin, and the case file was buried ever deeper. The FBI agents were essentially studying a cold case, and it would be up to them to solve it.

Once the FBI started examining the case notes, it became obvious that the scene of the shooting hadn't been processed the way they would have liked. There had been no witnesses, and the person who'd arrived first, the guide, had been hired by the shooter, or at least he got big tips from Winston Walker, so he wasn't completely credible.

Still, the guide had raised some interesting questions. For instance, he was perplexed that somebody like Walker would have been so sloppy as to allow his shells to spill from his vest. Walker always had blood in his eye when he hunted, and someone like that tended to keep a very close eye on the tools required for accomplishing his undertaking. He also hadn't been shooting the gun he normally did. In the past, he'd always shot a twenty-gauge, but on this hunt he'd shot a borrowed twelve-gauge, which anyone who hunted as often as Winston did would know was too much gun for the little birds.

Just to try and make sense of it all, he and the sheriff had even backtracked and hadn't found any spilled shells.

These were just circumstantial tidbits that didn't incriminate him but certainly raised eyebrows. The FBI made a living of chasing leads that caused their eyebrows to rise, but still, the good guys needed a break, if not a miracle, to help them prove that Winston Walker had killed Jim Hudson.

They'd learned early on that he'd changed his name from Fred Walker to Winston Walker when he was twenty-two years old. They guessed he felt the name Fred was holding him back, and Winston sounded more dignified.

Walker's reported income was higher than most but had been dropping off the last few years. They studied his house and his business deals, and each gave the appearance of somebody making more money than Walker was actually reporting.

The notes also revealed that Walker spent a great deal of time in Philadelphia, Mississippi, only about an hour from Meridian, where he lived, and assumed he was gambling at the Golden Moon Casino there. Gambling made sense for someone with his tendencies.

They knew that Walker was having financial difficulties, but just how bad they were was difficult to ascertain. The agents did know that many on the ad-sales team had quit soon after Jim's death, and that had made things even tougher for Walker. Jim had been his sales manager and worked directly with the sales team each day. He had been well liked, and once he was gone, several team members left immediately, not trusting Walker to honor their deals. The reps were pretty sure he hadn't paid for the printing of the last two issues, and that had them worried. With the printer calling daily, looking for his payment, the team was selling ads for a magazine that might not even get printed. Everyone held on to the slim hope that Walker would talk some printing press into printing the next issue on credit. If anyone could, it was Walker.

Another interesting discovery the agents made was that Walker and a select group of close allies were known to be buying and selling Indian artifacts to a group of Japanese collectors. The agents couldn't place a dollar figure on their operation, but as they dug around and talked to people, it became obvious that this was a top priority for Walker. The agents made a note to contact the Mississippi Choctaw Nation to see if they could learn more.

Chapter 10

John Allen was intrigued to meet with the FBI today at the tribe's offices. He was really enjoying his job. It was much more exciting than accounting.

The fact was, though, that purchasing artifacts for the tribe was proving more difficult than he'd thought it might be. People just didn't talk about their artifacts and generally didn't want to sell them. He'd come to realize that it typically took an owner passing away and the next generation not having any affection for the deceased's framed display of arrowheads or a shoe box full of what appeared to be just rocks. If certain individuals went to the trouble of searching fields and creeks for artifacts, then found some, they usually didn't want to sell them. They were immediately attached to them in a way that wasn't easy to explain. The people John Allen had met were like an underground cult when it came to their hobby. When they found an arrowhead and realized they were the first people to touch it for perhaps three hundred to two thousand years, it had a powerful hold on them. It was a hold that often cash couldn't break.

The chief of the Choctaw tribe had personally called John Allen and asked him to attend the meeting. When he'd received the call, John Allen had been meeting with a Mississippi Delta farmer whose family had been farming the same ground for three generations. Though the man had shown John Allen a few artifacts, he sensed there were more that the man was keeping to himself, a hidden stash of the best stuff. But since corn and beans were at all-time highs, the farmer wasn't interested in selling. John Allen made a note to watch commodity prices and farmer input costs. At some point in the future, the man would need some cash to help pay the bills.

The FBI meeting was held in a secure room in the third story of the Tribal Council's office. The security there was on a par with that of any federal judicial building, complete with walk-through metal detectors and a pair of security officers who searched briefcases and purses. One entire floor of the building was dedicated to processing and storing all the cash from the casino and the tribe's other businesses. John Allen had been there several times as an outside auditor and accounting adviser.

The basement held a giant state-of-the-art, climate-controlled room with metal racks for the storage of artifacts. The room had password-protected entry. John Allen had been shown the room when he'd first started his new job, and several times since had been allowed access to store recently purchased artifacts. Struck by how much empty space was left in the room, he figured it was his job to fill it up.

When the phone rang in the conference room, announcing the FBI's arrival, John Allen sipped his coffee and watched the facial expressions of his boss. The chief smiled frequently, but John Allen could tell she carried a great burden on her shoulders. She took the job of representing her people seriously. He figured the fact that she was the first female chief in the history of the Choctaw tribe meant she had to work even harder to make sure progress was made. John Allen knew she didn't trust many outsiders, but one would never know it from her demeanor. She appeared very cooperative on the surface, but behind the scenes she vetted everyone through her contacts. John Allen was proud to work for her. She cared about her job, its responsibilities, and her people. But he could tell the job was demanding more of her than anyone could likely imagine.

The two other Choctaw tribal executives in the room were often seen with the chief. They were trusted advisers, each responsible for various programs the tribe ran. John Allen had met one of them, the head of security, several times.

"Escort them up," said the head of security into the phone, then hung up. He turned in John Allen's direction. "Be careful what you tell these people. I don't really know what they want yet, but the governor's aide called, asked that we meet with them, and hoped for cooperation."

John Allen nodded and took another sip from his coffee, which was growing cold. "I'll follow your lead," he said, then looked at the other two and nodded again.

There was a brief knock on the door. Everyone stood as it opened, and two FBI agents walked through. The first person to come in was a remarkably pretty female who appeared to be in her midthirties; the second person was a balding man whom John Allen guessed to be in his early fifties, which meant he was probably getting close to retirement in the federal system. A security guard with dark skin and classic Native American features nodded at the chief and closed the door.

Introductions were made, and the chief extended a welcome. In John Allen's previous career, at the beginning of a business meeting everyone would typically introduce themselves and tell a little about what they do, then there would be a few minutes of polite chitchat before any business was discussed. He'd always hated the chitchat. Today, names and cards were quickly exchanged, then everyone got down to business. It was refreshing.

John Allen studied the two FBI business cards. Though Special Agent Emma Haden was all business, he thought he saw a special smile pass between her and the chief. Perhaps it was a female-to-female acknowledgment of respect.

"Thank you for seeing us," Agent Garner began. "We have a frustrating case that we think you can possibly help us with."

"We always want to help where we can," the chief said with a smile.

As Agent Garner bent down to retrieve some paperwork from his briefcase, John Allen caught Agent Haden looking at him. She smiled and looked back at the chief. *She's wondering what a white man is doing in here.* John Allen got that a lot.

Agent Garner straightened up and passed out four folders, one to each of them. John Allen was impressed that they'd done their homework and had known how many would be in attendance.

"We've been investigating a man from Meridian named Winston Walker," Agent Garner said. "We understand that he frequents this area, probably to gamble."

"That may be," the chief agreed, "though lots of people spend time here, for all sorts of reasons. We have great restaurants and attractions."

Agent Haden smiled. "Yes, but let me tell you a bit about this man."

So for the next ten minutes she spoke without interruption, painting a thorough picture of the man's activities, which were both criminal and unpleasant. John Allen took notes. When the agent began discussing Winston Walker's stolen artifacts possibly being from the Moundville Museum, John Allen heard the chief take a deep breath. It was as though the air had been sucked from the room.

"And how do you know about the Moundville artifacts?" the chief asked.

"Jim Hudson's widow told us about it. So far she's proven to be a very credible source."

"That's interesting to us," the chief replied, looking at her advisers, then at John Allen. "John Allen, have you heard of this theft?"

"No, ma'am."

The chief leaned back in her chair. "Thirty or more years ago, the Moundville Museum was robbed of its most valuable pieces. Something like two hundred and fifty culturally significant artifacts were stolen, and to my knowledge have never been recovered. They say it's the largest crime of its kind in the South, and everyone believes it was an inside job. The thieves basically stole the best of the best and were coming back for more when someone discovered the stash of artifacts in boxes ready to be moved. We are reminded of the crime and try to take precautions to protect the treasures that we have. The FBI investigated, but nothing ever turned up, and no one was charged."

The Indian advisers nodded in agreement. Clearly everyone remembered or had heard of the unfortunate crime.

The chief nodded slowly, thinking. "And you say this man with this connection to the Moundville heist, this Winston Walker, is from Meridian, Mississippi?"

"Yes, ma'am," said Agent Haden.

"That is also very interesting to us. We have a frustrating case of our own. Mr. Harper's predecessor, Wyatt Hub, has been missing for almost two years now. It's like he vanished into thin air. And the last place he was known to have traveled was Meridian."

"Do you guys have any leads?" Agent Garner asked with a furrowed brow.

"No, nothing at all. We suspect he may have run into some unsavory folks, who we have since learned frequent the black-market artifact business. Your office should have a folder on him. We petitioned your assistance for our missing man."

"What did this man do for the Choctaw Nation?" Agent Haden asked the chief.

Looking at John Allen with a confident, prideful air, she explained, "Just like Mr. Harper here, he was employed to act as our agent and to recover any Indian artifacts from Mississippi or wherever they may be located. We want to get back as many as we can. These artifacts hold great spiritual significance for our people."

"So how do you recover them, exactly?"

"We purchase them with cash. We probably overpay, but we want them all. They are very important to our culture."

"I could see how this could put your man into contact with some potentially dangerous people," Agent Haden said, looking again at John Allen.

The chief nodded. "Yes, and we didn't train our first man properly. We didn't think it was necessary. It was a foolish decision on our part. We have since learned better and have trained Mr. Harper here on how to protect himself. And he has full police authority on tribal lands. This may be a surprise to you, but there is an entire criminal subculture that digs in our sacred burial mounds and village sites at night, looting our heritage and selling it to collectors."

"Are these artifacts valuable?"

The chief smiled. "We hear of handmade pots selling to Asian collectors for $10,000 each. Ceremonial spear points called turkey tails sell for one hundred dollars per inch, and they can be eight to ten inches long. A warrior might have a cache of twelve to fifteen buried with him."

"That adds up!" Agent Haden and Garner looked at each other. "We had no idea."

"All our sacred places have been pillaged while under the watchful eye of the park rangers—who are there to interpret and tell our story—by clever thieves who use the cover of night to extract what they want. Now they are destroying the sites on private land, stealing from owners who have no idea these criminals are out there."

"What can be done?"

"There are stiff laws to protect these antiquities. But there is very little manpower to enforce those laws. It's a shame," the chief explained. "But let me assure you we would cooperate with your investigation and would offer Mr. Harper as our liaison to assist you. I think you will find he is quite capable, although still new to all this."

"Thank you, ma'am. That's exactly what we were hoping to hear."

"All I hope is that you permanently disrupt the group that's selling these artifacts, and that you can determine what happened to our man so that we can bring some closure to his family."

"Yes, ma'am. Absolutely."

"And if any artifacts are found that may belong to the Choctaw Nation, that they are returned to us. The same goes for the Moundville collection."

"Of course," the agents said at the same time.

"I'll leave you to work with Mr. Harper, and he'll keep us informed of your progress. And I expect my security chief will ask around discreetly and determine why Mr. Walker is a frequent visitor." The chief rose gracefully and shook each agent's hand.

"Thanks again," Agent Haden said.

John Allen Harper stood, out of respect for his boss. He was excited to be working with the FBI and to have a chance to find the missing man. He took a deep breath, privately hoping he would prove a worthy asset to the investigation. This was a big deal, but he was ready.

Chapter 11

After the chief and one of her advisers left, the agents shared a few more details with John Allen and the tribal head of security. The acronym for his title was "HOS," and since he was a big guy, everybody just called him Hoss. He looked like a full-blooded Indian, and he always had a scowl on his face. Evidently security for the tribe was a worrisome job. John Allen realized he didn't even know the guy's actual name.

Each little bit of information further energized John Allen. He wanted to catch this guy for so many reasons. He wanted closure for Wyatt Hub's family, he wanted to see Winston Walker convicted for the murder of Jim Hudson, and he hoped to stop the illegal sale of Indian artifacts. With luck he might even find some that he could bring back to the tribe.

Garner and Haden acted interested in John Allen's retelling of the events surrounding Hub's disappearance. John Allen told them everything he knew, much of it learned from reading reports, and Hoss filled in more details. Everyone seemed to think it worth investigating while they pursued Walker for the murder of Jim Hudson. John Allen also shared his recent experience at the gun show. All he knew was that the young man had a Meridian phone number, but he thought that might be significant. Maybe he had a lead into Walker's criminal operation.

Hoss silently studied the photo the FBI had provided of Winston Walker. While there was no way he could know everyone who visited the casino and the many businesses the Choctaws ran on their thirty-five thousand acres sprawled across ten counties, he suggested it was likely that Walker was a regular at the casino, which boasted the greatest flow of repeat customers. He promised he would meet with casino security to see whether anyone recognized Walker's face or whether he'd signed up for any VIP programs. If he frequented the casino, someone would know.

John Allen became aware that Agent Emma Haden was studying him. "If you don't mind me asking," she said, "how long have you been an agent for the Choctaw Nation?"

He blushed a bit. To him, the phrase "agent for the Choctaw Nation" made him out to be something more than he was. He hoped she didn't ask what he did every day. He suddenly didn't want to admit he traveled around and bought arrowheads. And if he wasn't doing that, he was hunting for them on eBay or hanging out in Internet chat rooms that discussed Indian artifacts. Some days he even spoke to elementary school classes around the state, when he couldn't make contact with anyone else. He'd been issued a pistol, but he hadn't been carrying it every day, and of course he'd never arrested anyone.

"A little over a year," he said, then took a sip of cold coffee.

Agent Garner had also turned his attention to John Allen. "What kinda background do you have?"

"I was an accountant and ran the Columbus branch office for a good-size accounting firm. We did some work for the tribe. They had a need, and I wanted a new career, so here I am."

Agent Haden seemed about to press him for more details, then appeared to think better of it, saying instead with a reassuring smile, "We actually have a lot of accountants on staff with the Bureau. They're a huge help with white-collar crime."

John Allen sat up a bit straighter and tried to think of something to say, but his mind was a blank. Agent Emma Haden wasn't just pretty, but flat-out beautiful, he decided.

"So tell me," she said, leaning forward, "if Walker was selling artifacts, what would be something that he couldn't resist? Is there a *Mona Lisa* of Indian artifacts?"

John Allen hesitated. He knew the answer and knew Hoss did, too. Hoss always preferred to listen rather than to speak, but that wasn't the reason John Allen knew Hoss would be reluctant to provide the answer. Like any Choctaw, he would have trouble speaking about the artifacts Emma Haden was asking about.

John Allen sighed and leaned forward. "Skulls. The guys that are really into selling the artifacts value skulls."

"Oh, my. Are they still around? I would have thought they would have deteriorated by now."

"Most have, but as I understand it, every now and then the conditions are just right to preserve one, and they're considered a trophy. They're pretty rare."

"Are they legal to possess?" Agent Garner asked.

"It's complicated," John Allen hedged.

"Very complicated," Hoss added, his disgust at the idea coming through clearly in his tone. "Most folks don't want anything to do with them, but there are those who do want them, for whatever reason."

"Do y'all have any here?" she asked.

"No, we bury all the bones we come across at a sacred site," Hoss said. "They are never stored like a souvenir."

"Okay," she said. "I'm just trying to think of a way to get Walker's attention."

"You should think of another way," Hoss replied. "That's not a good idea."

Agent Haden nodded, then looked at John Allen. Clearly she hadn't meant to offend anyone.

John Allen went on to say that the remains of anyone, particularly Indians, were treated with the utmost respect. The Indians believed that the artifacts, especially the bones of buried Indians, held great spiritual value for them as a people. He knew his reply was long-winded, but he felt she needed to hear their stance with respect to a tribal member's remains—and Hoss needed to hear it delivered to her.

"Look," John Allen said to her, "we'll be working together on this, I hope, and I can explain further if you have more questions."

"Yes, I'm sure I will have more. For now, though, let's return to Jackson and discuss how we want to proceed, then get back to you. In the meantime, if you have any ideas, let us know. You have our numbers."

Hoss stood and shook their hands. He didn't speak to John Allen as he left the room, and that made John Allen curious. Had he managed to offend the man with his explanation? Then, when Agent Haden shook his hand, he thought she held his gaze a bit longer than normal. He didn't have any idea what to think about that, so he just pushed it aside. He genuinely looked forward to working with them.

Chapter 12

It had been almost two years since Sadie's accident. John Allen had settled into a routine during the day that was comforting to him, but nights could still be tough, dredging up memories of his past life. He was alone, and the television was the only thing keeping him company. Lately he'd been binge-watching *Game of Thrones* on HBO and some fishing shows on Pursuit Channel. Some nights he listened to Pandora and sang to himself if the songs weren't too sad. He tried to remember Sadie's regimen of healthy suppers but wasn't doing a very good job at that. Tonight he'd prepared a tuna sandwich, though at least he went light on the mayonnaise—something else he'd learned from Sadie. He chased it with a cold Corona. He'd noticed that his pants were fitting a bit tighter and realized he wasn't getting any younger and that his metabolism was probably slowing down. He'd seen an ad for Anytime Fitness. Maybe he would join, he thought as he enjoyed the beer.

After he turned off the TV, the barn was quiet. It was May in Mississippi, and the air conditioner seemed to always run except late at night. The daytime temps were inching into the nineties, and every afternoon there was a small shower that popped up on the radar. But everything was dry—the crops, gardens, grass, and even blooming daylilies needed the moisture. While he considered whether this would be a good month to get back into bass fishing, his mind drifted back to Winston Walker.

He had read everything the FBI agents had given him. After that he'd Googled the man and found a very basic website for Winston Walker Publishing. There were several pictures of him in a coat and tie, looking like a wiz at business. His site praised the quality of his magazines and their readers and touted the rewards of advertising with them. None of the magazine titles interested John Allen in the least, and he'd never heard of them. John Allen knew there were a lot of costs to publishing magazines. There were graphic artists, editors, and writers to be paid, plus printing costs, postage, and just general overhead. Magazines that couldn't adjust to the new digital age were folding every month across the country, but John Allen also knew a well-run magazine with a solid ad base and lots of subscribers could still be very profitable. Accountants always admired magazines because subscribers gave their money up front on the promise you would later deliver magazines to them. But it was a setup ripe for a con artist to exploit. Winston's favorite angle appeared to be to mail letters to potential subscribers announcing a new magazine he thought they'd be interested in, then keep their cash and never publish the magazine.

Google also turned up an article in the *Meridian Star* newspaper that briefly mentioned the hunting accident, and a fund-raiser that had been held to solicit money for the victim's children's college fund. He found himself wondering whether Winston Walker still went on hunting trips. Had he gone out again that season, and did he intend to hunt this coming fall? A traumatic event like that could really have an impact on a man, he thought, then remembered that Walker had most likely committed murder. The hunt had only been the means to cover it up.

John Allen had grown up hunting with his father and had really enjoyed it. His father had been a member of a duck club in the Mississippi Delta, and they'd spent many weekends chasing ducks. He knew how to handle a shotgun and had never, ever felt uneasy or unsafe around any of the other hunters. It would take a cold-blooded person to aim at a man's head and pull the trigger. Taking another life would be a terrible burden, John Allen figured, but maybe not for someone like Winston Walker. John Allen studied the man's eyes in his photo and wondered what he was really like. He hoped for the chance to meet him and form his own opinion.

The idea Agent Emma Haden had suggested about using a skull as bait was a good one. The Choctaw Nation would never allow any bones they had in their possession to be used in that manner, but maybe they wouldn't even need an actual skull. If Walker was knowledgeable about Indian skulls, he would be well aware of their rarity, as well as their value to a certain kind of collector. Most diggers and mound looters were scared to death of bones and wouldn't have anything to do with them. Everyone in that world had heard stories of people taking bones home and having Indians visit them in their sleep, or of suddenly growing deathly ill or having some unusual calamity befall them. A few stories even ended in the death of the person possessing the bones. John Allen had no idea whether the stories were true, but they were plentiful.

On the other hand, he knew there were collectors who craved that sort of thing, and if they were interested, middlemen like Walker would be more than willing to turn a fast buck. John Allen was highly motivated to learn more about Winston Walker. He just might help solve a murder, possibly two. Right now he knew there were more questions than answers and that there were families hurting. John Allen understood hurt, and he wanted to help ease their pain. Tomorrow he would call Agent Emma Haden to discuss his idea of using a counterfeit skull.

◆ ◆ ◆

That same night, Winston Walker sat in his den and checked the text messages on his iPhone for word from his team that was out night-digging on a farm two counties south of him. When he found no messages waiting, he composed a text asking whether they were finding anything. The team reported they weren't, and that pissed him off. It also made him wonder whether they were telling the truth. The team leader's name was Runt. Winston trusted him, but only so far, as Runt was addicted to meth. Runt assured him there wasn't much more he could do. The topo map he'd studied had indicated the location had promise, though.

Winston ran his fingers through his hair and swallowed a big swig of scotch. He needed some money. Not a huge sum, but not a small one, either. After doing some calculations, he figured he needed about seventy grand to keep everything afloat. He was badly overextended on his home mortgage, and his ex-wife was threatening to sue if he didn't catch up on her alimony payments. He was two months behind on his Suburban payments and on every other monthly bill except the electricity. The power company was one of the few he couldn't bullshit for a little more time.

His publishing business was tanking, and the last of the advertising-sales guys, the lifeblood of the company, were about to leave. This was hardly surprising, as he hadn't given them a full paycheck in a long time. With great effort he'd successfully talked them into staying on, hoping they could sell more than they cost him, but it had been a break-even strategy at best. However, with them gone he'd have no hope of generating any revenue at all through the magazine.

He had already stiffed the printer for the last two issues of the gardening magazine, and he couldn't use that print shop again until he paid up, which he had no intention of doing. For the next issue, he planned to print only enough of to send one copy to each advertiser, to make them think he'd printed a full run. That would buy him some time, if the advertisers would pay their bills promptly.

He plopped down on the couch and stared at a rerun of *The Big Bang Theory* while he considered his alternatives. *Maybe I should get into television production or make a movie. That's where the real money is.*

After only a few minutes, he snapped off the TV. He needed to do something. He thought about any assets he had that he could sell to raise some capital, but none came to mind. His best hope was discouraging as hell to contemplate: a group of drug-addicted diggers who worked days in a chicken-processing plant and spent several nights a week digging artifacts for him. He needed them to find some good stuff. Something he could sell fast.

He lit a cigarette and thought about where they could dig next. It was time to take some chances and go back to the place he knew had what he needed. It was a risky plan, and in order to pull it off, he'd have to make Runt some big promises.

◆ ◆ ◆

Also that same night, Agent Emma Haden was working late.

She'd been an FBI agent for ten years now. She'd grown up in Lakeland, Florida, and attended the University of Florida, where she'd studied criminology. She'd always been interested in law enforcement, and the events of September 11 had sealed the deal for her. She wanted to catch criminals and do her part to make America safer. Her time at Quantico had been the most difficult experience she'd ever been through, but she'd managed to pass. Emma hadn't been at the top of the class, but she hadn't been at the bottom, either.

The Bureau had moved her several times, but no move had yet allowed her to be close to her home state of Florida. She'd done a stint in Seattle, then Bozeman, Montana, then Salt Lake City, and now Jackson, Mississippi—a step in the right direction, anyway. She was glad to be back in the South for a variety of reasons. While in Seattle she'd met a Boeing engineer who'd found her sassy and tart while they were dating. But once they were married, he'd claimed she'd developed an attitude. She hadn't felt she'd changed, but *he* obviously had—or maybe he'd never really understood the concept of monogamy. The end of their marriage after only two years had been an embarrassment for her, as it turned out he'd been having an affair with her best friend, who also happened to be his personal trainer. Fortunately, the Bureau had offered her a chance to move, and she hadn't had to remain in the same zip code as her ex-husband and ex–best friend. Since they'd had no kids, the split had been pretty simple, except that he'd kept begging her to take him back. Emma hadn't been even remotely interested and had poured herself into her work and wine.

There was no shortage of work to do in the Jackson office, or for that matter in any FBI office. It was difficult to manage the workload and to give every case its due. There honestly weren't enough hours in the day. She hated that she disappointed people who expected justice like in the movies. It just didn't happen like that. There were court battles and endless protocols to follow, not to mention sick days, vacation days, school plays, and a myriad of other normal things that interrupted a week's normal work flow for her and her partner.

Emma had a reputation for being a tough agent, much of it earned by having once saved her partner's life in a shoot-out in Salt Lake City. They were chasing a bank-robbery suspect in a mountainous area, and her partner had lost control of their car, which had flipped down a ravine. Her partner had been knocked unconscious and hung upside down in his seat belt. She had somehow cut him loose and dragged a man a hundred pounds heavier than she was to a safe distance before the government sedan exploded into flames. She'd earned respect that day, and the story of the event had followed her around. The other agents had taken notice, and her partner's wife was eternally grateful. The bank robber was later apprehended at a roadblock.

Emma always stayed late, then hit the gym for forty-five minutes of spin or yoga before coming home to her cat. She hadn't dated anyone since the divorce because she just wasn't ready. She had offers almost every week. Several of the gym rats had hounded her when she'd first arrived, but they'd finally gotten the message that she wasn't interested.

Tonight she'd skipped the gym and stayed even later than usual at the office. She was the only one in the building as she searched the Internet for more information on Winston Walker. She'd been touched by the story the victim's wife had told, and she believed it. But there just wasn't enough evidence to pursue a charge of murder or even manslaughter. Walker had been slick in planning the circumstances surrounding the "accident."

She didn't know much about the Choctaw Nation's artifact issues, but she did like the idea of trying to catch Walker or his crew on at least one charge, then leveraging somebody into talking. That seemed like their best bet. This train of thought led her to John Allen Harper. It was her habit to research everyone she met in a professional capacity. Knowledge was power, and the Internet revealed lots of secrets. She typed in his name and "Columbus, Mississippi," and found the story. As she read the article, she felt sadness for the man she'd just met. He'd lost a wife and an unborn child. After another few clicks, she was on Sadie Harper's Facebook page. It was still up, and there were hundreds of grieving posts.

She remembered his wedding band. Had he remarried? The accident had been almost two years ago. She then wondered whether that was enough time to grieve before a person could be expected to move on.

She circled back to the Indian artifacts. Since the victim's wife had told them about the ones her husband had placed in the storage unit under Walker's direction, Emma figured that information provided enough corroborative evidence to run a sting on him and see whether they could get him to buy something illegal. But would that be enough to leverage him to talk? Probably not, she thought, but they might get lucky. Perhaps a search warrant would reveal something else that might assist them. At the end of the day, if the man was locked up, it was a win for the good guys. But deep down she wanted to bust him for murder. She wouldn't feel satisfied unless she did. Winston Walker was a scam artist who operated just enough inside the law that he couldn't easily be caught. She'd seen it many times before. People were always looking for the easiest way to a payday. But Winston Walker was most likely a murderer, and that elevated him to cold-blooded status. He needed to pay for his crimes.

She would call John Allen and see what ideas he might have uncovered. He had seemed much more agreeable to working with them than the Choctaw tribe's head of security had.

◆ ◆ ◆

After showing the photo of Winston Walker to two different security officers, Hoss determined that the man was a regular at the casino tables. He rarely won big, but he had once—$6,000 on Christmas Eve. He played most everything but seemed to enjoy blackjack the most. The video showed that Walker obviously tried to talk dealers into pushing the envelope and helping him. None apparently had. All had turned disdainful looks up at the cameras and shaken their heads, alerting the monitor watchers that they had a "pain in the ass" at their table.

There was one alarming item of note that Hoss had noticed as he reviewed footage of Winston sitting at a blackjack table. Several times he was seen playing next to a janitor who worked at the Choctaw Nation's administration building, the one where the previous day's cash is counted, as well as where they stored the sacred artifacts.

One random encounter at a table could be overlooked, but three separate encounters during which they'd clearly talked to each other had Hoss uncomfortable. Now he had to think about how to handle the situation. Should he interview the custodian? Place him under surveillance? The first thing he planned to do in the morning was ask Personnel to pull the custodian's folder so that he could learn about the man. Hoss was paranoid about asking any questions of the other custodians. For all he knew, there could be a conspiracy to rob the cashier's office or empty the basement of artifacts.

The security head exhaled and dialed John Allen's cell number. He would call the chief at a more civilized hour when he had more information. She didn't appreciate midnight calls without all the facts, but John Allen would.

John Allen answered on the first ring, as if he'd been waiting for the call. "Hello?"

"You got a minute?"

"Yeah, man," he said, clearly recognizing Hoss's voice. "Talk to me."

"That man Winston Walker is a regular at the casino, all right."

"That doesn't prove anything, does it?"

"No, but he has met someone three different times at a table. Someone that works in this building."

That got John Allen's attention. "Who?"

"One of the night custodians, Rosco Jones."

"I don't know him," John Allen said.

"I don't, either. I just see him around. He's been here a few years."

"And Rosco has keys to sensitive areas in the building?"

"Rosco has electronic keys to everything except the cash room. I'm in the process of changing his access to the basement area. That's the room that scares me. I can also monitor where he's been. I can shut him out of anything important, but I hope he hasn't already done something stupid."

"Like stealing artifacts from the tribe's collection!"

"Exactly. I haven't told the chief yet. I'm sure she's asleep."

"Anything like this ever happen before?"

"Nope."

"So should we tip our hand and talk to him, or just monitor him?" John Allen asked.

The head of security sighed, still trying to make up his mind. He finally said, "I vote we monitor him. There might be more folks involved. If we talk to him, they'll just shut down and we'll never know."

"Good point."

"I'll find out how often he's been in the basement storage area."

"Yeah, that will shed some light." John Allen exhaled. "So do you know anything at all about Rosco?"

"I know he had to pass a background check to be employed here."

"How thorough?" John Allen asked.

"More thorough than yours."

"That's a relief."

The head of security groaned. "We'll talk in the morning when I have more details, and you can bring the FBI up to speed."

"Gotcha."

"And . . ." Hoss paused to make sure he had John Allen's attention.

"Yeah?"

"Don't do anything without telling me about it first."

Chapter 13

John Allen was up at daylight, thinking about the Winston Walker case. What if Walker had an inside person stealing artifacts from the basement storage area? It would be a simple crime, as he'd be surprised if anyone inventoried the items with any regularity. Some of the artifacts were museum quality and very valuable. He had a knot in his stomach. It would be so easy for Winston Walker to accumulate a great cache of artifacts or sell them to an investor.

Deciding to go for a jog, John Allen searched through his pile of folded T-shirts, which numbered at least forty. There were five he regularly wore, but he wouldn't get rid of the other thirty-five. After picking one of his favorites, he walked outside and commenced exercising without stretching. Back when he'd jogged regularly, it had always helped him think through problems. The cool morning air felt good in his lungs. It had been a while since he'd exercised, and he vowed to get back into a regular routine. His stamina, or lack thereof, freshened that resolve.

He held his cell phone while he ran in case the tribal chief or Hoss called him. His plan included a brief workout; then he would speed down to the administration building and try to conduct some sort of inventory. He didn't have a list, but surely someone did.

Running back toward home, he was struck once again by how the barn looked like an old, worn-out farm structure, revealing not a clue as to what was inside. He wiped sweat off his face and wondered whether Sadie would have liked his setup. Probably not, he decided. She'd loved traditional houses with shutters, window planters, and porch swings. She also would have given him grief about driving a Porsche, though she would certainly have asked to drive it to her tennis matches.

His life had changed drastically, but he'd stopped feeling sorry for himself. Lots of people's lives changed, and it didn't take a tragic accident to spin someone's world upside down. Sickness, divorce, depression—all occurred every day. Why should he expect his life to be any different?

Sadie's parents were hurting, also. They called, checking on him regularly, the pain audible in their voices. They lived in Memphis and were good people. Sadie had been an only child and the love of their lives.

He thought about where his life would be now and realized they would probably be talking about a second child. Sadie had wanted two or three. John Allen had just wanted whatever she had. She probably would have been thinking about a bigger house by now, too.

As he approached his barn, where the Porsche was parked in a converted tractor stall, he couldn't help but smile. No doubt Sadie, with her sarcastic wit, would have said he was now a cross between Indiana Jones and James Bond, or at least thought he was.

◆ ◆ ◆

There was tension in the air at the office when John Allen arrived. Hoss had pulled reports on Rosco Jones's movements within the building for the last six weeks, and Hoss's concern was clearly reflected on his face. He quickly motioned John Allen in and began to bring him up to speed.

"Thirty-eight years old. He was hired on three years ago and has been a dependable employee. He works the night shift, and aside from using lots of sick days that seem to coincide with Thursday NFL football games, I don't see anything out of the ordinary. Prior to working here, he ran a chainsaw for a logging company for five years until he hurt his back. He was born and raised in Lauderdale County near Meridian. High school graduate, no college."

John Allen sipped his coffee and stared at the computer screen displaying Rosco Jones's image. John Allen had seen him a few times, but he was embarrassed to say he hadn't paid the man any attention.

"His wife works at Peggy's Restaurant in town. She's a cook," Hoss said. "I've never been there. You?"

"I eat there all the time when I'm in town. It's just a house. You pay with the honor system and go through a buffet line; then all the rooms have tables. You may end up sitting with folks you don't know, but the food is out of this world."

"There is nothing I can see that would suggest he is involved with the wrong crowd or ever has been. He has a kid. She's a senior in high school. I called a source of mine at the high school to ask about her. You know, maybe she's driving a Porsche." Hoss said this with an attitude, like maybe he didn't approve of what John Allen drove. "I'm told that she is a smart kid with ambition and has applied to several expensive colleges. She'd get some scholarship help for sure, but the cost to our friend Rosco would still be staggering. My source didn't know how he was gonna be able to do it. This could be a motive."

"Yeah, helping his kid."

"You siding with him?"

"No, not at all. Just saying a father's love is pretty strong."

"Still don't give him any right to steal from us."

"I agree. I need to check the basement. Do you have an inventory list of what's down there?"

Hoss exhaled, reached across his desk, and picked up a notebook. "Yeah, about that," he said, handing it to John Allen. "I talked to the chief this morning. She is upset that someone could have access to our treasures and wanted you to personally inventory the room. She also gave clear instructions that she wants us to catch them all, and especially Mr. Walker. She said to tell you she would call you later."

John Allen thumbed through the inventory list. This would take some time.

"I think we're all on the same page," he said. "I assume you locked Jones out of some areas?"

"I did."

"What will you say to him when he asks?"

"He was off last night. When he gets back tonight, he'll be told that we have a glitch in the system that will soon be repaired, and he can have access when the issue is resolved. It's pretty common for the electronic keys to fail. They are very similar to the keys you swipe at a hotel."

John Allen placed the folder under his arm and nodded in an approving way. Grabbing his coffee, he drank the last of it and tossed the cup in the trash beside Hoss's desk.

"Can I get in?"

"Come with me," Hoss said as he stood up, then headed to the door.

◆ ◆ ◆

The basement was a quiet, sterile room that would make a thoughtful person think or make a worrier worry. Some people even referred to it as spooky. John Allen had been in it several times before to stack what he had recently purchased. The concrete walls were cold and bare. Standard-issue brown boxes stacked on the gray metal racks provided the only color. Each box contained numbered artifacts along with a statement as to where and how they'd been found, or as much of the story as was known. To the Choctaw Nation every artifact was sacred and had a story to tell.

Hoss unlocked the door and allowed John Allen to enter.

"I hope it's all there," Hoss said drily from the doorway.

"You're not gonna stay?" John Allen asked as he looked around the room.

"I have a bunch to do. This is your department."

"Yeah, thanks."

Hoss stepped out, and the door slammed shut. John Allen walked over to the last box he'd placed in storage. He had purchased it from a college student in Oxford, Mississippi, and knew exactly what was supposed to be in it. The shoe box full of arrowheads had originally belonged to the student's grandfather, but as far as the kid had been concerned, it was just a box of rocks. He'd wanted cash, and John Allen had been happy to pay once he learned the arrowheads had all come from a farm near Itta Bena, Mississippi, a location that guaranteed they were Choctaw artifacts. There were eighty-seven pieces in all, and some were quite good, in John Allen's opinion. There were two excellent Dalton points.

He unfolded the box lids and saw that the shoe box inside was intact. Lying on top was the list of artifacts and the location in which they supposedly had been found. John Allen had learned that from the point of view of archaeologists and historians, location was critical to establishing the authenticity of any artifact. The Choctaws supported efforts to uncover this information, but primarily they just wanted to get the artifacts back into their possession.

The shoebox was full and appeared to be the same as he'd left it. He hadn't really expected these arrowheads to be gone, though, as they were probably worth no more than forty dollars each.

He moved on to other boxes he had secured in the room, and they all seemed to be intact. A flush of relief went through him as he continued to the next aisle. He had no idea what was in these boxes, since he hadn't been a part of securing any of the artifacts within them.

John Allen's cell phone rang, and he studied the number before answering the call. It was from the Jackson, Mississippi, area. Wondering who it could be, he cleared his throat and answered the call. "Hello?"

"This is Agent Emma Haden. Have I caught you at a bad time? Do you have a few minutes?"

"No . . . I mean, yes, it's a good time, and I can talk. I'm glad you called. We've got some information on your suspect," John Allen said, shaking his head at his own awkwardness. He did enjoy saying the word *suspect*, however. It sure beat saying *tax-deferred credit*.

"Good," she said. "What did you find?"

"Our head of security found some members of his team who recognized Walker's picture. Evidently he's a pretty steady player in the casino. He's won about $6,000 that we know of, but Hoss is checking some other payout records. I bet he's slick enough that if he wins, he cashes in just enough chips to stay under the IRS radar."

After a pause, she said, "I hope you have more info than that!"

Her bluntness caught John Allen off guard, but he quickly recovered. "Oh, yeah, here's the good part. He was seen on security cameras talking to one of the custodians of our admin building. They were seen at least several times together."

"Uh-huh," Agent Haden said, sounding unimpressed.

"That probably wouldn't have raised any concerns," he went on, "but based on your comments that Walker was suspected of trafficking in the sale of artifacts, maybe stolen artifacts, seeing them together scares us."

"I'm sorry, but why is that, John Allen?"

"The custodian's name is Rosco Jones. We are running a background check on him right now, but he has access to almost every room in the building where you met with us. Including the artifact storage room."

"Oh, wow, now I see what you're saying." Agent Haden finally sounded like she didn't think he was a nitwit. "Have y'all talked to him?"

"No, not at all. Hoss has locked him out of the artifact room and told him it's due to some key-card malfunction. I'm inventorying the artifact room right now."

"You're right. That's an interesting connection, considering Walker's alleged history with artifacts."

"Let me tell you," John Allen said, "if you can get him for selling stolen artifacts, ones taken from a federal Indian reservation, you could put him away for a while. They take that pretty serious."

"That would be a step in the right direction, all right," she said. "And it'd maybe help us put some pressure on someone to squeal on Winston for murdering Jim Hudson. I bet someone close to him knows or at least suspects something."

"You should know that the chief was very emphatic that she wants this guy caught. It's disturbing to her, and to everybody, not knowing what he and this Rosco have been meeting about. I mean, they could be plotting something even bigger, like robbing the cash room or the vault. It's all in this building."

"We need to make a plan," Agent Haden said. "Ideally, the fewer people up there who know about this, the better. Those two could have others on the inside who could tip them off."

"I don't think Hoss has told anyone but the chief."

"Great. Listen, let me check my schedule for a minute," she said. There was silence, then she was back. "I can move some things around and be there after lunch. Can your team meet off-site at a private location?"

"Yes, I know I can, and I expect Hoss can, also."

John Allen was a little embarrassed by how excited he knew he sounded, but when Agent Haden answered, there was a charge in her voice, too.

"I'll be there," she said. "I'll call when I'm close, and you can tell me where to meet."

John Allen stared at his phone when the conversation was over. He had just hung up with the FBI. They were going to be working on a case together. He took a deep breath and called Hoss, who quickly agreed to convene whenever she arrived.

As he slid his phone back into his pocket, John Allen's mind raced with possibilities. The law-enforcement aspect of his job was all so new to him. Protocols, procedures, discretion, and attention to detail were all paramount to success, and the stakes were high. His adrenaline was pumping.

Checking his watch, he realized he needed to finish his inventory of artifacts and walked to the next aisle. The boxes were stacked neatly and looked as if they hadn't been touched since they'd been placed there.

Opening the folded top of the first box and looking inside, though, he saw that it was empty.

"Holy shit!" he exclaimed, and quickly began checking other boxes.

◆ ◆ ◆

Runt listened to Winston explain his plan. It sounded pretty feasible to him and a lot easier than working all night probing the soil and digging. He liked digging once they located a good site, but finding the site sometimes was drudgery. He also liked when Winston was desperate, as that meant there would be lots of incentives. Whenever Winston was in a bind, he would entice his crew with meth and the promise of extra money, which never failed to motivate them. Winston took an unusually long drag off his cigarette, and Runt knew he was approaching desperation rapidly.

"So," Runt said, "how many boxes we talking about?"

"Several," Winston said, then exhaled a stream of smoke. "Probably four to five."

"They may miss that many," Runt said as he nervously checked his text messages. His girlfriend hadn't responded to his recent message, and he could all too easily imagine reasons for that. Like, that she was texting someone else. Or worse.

"He's leaving the boxes, Runt. The rocks and stuff will be put into trash bags and hidden in the dumpster."

"Sounds like a big haul."

Winston smiled, and the cigarette dangled. "Oh, yeah."

"You got a buyer lined up?"

"Hell, yeah. All I need is for you to back up to the dumpster and grab the garbage bags. The only worry is my contact is acting jittery lately. I hope he ain't getting a conscience."

Runt thought about what Winston wanted him to do. In the past their contact had just slipped the artifacts out in his lunch box. The volume Winston wanted forced a new plan that would temporarily expose Runt or whoever retrieved the stolen pieces. Their contact knew the routines of the building's security officers, and there wasn't a camera on the backside of the building. The unknown factor was the possibility of a random patrol by the Choctaw police. But Runt knew a good diversion could take most of them out of the way for a few minutes. It really didn't seem that bad. Runt was used to taking risks, and the meth would make him fearless. The whole concept of stealing something excited him and made him feel alive.

"So what's in it for me?" he asked, cussing his girlfriend under his breath. He knew she was seeing someone behind his back. He just couldn't catch them.

Winston twisted the top of a cold beer and took a sip. He seemed to be thinking about his response. "I gotta pay my inside guy for stealing the stuff, and he wants more than last time. He's getting greedy. So I am offering you twenty percent of what I sell it for."

Runt lit a cigarette and blew the smoke straight up. "When?"

"Rosco said he would let me know. I expect soon. Might even be tonight. You in?"

The television played in the background, and neither paid it any attention. Runt again checked his text messages, but this time he did so absentmindedly, aware that his slow response was torturing Winston.

"What about some up-front cash?" Runt said at last.

"How much?"

"Thousand bucks."

"No way."

Runt was thinking, which for him could prove dangerous. "You gotta do something for me. I need some money."

"How about I'll kill you if you don't?"

Runt raised his eyebrows. He knew what Winston was capable of doing when he was feeling pressured. He'd seen it several times.

"I'm in. But I need a favor."

"I don't usually do favors. What is it?"

"I wanna get my girl a big diamond ring. Maybe that will make her quit running all over town and settle down with me."

Winston grinned. He knew Runt's girlfriend intimately. When she needed drugs, they traded favors, and she frequently needed drugs. Runt had no idea.

"I need somebody that knows about rings and diamonds," Runt pressed. "You know about these kinda things. I don't have a clue."

"Yeah, I'll help you. The money you make on this haul, you can get her something really nice."

Runt was pleased. His girlfriend was making him crazy, and he thought a ring might warm her cold heart. He held out his fist, and the two degenerates bumped fists.

"You can buy her a big rock," Winston said, "but that ain't gonna make her love you. Trust me, I know."

"This one's different."

Winston chuckled, shaking his head. "You just gotta hope she don't pawn it when she needs some money."

Chapter 14

Hoss and John Allen appreciated the agent's idea to meet someplace off-site. There was no doubt that multiple visits by an FBI agent to the admin offices would attract interest, and try as they might to keep it quiet, someone would find out.

They decided to meet Agent Haden on the backside of the bleachers at the Choctaw High School baseball field. No one would be there, and they could freely discuss everything. John Allen called her with directions and again admired the energy in her voice. The modern sports annex was a half mile from the school. They were guaranteed to be able to talk without an audience. The only motion was a sprinkler system watering the grass.

The day was well on its way to being the hottest so far of the year. From now through September the temps would climb high into the nineties and occasionally jump to triple digits. An outside meeting wasn't ideal, but Hoss had insisted on it, and Agent Haden hadn't questioned the venue.

She pulled into the parking lot in her government-issue silver sedan, parking next to John Allen's Porsche, and he noticed she looked it over as she exited her car. She was dressed fashionably, and John Allen looked for a bulge indicating her firearm but didn't see one.

Hoss wore mirrored Ray-Ban sunglasses and was sweating like he'd sprinted to the meeting. He had a bandage wrapped around the knuckles on his right hand. When John Allen had explained to him that three boxes of artifacts were missing, he'd slammed his fist into a wall in his office. He had wanted to go straight for Rosco Jones and beat the truth out of him. John Allen had been able to calm him down, but it had taken a while. It infuriated Hoss that his people's sacred artifacts had been violated again.

"Agent Haden," John Allen said as he extended his hand. "We've been anxious for you to arrive."

"Good to see you two," she said as she shook his hand. As she reached to shake Hoss's hand, he declined, pointing at the wrapping.

"Anger issues," John Allen explained.

Agent Haden nodded, clearly curious, then glanced around, wincing a bit at the intense sunlight.

"We needed someplace to meet that wouldn't raise suspicion," Hoss explained. "Right now I don't know who I can trust."

"You don't have a room with air-conditioning?"

Hoss shrugged, obviously in no mood for humor after the news he'd just received about the artifacts.

"Let's go sit on the bleachers in the shade," John Allen suggested, trying to be accommodating.

Hoss immediately turned and started walking in that direction while John Allen fell in beside Agent Haden. He'd dressed up a bit, but she was dressed more casually than he'd expected.

"Where's Agent Garner?" he asked.

"He had to testify in court today."

"So you guys don't have to wear dark suits every day?" John Allen asked as they walked. "You're not really dressed like the agents I see on television."

"You watch a lot of TV?" she asked, looking like she was trying not to smile.

"I guess maybe more than the average guy."

"Well, don't believe everything you see on those shows. The FBI is more progressive than it's portrayed as being."

Hoss arrived at the shade first and wiped his forehead with the back of his uninjured wrist. "Thanks for meeting us here," he said, which for him was a big effort at civility.

"No, I understand," she said. "It's smart." She glanced to John Allen, then turned back to Hoss. "Tell me, what did you guys find out?"

Hoss nodded at John Allen and folded his arms.

"Since we talked earlier," John Allen said, "we found three empty boxes in the artifacts room. We think the two men may have already been working together. Our guy Rosco being the inside man, and your guy buying and probably reselling."

"Let me get this straight. These items or artifacts were stolen from the tribal administration building, and it's sitting on federal land, right?"

Hoss again nodded his head.

"That makes all this federal."

"Yeah," Hoss said. "We catch him, and you can burn his ass. There are actually several federal acts that this can fall under, like the Antiquities Act that is meant to protect historical artifacts. It carries a stiffer sentence than just stealing, say, a computer."

"Do you guys know the value of what he stole?"

"It's hard to say," Hoss replied. "Value to who? To us, they're priceless. On the open market the pieces they have would probably fetch twenty-five to forty thousand dollars. It just depends." He shrugged. "We just learned the pieces are missing. There may be more."

Agent Haden took off her jacket and folded it over the bench-style seat. John Allen couldn't help but notice her firearm and her figure. *The bureau must require them to work out,* he thought. He hadn't noticed a female in a while. A quick look at her left hand revealed no ring, but then she had no jewelry on her hands at all. Maybe she just didn't wear a ring while she worked.

He forced his mind back to the matters at hand. "We don't know if they're planning anything else," he said, "but it's a good bet that since they were successful once, they'll want to do it again."

Hoss nodded. "Greed."

"Right," Agent Haden said. "Have you told anyone about this yet?"

"Just the chief. She was upset."

"I'm sure. You know, we should quietly dust for prints and secure the area, if only for a brief time. You said you blocked his access?"

Hoss nodded.

John Allen was enjoying watching her analyze the situation. She gazed at the horizon while she appeared to weigh options. "It may take some time, but I think we should set a trap."

"We just don't want to lose any more artifacts," Hoss said with absolute certainty.

"Oh, I agree. Don't want that at all. He just needs to feel like he's gotten away with it, then either we need to let him think you guys have acquired something really valuable or we try to go and buy something from him." Again she paused, her expression pensive. "What's Rosco's schedule?"

"Works at night from six to after midnight, five days a week," Hoss said.

"We gotta keep him thinking everything is okay. Your plan to make him think you're having problems with the keyless entry is a good one. Maybe even have a fake repair crew appear to be working on the system while he's there one night. I have a couple of agents that could use some overtime and would help us. You'd be surprised what they might learn in the break room over coffee."

Hoss scowled. John Allen knew he wasn't excited about having more people in his building, but he apparently couldn't come up with any strong reason to deny them access. "As long as you vouch for them, we can make it work."

"Do we need to put Rosco under surveillance?" John Allen asked.

Agent Haden gave him a quick but thorough once-over. John Allen wasn't sweating as much as Hoss, but he was plenty hot. "We don't have that kinda manpower available," she said. "Do you guys?"

"No," was all Hoss said, then for John Allen's benefit added, "It takes a lot of men to watch someone twenty-four hours a day."

"We can get a search warrant when the time comes," the agent said, "but I suspect the artifacts have already been moved. When is the last time anyone saw them?"

Hoss sighed. "We don't know. It could have been weeks, maybe months."

"So we really don't know that he stole them, but I'll bet we've stumbled onto an ongoing crime," Agent Haden stated.

"Yeah, I was afraid of that. This could have been going on a long time," she said, then stared off into the distance again. John Allen and Hoss looked at each other, then back at her. "We have to bait Winston out," she said, finally. "That's probably the surest way. A trap."

As the group stood silent, John Allen thought about what had been discussed. He knew they all wanted to catch the criminals, but if they were going to catch the whole group, they needed to make good decisions.

Agent Haden studied John Allen and said, "Do you think you could act as an undercover agent with us? You look more civilian than any of my team."

"I'm glad to help."

"We'll be close by. You'll be wired. Anything gets fishy and we'll rush in."

John Allen nodded, feeling his heart pound. "Anything I can do."

"Have you ever done anything like this before?"

Hoss snickered. "He bought some arrowheads off a college student last week."

John Allen rolled his eyes. "No, but everybody has to start somewhere."

"I'll work with you. I haven't lost an agent yet," she assured him.

"All right, then," he said, and they smiled at each other.

Then John Allen turned to study Hoss, who clearly appeared to be uneasy. John Allen didn't know for sure what the head of security was thinking, but he was probably trying to acclimate to the idea that this project would have the two of them working together closely. Hoss was a loner, and John Allen was an outsider as well as a law-enforcement rookie in clear need of some support. It didn't help matters that John Allen was pretty sure Hoss didn't think much of him.

"Sorry to say it, after us sweating out here in secret like this," Agent Haden said, "but I'd really like to see the basement. Discreetly, of course. Think you can slip me in there?"

"We're pros at that," John Allen said as he wiped sweat from his forehead.

Hoss thought for a second, then nodded. "We should be okay. You don't exactly look like a typical federal agent."

"I'd just like to see what this room looks like," she said. "I may get an idea that will help us."

As they walked toward their vehicles, John Allen's mind was racing, thinking about going undercover and trying to trick Winston Walker. Could he do it? He didn't know, but he knew he would try.

"Will the chief allow us some freedom to work a sting?" Agent Haden asked. "I'm sure she'd like to search Rosco's house and try to find the artifacts, but I really feel that would be in vain."

"She'll do whatever I recommend," Hoss said, wiping his forehead as he moved toward an unmarked sedan similar to her own.

"That's good. I like her," Agent Haden added, then turned to John Allen as he headed over to his Porsche. "Is that yours?" she asked. "You got some kinda midlife crisis going?"

Hoss laughed out loud.

"It's part of my cover," John Allen said sheepishly.

She chuckled. "Really? I love it. That's going to be perfect for Winston Walker."

"Let's roll," Hoss said. "I need some air-conditioning. Agent Haden, leave your car here and ride with Speed Racer, and y'all can talk more. Follow me. We'll go in the back door of the building and avoid some prying eyes."

Agent Haden nodded her head in agreement, and suddenly John Allen was nervous. The kind of nervous you get when you're sixteen and picking up your prom date. He hoped his radio wasn't tuned in to something that would embarrass him.

Chapter 15

That night, John Allen spent a long time turning over the events of the day in his mind.

Once they'd slipped in the back of the admin building, he'd spent a couple of hours with Agent Haden and Hoss, trying to determine a plan. The chief had dropped by just as they were winding down to pledge the full support of her staff to take down the thieves. She'd been extremely pleased that John Allen was proving to be an asset.

They'd spent another hour showing Agent Haden the artifact room and explaining to her the complicated laws surrounding the acquisition, retrieval, and sale of artifacts. Anyone could surface-hunt for arrowheads and other artifacts on private land, but it was strictly forbidden on federal properties and in national or state parks. It was also legal to dig on private land with the landowner's permission, but once a bone was discovered, the diggers were required to shut down the dig and notify the proper authorities, since bones were illegal to possess.

Agent Haden had paid close attention to everything that had been said, but it was obvious she wanted to get Winston Walker on a heavier charge than stealing artifacts, and simply viewed them as a means to that end. Once she had someone close to him facing federal charges, she hoped to get him to break and point the finger at Winston.

John Allen kept finding himself wondering about Agent Haden in other than a professional capacity, and this bothered him. There was something about her he liked, and he felt guilty for having those feelings. He hadn't expected to feel this way again, or at least so soon. She was smart and attractive. He found her very interesting, and she smelled good. He sat staring at the television, thinking about his situation. It had been almost two years since his wife's accident. He missed her companionship every day, but tonight he was thinking of another woman. This was an entirely new emotion for him, and it knocked him sideways. He sipped a bottle of water and watched a rerun of *American Ninja Warrior*.

◆ ◆ ◆

Agent Emma Haden was walking at a fast pace on her treadmill. She had planned to walk two miles, which was her goal five nights a week. She was motivated to stay fit. The Bureau expected it of her, but she also enjoyed being healthy. She walked, jogged, took a paddleboard out on the local lakes, worked out with free weights, and sometimes did yoga. She'd learned to exercise during her twenty weeks of training at Quantico, Virginia. That had helped her get into the habit of exercising, and since then, she'd kept it up.

At least once a month she went to the firing range and shot a hundred rounds. She could load each of her pistols blindfolded. There were many male agents who weren't as proficient with their firearms as she was. She owned several guns. One agent who considered himself a wit liked to joke that she had as many pistols as purses, but the fact was, she had more pistols.

As was her habit while she walked, she mentally reviewed the details of several ongoing investigations, but the Winston Walker case was front and center in her mind. She really wanted to take him down. When she'd interviewed him about the hunting accident, he'd shown no signs of remorse. He'd known nothing could be proven and had been very full of himself.

Sting operations were difficult to pull off, however. They required forethought. Trying to anticipate what criminals would do or how they would react was a challenge. There was little room for mistakes. Mistakes could get people injured, or even worse, killed. The goal was to get all team members back home to their families at the end of the shift.

Her thoughts kept turning to John Allen Harper. She needed him for this operation, but she didn't want to put him in too much danger. The Choctaw Nation may have given him some training, but from what she could tell, he was a glorified security officer with a pistol and a really cool car. She had enjoyed meeting him, though. He was polite, soft-spoken, and handsome. She wished she could meet a man like him who wasn't married. While driving with him, she'd confirmed that he had a gold wedding band on his left hand. That ended any further thoughts she had of the man, except wondering how he'd dealt with losing his wife and unborn child. That was a heavy burden.

Agent Haden appreciated that John Allen genuinely wanted to help them and that he had been personally chosen by the chief of the Choctaw Nation. Hoss was a more complicated person. He was hard to read. He appeared to be a seasoned security professional, and so far he had been helpful, which was a bit unusual. Oftentimes men in his situation resented the FBI being involved or even coming into their jurisdiction. She would reserve judgment on him until she'd spent more time with him. So far, so good. But there was something about him that made her uncomfortable. Then again, she had to admit she'd misjudged men before.

Adjusting the treadmill speed down to 3.0, she wiped the sweat from her face. The hair in her ponytail bounced slower now as she continued to walk. The sun was beginning to set on the Ross Barnett Reservoir as she wound up her exercise routine. She loved her condo's view of the "Rez," as everyone called it, a thirty-three-thousand-acre lake created by damming the Pearl River. Formed to provide a permanent source of drinking water for the city of Jackson, the lake now had a tremendous economic and recreational impact on the area. She lived in one of the four-thousand-plus residences on the lake's edge and loved the water and its relaxing effect on her.

Stopping the treadmill, she stepped off it, then went out onto the little patio to cool down and enjoy the last of the sun's light over the Rez. Then she planned to eat something healthy and have a glass of red wine before the 10:00 p.m. call she expected from the two agents posing as the keyless-security-repair team. She hoped they'd learned something that would help the investigation.

Chapter 16

It was a cloudless summer morning in Philadelphia, Mississippi. Hoss sat at his desk and stared out the windows, trying to make sense of all that was happening.

Everybody had called him Hoss since accepting his job, but his real name was Martin Appletree. His mother was Native American, and he had never known his father. His mother explained that his father was a civil-rights activist from New York City who'd come through the area in the mid-1960s. They'd met at a civil-rights rally, and while she'd thought it had been love, he'd just been passing through on a summer mission to make the South a more equitable place. They had not remained in contact.

Hoss had been raised about as poor as one could imagine, but with all the love a mother could give. As the tribe organized and started trying to better itself by building casinos, hotels, and other businesses, he'd been hired on to do whatever he could. His good work ethic was noted, and coupled with the fact he'd grown up in the community and was known to almost everyone, he eventually worked himself into the current position of heading up security for the tribe. One outstanding characteristic that made him the perfect candidate was that he intimidated most people. He wasn't a tribal police offer, but as the head of security for the tribal headquarters, casinos, and other associated businesses, he was allowed to operate outside of the normal protocols that often hindered police departments. He was a free spirit, and his security force and the tribal police officers revered him.

Martin "Hoss" Appletree was not a very friendly person and was suspicious of everyone. He knew lots of secrets about people and considered that knowledge to be power. His cameras revealed almost everything, and his crew of security officers provided him with information that filled in the gaps. He knew who worked hard and who didn't, who stole toilet paper and lightbulbs, and who put in extra work for no pay. He knew who had a gambling problem, who didn't know when to stop drinking, and who was seeing whom on the side at their hotels. He had too much knowledge. Most of it didn't help him with his daily duties; it was just a burden that made him express a visible disdain for people in general. However, occasionally knowing someone's troubles provided a glimpse into their needs and motivations, which was proving to be quite valuable.

When the phone had rung earlier this morning informing him that Rosco Jones had been found dead from an apparent suicide, he'd begun staring out the window. Anyone watching would have thought him to be contemplating something deep, like the circle of life. With the knowledge that Hoss had, knowledge that only a few others shared, he had much more than that to consider. This could seriously impact the FBI's investigation. Rosco had been their only direct link from Winston Walker to the artifact room.

Hoss had understood he would be deeply involved from the moment he received the call. He immediately alerted the chief, who generated more questions than Hoss had answers to.

Only a few miles away from him sat the city of Philadelphia. The city that had been known for racial tensions was waking up slowly, and today would prove to be a sad one for part of the community. This time the national media wouldn't converge on the city, like in 1964 when the three civil-rights workers went missing. Today's event would include the Neshoba County Sheriff's Department and the city police all moving quickly to close out an ugly situation that no one wanted to deal with.

Rosco Jones had been found in his car, parked under a bridge that spanned the headwaters of the Pearl River. A fisherman found him and called the police immediately. Everyone considered it a suicide except a Neshoba County detective who happened to know Rosco. According to Hoss's contact, the detective arrived just as the coroner was preparing to take the body and ranted until they agreed to come back later. The extra time allowed him to investigate the scene. Though the scene had already been contaminated, he ordered that it be taped off so that it could be studied, and he cussed several police officers for not calling him earlier.

The suicide would complicate the FBI plans, Hoss knew. Nothing ever went as planned.

Hoss grabbed his keys and started for the door. He wouldn't have any jurisdiction at the site, but he had an imposing presence, and his opinion would carry some weight. The chief wanted the tribal police to be involved, and with this latest twist, she now wanted a search warrant for his house in the hopes of finding stolen artifacts.

Chapter 17

The shade cast from the bridge over the Pearl River was the only relief from the worsening heat. There were a half dozen law enforcement and emergency-response vehicles parked around the scene. A boat ramp with parking bordered both the river and the bridge. Hoss had been here many times. Growing up, it had been a popular teenage hangout. He parked and headed over to learn the latest information about Rosco Jones's death. Hoss had decided he would play dumb about Rosco and not mention anything concerning the stolen artifacts unless he was forced to do so.

The Neshoba County detective who'd taken over the scene was well thought of in the rural community and by the local law-enforcement officers. He had solved several cases that endeared himself to the locals and impressed his colleagues. He was tall and thin and looked like he might have played sports as recently as a few years ago. Hoss hated sports. The two men had seen each other at functions but had never worked together professionally. His name was Jamarius Reed, and he was intently studying what clearly still appeared to Detective Reed to be a crime scene.

Hoss watched the man work for a few minutes before interrupting. "He worked out of our tribal offices."

Jamarius looked up, recognizing him. "Yeah, it was a good job for Rosco since he'd hurt his back cutting pulpwood," Jamarius replied.

"You knew him?"

"He was my Sunday-school teacher. Good man. Real good man."

Hoss shook his head, bent over to look inside the vehicle, and saw Jones slumped in the driver's seat. "So what happened? Why did he do it?"

"That's a good question. Good question."

"Was he depressed?"

Jamarius stood up and wiped his forehead. "He was a janitor at night and cut grass with a push mower during the day, even with his bad back. But I never heard him complain, not one time."

"Something must have set him off," Hoss insisted.

"Not that anybody close to him can recall. It doesn't make sense to me."

"He gamble? Maybe he lost big—you know, bet the farm?"

"Not that I'm aware of. He went to the casinos to hand out flyers and invite folks to come to church on Sundays."

"Do you see any evidence of foul play?"

"No, not really," Jamarius sighed, then looked at Hoss. "The man had a daughter and a loving wife."

"Yeah, I read his personnel file. The tribe will probably do something to make sure there's a college fund for the girls."

"That would be real nice."

"There a note?"

"No note here, and they haven't found one at home."

"Anything I can do to help you?"

"Let his boss know he won't be coming in tonight."

"I can do that. But I was thinking that maybe I could get the tribal police to help you check all this out. I can tell that you don't think it's what it appears."

"No, I can handle this," Jamarius said as he stared at the body.

It sure looked like a suicide to Hoss. He had seen a few in his career. "So, Detective," he said, "if you don't see any signs of foul play, what makes you think this was a not a simple suicide where a depressed man wanted to check out early?" He was considering telling Jamarius that he could have the FBI investigate if he wanted.

"I knew him. This wasn't something he would ever consider."

"Do you ever really know someone?" Hoss asked, walking to the other side of the Chevy Caprice to study the scene from a different angle.

Jamarius pinned Hoss with a look, then pointed at the body. "That man right there had a daughter that was about to compete in the Miss Mississippi Pageant. He bought her a fancy violin, and he listened to her play every morning. He drove to somewhere in Alabama to rent a dress that he couldn't afford to buy, and he already had a hotel room reserved in Vicksburg for two nights. He was so proud of her and wanted to see her compete. He was convinced she would win. There is no way he did this prior to the big night, and no way he would break his girl's heart right before it."

"From what I've heard, he was headed into some debt. Deep debt, to send that girl to college."

Jamarius quickly shook his head. "He lived in a paid-for house and really didn't have many bills. His kids were everything. His girl is going to get scholarships, then they'd see about funding the rest. The church did a bake sale to raise money for the family's hotel room during the pageant."

Hoss made a decision. It was out of character for him to reveal information, but this situation had direct bearing on important artifacts of the Choctaw Nation. He needed answers. "I think I can explain what happened."

Jamarius looked at Hoss, who glanced at two other deputies searching the edge of the parking lot, presumably for anything that might make their colleague happy. They appeared to Hoss to be out of earshot.

"I'm listening," Jamarius said.

Hoss lowered his voice. "You can't talk about this, it's an ongoing federal investigation. But we have a strong suspicion that Rosco was working with another person to steal artifacts from the Choctaw tribal office."

"Artifacts?" Jamarius's brow furrowed.

"Yes, they are quite valuable."

"Your suspicion? You got any evidence?"

"We have him on video, talking to a known artifact reseller," Hoss explained. "There are several missing boxes, and he had keys to where they were stored."

"The FBI?"

"It's a federal crime."

Jamarius remained silent for a moment. "How would that turn him to suicide?"

"Haven't you ever heard the stories about people finding Indian artifacts or bones and taking them home and feeling like they're being haunted by Indians?" Hoss asked seriously.

Jamarius stared at him for a few seconds, then said quietly, "I once knew a guy that found some stuff and took it home, and he said a hawk perched in a tree outside his house. He had never seen the hawk before. The next morning the hawk was still there, and when he got to work, the hawk was sitting in a tree next to where he parked. He freaked out and went home and took the pieces back to where he found them and never saw the hawk again."

"That's a mild case," Hoss assured him. "I've heard stories all my life, hundreds of stories, and some much worse."

"You think Indian spirits drove him to commit suicide."

"Something like that."

Jamarius sighed. This wasn't what he wanted to hear, but he did believe in spirits and hauntings. All his life he'd been a bit spooked about old houses, cemeteries, and funeral homes. It took all his mental strength to work investigations with bodies. "If the mind believes it, then it be real," he said, shaking his head.

"Can you get me into his house to look around?" Hoss asked.

"You think something's there?"

"There might be. The FBI can get a search warrant, but I would like to keep this quiet within our community."

"Tell me this, if you take the reseller down, do you have to drag Rosco into it?"

"Maybe not. We just want our artifacts."

"Is this reseller guy from around here?"

"Nope."

"I see." Jamarius exhaled loudly, his expression turning grave. "I'd like to keep Rosco's name clear, for his daughter's sake. I'm telling you, he was a good man."

"You help us and we'll help you," Hoss said. "Let's go look."

◆ ◆ ◆

John Allen woke before dawn and decided to do something he hadn't done in well over three years. He walked into his extra bedroom where he kept his fishing tackle. Grabbing a bait-casting setup, he looked through his tackle box until he found a floating frog lure and tied it on. He worried that the line might be old and rotten, but he slipped on rubber boots and walked the two hundred yards to the pond's edge.

The sun hadn't yet poked its head over the horizon, but the birds were singing, and the early false light was beautiful. The water was warmer than the morning air, causing a layer of thin fog to swirl over the dark surface. The weight of the rod and its cork handle felt surprisingly good to him. Like shaking hands with an old friend.

At the water's edge he looked for snakes but really didn't expect to see one this early in the morning. He eased closer until he was within casting distance of a big stump that sat quietly in the water. The water depth had to be three or four feet there, which was ideal. Checking the frog lure, he noticed rust on the hooks. And the rubber body was partially dry-rotted, but it would have to do. As he flexed the rod tip a few times, the physical memory of what he needed to do was still there. He intended to land the frog on the exposed top of the stump, then gently pull it off into the water. This would simulate a frog jumping into the pond, looking very vulnerable.

The hooks weren't the only things that were rusty, as his cast missed its mark and bounced off the side of the stump, then plopped into the glassy-smooth water. John Allen smiled at how good this felt. The surface ripples expanded quickly away from the frog, and as the biggest of them approached three feet wide, he twitched the rod tip. The frog responded with a quick jump, then rested again. John Allen had missed this part of his life. Topwater was his favorite fishing method for catching summertime bass. There was nothing quite like a bass exploding onto the surface.

He was still holding that thought in mind and hadn't even twitched it a second time when the frog disappeared and the water erupted in a vicious strike. John Allen reflexively set the hook. The fish felt good, really good, and he let out a little line when it made a run for deeper water. The rod bowed under the pressure of the bass as it circled just under the water's surface. *Too fat to jump,* John Allen thought with excitement.

The fish continued to fight until John Allen worried the old line would snap under the stress. There was nothing to do but keep his rod tip up and allow the fight. After a few minutes he could tell the fish was tiring, and he gained ground by walking a bit closer and reeling the line in as fast as the bass would allow.

A moment later, a giant largemouth bass was lying on its side at the water's edge. John Allen bent down and grabbed the fish by the lower lip. It shook its head one more time, then calmed down enough for him to raise it out of the water and hold it up to admire. It had to weigh seven pounds. The fish was healthy and beautiful, its emerald-green upper body tapering down to a pale-white underside, gills flaring bloodred in contrast. Then, John Allen quickly unhooked the fish and admired it one more time before releasing it back into the water.

Satisfied with himself, he watched the fog float over the water and realized just how much he had enjoyed that moment. He'd needed that fish. He hadn't fished since the accident. That was a long time to deny himself such pleasure.

With one last look at the water, he started back to the barn. He'd accomplished what he'd come out to do. Suddenly he felt like he was living again. In the brief few moments he'd been fighting the fish, while his rod had bowed and the line had stretched, he hadn't thought about any of his problems or worries. He hadn't thought about anything but that fish, and that had felt good.

"Thank you, Sadie," he said as he looked up at the rising sun and walked to the barn.

◆ ◆ ◆

John Allen started his workday by giving a talk on local Native American history to the sixth-grade students at a nearby school. After showing them some artifacts, he wrapped up and was driving to the office around midmorning when his cell phone rang. Hoss explained the situation regarding Rosco Jones.

John Allen was stunned. "Do you think that Winston Walker could have killed him?"

"I thought about that, but it sure looked like a suicide to me," Hoss said, his tone firm. "Plus, I have an explanation, and I'll tell you about it when I see you."

"You can't tell me on the phone?"

"We need to do it face-to-face so I can see if you believe me."

"Okay, I'll be there in thirty minutes," John Allen said, then added, "Hey, we need to tell Agent Haden."

Hoss grunted. "I'll let you do that."

John Allen was still excited about the morning's catch. He planned to eat a fried honey bun for breakfast to celebrate.

Chapter 18

Hoss spent an hour with Jamarius, searching Rosco Jones's house. Rosco's wife was distraught and welcomed the search because she wanted answers. They didn't toss sock drawers out onto the floor and make a mess like they usually did in a full search. They looked in the obvious places—in closets, in corners, behind the drapes—while they tried to disturb as little as possible for the sake of Rosco's wife. They did check the storage building out back, and they even looked in the chicken coop.

Hoss convinced Jamarius that if Rosco had kept any artifacts at his house, they would be in boxes, stashed someplace like a box of old vinyl records. The house was immaculately clean and had the feel of the home of a hardworking couple who lived within their means and were proud of what they had.

The two men didn't tell her what they were thinking but rather gave the impression they were trying to determine what might have pushed or caused Rosco to do what he'd done. Jamarius wanted to provide her with some better answers but not create more pain. Knowing Rosco had committed suicide was obviously just pure pain and raised a lot of terrible questions for her. Hearing that he might've been murdered would have been just as painful and would have created just as many difficult questions. It was a no-win situation for both of them. She couldn't believe her husband had killed himself.

She answered every question, and both men could tell they were truthful answers. Rosco had been acting differently. Something had been on his mind, but she didn't know what it was. Her husband had been a very private person. She did explain that just before the ten o'clock news, he'd received a phone call and said he had to go meet someone about work. He never came back. She said he'd received other such calls occasionally. This information intrigued both men, and Jamarius made a note to check Rosco's phone records.

Hoss asked questions that might give insight into Rosco's relationship with an artifact reseller, and Jamarius listened carefully, observing the woman's body language. But neither man came away with an answer that yielded any serious insight into the situation. They wrapped up the search after Rosco's wife received a call saying she was needed down at the funeral home, as it would take the home a while to prepare the body, and they had questions, too. Money would be one of them, Jamarius knew, and he assured her the church would take up a love offering to help. He would personally call the preacher and see that it was done. She cried and hugged him while Hoss stood awkwardly to the side. His only offering was that he would check with the tribe and make sure she got any pay Rosco was owed. She thanked him, also.

The men walked to their vehicles, promising to stay in touch and to share information. Jamarius wanted to trace that incoming phone call before making any decisions. But he had to admit that he'd been spooked the whole time he was in there, a fact that made Hoss's theory feel more plausible to him. The thought even occurred to him that the spirit had lured Rosco away from home with that call, but he quickly dismissed it. He didn't want to investigate anything that was in the same league as voodoo.

Standing in the gravel driveway and looking at the modest house, the detective thought about where Rosco would hide something. They'd checked only the obvious places. Maybe Rosco had returned the artifacts, but that scenario felt like wishful thinking. Maybe Rosco had thrown them into the river. Then Jamarius's eye fell on the garden on the side of the house. Tomatoes, okra, squash, and corn. The ground would be soft and easy to dig in. *I would have buried them there,* he thought. He would come back without Hoss and look, but it was a huge garden. It would take time.

◆ ◆ ◆

Once John Allen heard Hoss's explanation for Rosco's suicide, he spent some time thinking it through. He didn't know whether he believed in spirits. The spooky stories were common enough, though—he'd heard many during his short time working for tribe. While growing up, John Allen had heard all sorts of tales about ghosts that supposedly resided in many of the old southern houses, and he hadn't known what to make of those, either. He'd never encountered a ghost, but that didn't mean they didn't exist. Indian spirits making someone commit suicide, though, was pushing the limits of credibility.

He sat staring out the window in his office, wondering what to believe. He also wanted to know who'd called Rosco the night before. Obtaining that information sounded like it could be a promising lead.

As he contemplated the scratches the bass's raspy teeth had left on his right thumb, he realized he still needed to call Agent Haden and bring her up to date. He was glad to have an excuse to contact her.

Agent Haden answered on the third ring, and he explained the whole Rosco situation to her. He went on to say that if there had been a crime scene, it had already been processed and disassembled by the sheriff's department. Her response was a bit saltier than he expected, but her spunk made him smile.

"He wasn't the big fish," she said. "We still gotta get Winston."

"Let's do it," John Allen said, realizing he was trying to impress her with his enthusiasm. That's really all he had—he didn't know what else to do.

"I'm glad you called," she said. "I think I have the perfect bait. I called in a favor with an FBI contact, and I got hold of an old skull. It was never identified, and they think it's at least a hundred and fifty years old. It's just been sitting in storage. It's stained and partially fragmented."

"That sounds perfect. There was no way I was going to get one from the tribe."

"I suspected that," she said. "Can you can come down here so we can work out a plan to get you in front of Winston? You might need to spend a few days."

"Let me touch base with the boss, but I don't think it will be a problem." John Allen made an effort to keep his growing excitement in check.

"Make whatever preparations you need. The Bureau will put you up in a hotel."

"When do you need me?"

"As soon as you can get here. Let me know when you're an hour out. I'll be here at the office unless something comes up."

"Unless the chief surprises me and puts on the brakes, I'll be there in a few hours."

"Oh, and John Allen? Be sure you come in that fancy sports car."

John Allen smiled. "No problem."

◆ ◆ ◆

Hoss and the chief sat in her office and discussed the latest events, including Hoss's thoughts regarding them.

She knew of the stories about people being haunted by the spirits attached to the artifacts. She believed in those spirits and knew that if they had, in fact, scared Rosco Jones enough to commit suicide, he'd been doing something that caused him to deserve it.

The belief in spirits was a fundamental part of their culture. But of all the stories she'd heard, none had included suicide. Most could be passed off as a dream or a figment of a tortured imagination. And as far as non–Native Americans were concerned, there had always been a reason to doubt such an explanation and provide an alternative theory.

The fact that something like this was happening under her watch concerned her, and it wasn't like she didn't already have a full plate of responsibilities. While in the last twenty years unemployment among members of the tribe had gone from 4 percent to over 90 percent, the poverty and despair that had not so long ago plagued her people had abated under the watchful eyes of past chiefs. She was committed to improving on that progress, especially regarding education and health issues, which were her passions.

The chief swirled her Starbucks coffee pensively. "You don't think the artifacts are at Mr. Jones's house?"

"I don't know, ma'am. We looked in the obvious places. I don't think he knew we were on to him, which makes me think they would have been tucked away somewhere we could find. That's assuming he still had them. And I expect to know about the phone call sometime soon."

"I respect your agreement with the detective, and I understand protecting family. The daughter, she sounds like a good girl—and I don't want to unnecessarily tarnish her daddy's image even if he was stealing from us. That could have a big impact on her. But right is right, and we have to protect what is ours. Let me know who called him."

Hoss slowly nodded and agreed with the chief's wisdom.

"I'd tell you to search the house again during the funeral, but if you were caught, it could get ugly for us," she said.

"And, anyway, they live in Philadelphia and not on the reservation," Hoss pointed out. "We don't have any jurisdiction there."

The chief nodded. "While John Allen is working with the FBI, go talk to the tribal police, the Philadelphia police chief, and the sheriff, just so they know what we have going on. The only ones who will care will be the tribal. The rest are too busy with their own crimes."

"Yes, ma'am." Hoss stood up to leave.

Chapter 19

John Allen walked into the FBI office in Jackson, Mississippi, brimming with anticipation. He was about to play a role in apprehending a suspected murderer and artifact trafficker. He would also get to spend time with the woman who'd been on his mind for the last several days. She'd stirred something in him, but he didn't even know whether she was married. He really didn't know anything about her. As he waited for her in the secure lobby, he wondered what lay ahead for him. The generic government wall clock showed that it was almost 3:00 p.m.

A heavy door cracked open, and Agent Emma Haden stuck her head out. "Hey, you," she said with a smile. "How was the trip down?"

"Thank goodness for air-conditioning."

"Come on back to our conference room. I have two other agents I had hoped would be here to help us, but they just got called to the capitol. An unknown substance was found on an envelope." She shrugged. "It's the world we live in now."

John Allen nodded and glanced at her left hand. Still no ring. He thought she noticed him looking, but he wasn't sure. She didn't break stride.

A brown box that had been opened sat on the table in the glass-walled conference room. The agent reached in and gently removed a skull. It looked as if it had spent the last hundred years in a swamp.

"It looks real."

"It is real," she replied.

"I meant—"

"I know. It's real; it's just not an authentic Native American."

"It sure is creepy-looking," John Allen said, not wanting to touch it.

"Do you think he'll be able to tell the difference? You're an expert at these things, aren't you?"

"Well, I wouldn't say 'expert.' I've had a crash course in arrowheads, spear points, and pottery, but not bones, and especially not skulls."

Agent Haden gazed down at the skull in her hands. "I don't see how he could tell. Not immediately, anyway." She placed it back into the box. "It's not every day that you handle one of these."

John Allen's phone vibrated, and he read a text message from Hoss saying that the call to Rosco had come from a burner phone, but that they were still trying to trace it. He told John Allen to keep him informed about what their plans were for the sting.

Agent Haden noticed the look on his face and pulled out a chair. John Allen placed his phone on the conference table and sat down, repeating the gist of the message for her.

"Dammit. I'll bet you money it was Walker."

"Can you guys step in and help?" John Allen asked. "The local sheriff would probably welcome your assistance."

"Don't be so sure. We can't get involved unless they ask us to," she said with a sigh. "But I'm betting our current investigation eventually comes back to it, and then we'll get involved with both feet."

"Good."

"Thank you for doing this, John Allen. You know it could be dangerous. Is your wife okay with you doing this undercover work?"

"I guess you don't know," he said, exhaling deeply. "My wife was killed in a car accident about two years ago."

"Oh, I'm so sorry," she said. "That's awful. I just assumed when I saw your ring."

John Allen looked at his wedding band and spun it around on his finger. "Yeah, I know. I just haven't taken it off."

"I'm sorry for prying."

"That's all right." John Allen saw this was his chance to learn about her. "What about you? Does your husband mind what you do?"

She rolled her eyes. "I'm not married. I got divorced a few years back. I don't make good choices in men," she added with an embarrassed chuckle.

"It happens," John Allen said, trying to calmly process the information.

Steering the conversation back to the matters at hand, Agent Haden opened a folder that had Winston Walker's photo clipped to the edge. Inside was a stack of papers.

"How are we going to make contact without him getting suspicious?" she asked.

"That's what concerns me."

"We learned from Jim Hudson's widow that he hangs out at a bar every evening with a couple of guys who work for him. We have their names, and we think you could approach one of them in hopes they would take you to Winston."

"Okay. So who are these guys?"

Agent Haden shuffled through the folder to a photograph and slid it across the table to him. "This is a guy they call Runt. He's a meth head. Probably one of those diggers you guys refer to. He's Walker's right-hand man."

"I've met this guy before," John Allen said, staring at the picture. "At a gun show right here in Jackson a few months back. But his badge said his name was Billy."

"That's right, Billy Copeland. But his street name is Runt." Her brow furrowed. "Damn. Him knowing you could be a huge problem. Is there any way he might suspect what you do?"

"No, not at all. He knows I want to purchase artifacts is all. I've talked to him in person once and tried to call his cell a few times, but he's never brought anything to me."

"You're sure he might not be suspicious?"

"I don't know. I don't think so. But I think he's paranoid."

Agent Haden got up and walked to the far end of the room, thinking. "If he traced your cell-phone number, would it go back to the tribe?"

"Nope, it's mine."

"So he thinks you're just an avid collector."

"That's right."

"Maybe this isn't necessarily a bad thing that you already have a relationship with him." She came back to the table and pulled another photo from the file. "Here's another one of his thugs. He's a mountain of a man. It says here he played football at Southern Miss and weighs two eighty. But you can tell the drugs are taking a toll on him from this picture."

"Yeah, these guys don't exactly look like fitness freaks."

"Or geniuses. They're meth heads, and they always need money. We're hoping that their need for cash will pave the way. But listen to me now—these guys are dangerous, and capable of anything. Mostly they are two-bit hoodlums, but you can't underestimate them, especially if they are jacked up on drugs. They can be evil and surprisingly strong. I know the type, and unless you've had direct experience, believe me, you can't imagine."

John Allen studied each picture carefully, committing the men's faces to memory, then gave her a nod.

"Tomorrow we'll get you ready," she said, slipping the photos back into the file. "We'll travel to Meridian and bait the trap. We have a man that will monitor these guys on social media. You would be surprised what they post on Facebook, Twitter, and Instagram."

John Allen agreed. "I have a few folks I'm stalking on Instagram. They're posting pics of the arrowheads they're finding. I'm hoping to recognize a landmark one day."

"They can't help themselves. We'll have a good idea where they'll be."

John Allen glanced at the box. "Agent Haden, if he really is selling artifacts to some underground collectors, I expect that skull will be hard to resist."

"I hope so, and call me Emma."

John Allen felt himself blush and thought she'd noticed because she smiled. Which, of course, only made him blush even harder. He was making an utter fool of himself.

In the awkward silence, Agent Haden's cell phone rang. She suddenly focused like a laser beam on the call, her expression turning concerned. After a minute she disconnected.

"I need to have a meeting in here; then I may be out for a few days," she explained with trepidation. "We just got a call that there has been a suspicious person hanging around a crop-dusting operation north of here, near Yazoo City. This is a top priority with Homeland Security, and I need to get on it with them. But, look, don't say anything to anyone. I shouldn't have told you that, but for some reason I trust you."

"No worries, I understand. We can do this when you get back. Go get the bad guys."

"Hey, do me a favor," she said. "Take the skull and find a better box to show it off in. That box looks like it's straight from the evidence locker."

"You think maybe I should try Bed Bath & Beyond?" he asked with a smile.

"No, no. Try Hobby Lobby," she responded quickly, not catching that he was joking. She was used to solving problems in a hurry.

"We have a room for you at the Hampton Inn," she said. "Go ahead and stay tonight if you want. I hate that you drove all the way down for this."

Through the glass walls of the conference room, John Allen could see another agent getting ready for the next meeting. "It's fine, really."

She glanced at her watch. "This meeting could go on for a while, but I bet I could meet you for supper about eight if you'd like to?"

John Allen tried not to smile. Maybe this was just FBI social protocol when working with other departments. "That's sounds like a good idea. But don't let me keep you from something important."

"This will be a planning meeting. We already have two agents headed that way. They'll call in, and we'll deploy a bigger crew tomorrow, including me."

"Okay, um—just call me, then."

"I gotta get some files pulled. The agent at the front desk can let you out," she said as she grabbed her phone and hurried to the conference room door.

Through the glass, John Allen watched Emma and another agent speak excitedly to each other.

He liked Agent Emma Haden. He fiddled with his wedding ring and wondered what he should do next. It had been a long time since he'd chased a woman. He tucked the skull under his arm and left the Jackson, Mississippi, office of the Federal Bureau of Investigation.

Chapter 20

Winston Walker spent the latter half of the day trying to run a scam on a new company that made organic garden fertilizer. The husband-and-wife team were old-school hippies who knew how to compost and create fertilizer but had no idea how to advertise their business. They spent more time talking about a Phish concert than they did asking about the demographics of his magazine. Then they left his office with a signed contract they hadn't read and a promise from Winston that he would change their lives. Ironically, that wasn't a lie, since he had their credit card. They'd handed it over for him to write down the numbers, and he'd slipped it under some papers on his desk.

As soon as the hippies left, Runt slithered into Winston's office. He didn't even have to ask Winston how it went—he could tell by his boss's satisfied expression.

"They're selling shit, and I'm selling shit," Winston said with a grin.

"They just don't have any idea how much shit they just bought," Runt said with a laugh.

"We need that ad campaign more than they do." Winston lit a cigarette and sent a stream of smoke up to the ceiling. "So," he asked, "how are you and Sweet Thing?"

Runt sighed. Love was obviously not his strong point. "It's complicated." Now that Winston had brought up his girlfriend, he felt compelled to dig out his phone. No messages from her. Another sigh. "Hey," he said, "me and the boys are going to the Pop A Top and get a drink. You coming?"

"Yeah, I'll be there later. I'm trying to work on a new angle to get those artifacts I was telling you about."

"What about your inside man?"

Winston chuckled. "Yeah, he ain't gonna work out."

Runt was confused, which was a constant condition for him since Winston rarely shared details. "Just let me know. I'm sitting on 'go,' boss."

"I will. We need the cash," Winston said as he blew smoke at the ceiling. "Times are tough, Runt. We need all we can get."

"We haven't had any luck finding anything valuable lately."

"We need to start looking where we know the good stuff is. You know, the stuff that's already found. I know a couple of guys that are supposed to have incredible collections."

"What about that guy I met at the gun show in Jackson? I gave you his card."

"Yeah, I forgot all about him. I checked him out on Google, and it looks like he's an accountant in Columbus."

"He had a fancy car. He sure smelled like money to me. Plus, Columbus is an artifact-rich area. We got anything you could sell him?" Runt asked with a devious grin.

"If he does have money, he probably has some good shit. We should steal it. Think anyone would notice if an accountant overdosed?" Winston laughed as he looked through his desk drawer for the business card. "Damn, Runt. Every now and then you have a good idea."

Runt smiled. "A blind hog finds an acorn every once in a while."

◆ ◆ ◆

John Allen checked into the hotel, wondering about his dinner date. Ordinarily he would have just stayed with his parents, but he was doing what he was told. He didn't have any expectation that the night would end in any way other than a good meal and interesting company. However, he did wish he'd brought some nicer clothes and a sport coat. Having been depressed most of the time for the last two years, he'd rarely given any thought to making an effort to look good. Sadie had always jokingly called him a "mood dresser," and his mood since her death hadn't been up to par.

A quick check on TripAdvisor confirmed what he'd suspected—the Iron Horse Grill was the top-rated restaurant in the area. He wondered what Emma would be hungry for and assumed something healthy. She gave the appearance of someone who was into fitness and health.

At seven o'clock Agent Haden phoned, and they made plans to meet at the restaurant. She was fine with his suggestion. He arrived early, and while he waited, he texted Hoss that the project was going to be delayed a few days. John Allen would let him know as soon as it was back to "go" status. Hoss replied with "K." John Allen hated the brevity of texting. It was ruining people's ability to communicate, although he could see the value in it sometimes.

An appetizer of sour cream–topped tamales arrived just as Emma strolled over to his table. She certainly didn't look like a federal agent tonight. As he stood to greet her and pull her chair out for her, John Allen was shocked by her beauty. Before he sat down, he noticed several men staring at her.

"You look very nice," he managed to say. He wanted to say "beautiful," but something held him back.

"Thank you. You do, too."

"Would you like an adult beverage?" John Allen asked, holding up his Corona.

"I would absolutely love a glass of wine."

John Allen looked around for their waiter but didn't see him. He was nervous, and the only way he knew to work through it was to talk business. "That terror threat, is it legit?"

"We don't know yet. We've been monitoring crop dusters since 9/11. Our fear is that someone would steal a plane. I mean, think about it: low-flying, powerful airplanes that have the ability to haul and spray chemicals. This particular pilot has reported seeing someone observing them refueling and loading chemicals for several days, and we're gonna go set up surveillance, then try and pick them up. I just hope they show up tomorrow. Sometimes these types of cases can take days."

"Did the pilot get a look at the car or license plate, anything that could help?"

"All he knows is that it's an older silver Toyota sedan. The guy leaves quickly if approached."

"Well, good luck with it." John Allen finally flagged down the waiter, and Emma ordered a glass of red wine. She passed on an appetizer after eyeing the tamales suspiciously.

Unfolding her menu, Emma exhaled. "Yeah, we'll need the luck. These cases are ultrahigh priority for us and always difficult."

"It makes me feel better to hear that it's high priority," he said. "I hate that a portion of the American public seems to have forgotten 9/11."

"It's natural that we slowly forget. It takes an event to remind us all how important it is. It's just our job to prevent them in the first place. The problem is the workload. The constant investigations cost much more than they used to, and we all need more funding."

"I can't imagine the stress all that creates."

"It's real," she said, rolling her eyes. "So what are you ordering?"

"Filet mignon and some cheese grits."

"Wow, that sounds good. I just don't know what I want yet," she said, turning to the back page of the menu.

"Are there lots of threats monitored by Homeland Security?" John Allen asked.

"Well, there are lots of reports from citizens who see things they think are suspicious. We check them all out. People are very suspicious of any Muslims right now."

The conversation paused as the waiter arrived to pour the wine and take their orders. While Emma finally decided on a salad with grilled fish, John Allen sipped his beer and noted how good it felt to be out in the world. The energy Emma gave off made her exciting to be around. He admired her quiet confidence.

When the waiter left, Emma sipped her wine, then looked around the restaurant and smiled. "Nice choice, John Allen. This is one of my favorite places."

"Good."

"So," she said, "tell me about yourself."

John Allen related his life story while they waited for their entrées to arrive. He hadn't told it to anyone in a long time. She listened with interest and laughed at his story of being suspended from Mississippi State for a week after cleaning a deer in the dorm showers. He loved her laugh.

"That's the worst thing you've ever done?" she asked, continuing to laugh.

"Well, that I was caught doing," he added with a sly grin.

"That's hilarious."

"My mom was real embarrassed. A week of suspension wasn't too bad, though, I guess. It's now a posted rule. Imagine that."

"That's nice to know you left an impact on your college," she said, and kicked him gently under the table.

The food arrived and forced a timely break in the story. Once the waiter left, John Allen suggested that he bless it.

"Please," she replied with a small smile, and bowed her head.

After finishing the prayer, John Allen started slicing his filet and asked, "So what about you?" He was happy to divert the conversation away from himself, although he'd loved the way she listened to every word he said. She was a great listener.

Emma gave him her history while they ate. She'd graduated from high school and college with honors. After college she'd entered the police academy and worked for the Tampa Police Department for two years. As a junior detective, she'd solved a high-profile cold case that had involved murder, a popular doctor, and prescription painkillers. It had resulted in her being noticed, had kick-started her career, and had given her an opportunity to advance to the FBI.

"So you enjoy the job?"

"I love it. I love feeling like I'm making a difference. I've had a good life, except for a bad marriage. I'm so glad I moved on. Life's too short, and he gave me the best reason to leave." She took a bite of her fish and chewed it thoughtfully. "I think that all I've been through, though, has helped me become the person I was destined to be," she added, then smiled. "Which is someone who'll talk about herself for fifteen minutes straight, I guess. I must say you're a good listener, John Allen."

John Allen smiled, then took a sip of beer. He started to repress his response but decided to say, "All that is so true—experience makes you wiser. But all you have to do to be the person of your destiny is to just do it." He thought about asking what her ex-husband had done to make her want to leave but decided against it.

Emma eyed him as she sipped her wine and absorbed his comment. "You're right, you're absolutely right. It's just easier said than done."

"Look, I'll admit that I'm not a good example for doing what I say. I've been in a funk for two years, but I'm slowly crawling out of it. I know what I need to do. I'm just slow to do it."

Emma admired his honesty. After making eye contact, she placed her hand on his arm. "You've been through an awful experience. Only you can know when it's time to move on."

"Thank you. It's been tough. I wouldn't want anyone to have to go through what I did," he replied, looking away.

She changed the subject. "So, tell me, who's your favorite singer?"

"I have a lot of favorites, but I listen to James Taylor more than anyone else. Probably because I play the guitar a little bit, and I can play some of his songs. What about you?"

Emma laughed. "I can't play the guitar, or any instrument, for that matter, but I love Billy Joel. In fact, I have a cat named after him."

John Allen grinned. He had never really been around cats. She did seem like someone who would have a cat, though.

They finished their dinner and shared a dessert, both of them enjoying their conversation until Emma admitted she needed to get some sleep since she had an early morning.

"Let's hold off with setting a trap for Walker," she said. "I'm probably going to be hiding in a cornfield tomorrow, so you may not hear from me until I get closer to town and have service."

"No problem, I have plenty to do. Be sure you spray some bug repellent if you do hide in a field. The chiggers are bad right now, and they would love to chew on someone sweet like you." He flushed after he said that but didn't regret that he had.

"That's good advice. Aren't they the same thing as red bugs?"

"Yes, they are."

She grimaced. "I definitely know about red bugs."

As they walked out to the parking lot, she pointed at his car and laughed. "You know, that really doesn't seem like something you would drive."

"To be honest, I thought the same thing at first, but I really enjoy it now," he replied sheepishly. "It's fun to drive, and the women seem to like it," he continued with a touch of sarcasm.

Emma laughed again, and he realized he hadn't made a female laugh in a long time, and it made his heart feel good. He was wondering whether he should kiss her good night, but he decided it really wasn't a date, so he tried to shake her hand.

She hugged him instead and planted a quick kiss on his cheek. "You're a sweet guy, John Allen. Take care of yourself."

"You be careful tomorrow," he urged.

"Oh, and I want to hear you play that guitar one night," she said as she pressed the "Unlock" button on her key fob.

John Allen watched her drive off, his heart pounding faster than usual. She was special. He was going to need to blow the dust off his old Fender guitar. He hadn't touched it in well over two years.

◆ ◆ ◆

Winston waltzed into the Pop A Top as if he were gracing people with his presence. It was not an upscale bar by any means, but it had a regular clientele best described as a cast of characters. On most any night you could find whatever you were looking for in terms of trouble. If it wasn't already there, a quick phone call would bring it. Every town had at least one bar like the Pop A Top.

When Runt saw Winston, he waved him over. A Rascal Flatts tune was playing on the jukebox, and three girls in short denim cutoffs danced with one another for the viewing pleasure of some out-of-town construction workers. It was a typical Friday night. Runt and his girlfriend, Gina, were in a deep conversation about *Game of Thrones*. She loved John Snow and wanted him to live, and Runt was, predictably, a fan of the platinum-blonde Khaleesi.

Winston waved at the bartender, who automatically brought him over a Jack and Coke. He grabbed a handful of peanuts and watched the denim-clad girls dance.

Runt leaned in close to ask, "You hear from your boy with the tribe?"

"Nah, I told you that's not working out."

Runt nodded.

Winston took a big sip of his drink and squinted as it burned going down. "What we gotta do is make some scratch quick. I plan to call that preppy-shit accountant from Columbus."

"That's only an hour and a half from here. That ain't a bad road trip," Runt said. "He had a badass ride. Even if he ain't got no Indian rocks, we could steal his car."

Winston pulled the business card with the man's name and number on it from his wallet and looked at it, then decided he would call in the morning. Tonight he would drink—a lot—and enjoy the money he'd made today. The short denim shorts were looking good to him. The night was young. Maybe he would even venture over to the J & J shoe show and watch some strippers. *Why not?* he thought. He had some cash, and he was open to suggestions.

"Hey, boss, you're on a roll," Runt said, hugging his girlfriend, who wasn't hugging him back. "Let's do something big tonight."

"I am. I'm going to the casino," Winston said, making it clear that Runt and his girlfriend weren't invited.

Chapter 21

The morning started before daylight for Agent Haden and her colleagues. They met at a truck stop and familiarized themselves with the layout of the private airport, the crop duster's schedule, and where the observer had been seen. Two agents had scouted the location in the dark last night and had a plan for surveillance. So far a data search of silver Toyota sedans with Mississippi plates hadn't yielded anything of significant interest. Their best bet at this point was to catch the guy in the act.

The airstrip was north and west of Yazoo City at the edge of the delta. The area was as flat as the Gulf of Mexico on a calm morning, and its mosquitos were reported to be vicious. There was, however, a hell of a barbeque joint a few miles away, so lunch would be worth waiting for. Agent Haden, being the only female, rolled her eyes at the men's constant thoughts of the next good meal.

As they sat in the booth at the truck stop, she looked at the faded photos of Jerry Clower hanging on the wall. This was the old southern comedian's hometown. She recognized the photos and remembered her daddy listening to his stories on cassette tapes. She made a mental note to purchase one and send it to him. He didn't have iTunes, which would have been so much easier.

After the business at hand was finalized, she dosed her scrambled eggs with Crystal Hot Sauce and ate them while she listened to the other agents gab. They'd ordered bacon and pancakes and enough cholesterol to harden their arteries. Not a man among them had made anything close to a healthy choice off the menu. She knew at least a few would show better sense when they were at home with their wives.

Her mind drifted to John Allen. He looked to be in decent shape, and he hadn't pigged out in front of her last night like most men would have. She wondered whether he watched what he ate and exercised. That was important to her. She checked her watch. It was still only 5:45. She figured he was still deep asleep at the Hampton Inn.

She'd enjoyed listening to him tell his story last night. She had seen pain in his eyes, and he'd shown a cautiousness that wasn't exhibited by most men. He hadn't had a desire to rush anything, and she liked that. She didn't know for sure whether he liked her, but she thought he was interested. The presence of the ring demonstrated to her that he wasn't a playboy but was capable of loving one person. That thought was reassuring. And she could never remember another man blessing her food other than her father. She'd liked it.

"What are you smiling at, Emma?" the senior agent asked, startling her.

"Oh, nothing," she replied. "I was just remembering my daddy listening to Jerry Clower tapes."

They all chuckled. "That man's stories about Marcel Ledbetter were the best!" an agent said as he stuffed a sausage in his mouth.

Emma hadn't realized she'd been smiling. She shook her head. A man hadn't made her feel this way in a long time. Maybe forever. There was something special about John Allen Harper.

"Do they sell bug repellent here?" she asked, to make sure the subject stayed changed.

"I got us some last night at Walmart," the lead agent said. "And Cokes and bottled water for you, Emma. Hurry up. We need to roll and get into position. It's going to be a long, hot day."

◆ ◆ ◆

The alarm clock glowed 5:50 a.m. when John Allen decided he couldn't lie in bed any longer. His mind kept replaying last night's dinner. Sitting up, he wondered what Emma was doing right now. Then it occurred to him to wonder whether she might have texted him. He really didn't think she would have, but he grabbed his phone and checked anyway. The only text was from his mother, reminding him to send her his Christmas list.

Rummaging through his travel bag, he pulled out shorts, a wrinkled Adidas shirt, and his running shoes. He'd start his morning with a two-mile run, then visit his sister and parents before rolling back down the highway to the office in Philadelphia.

On his way out of the hotel, he noticed a lady who was setting up the continental breakfast. It wouldn't be great, but it was free. He put his earbuds in as the electric doors opened, then tapped Pandora and cued up his playlist.

Typical early-summer mornings in Mississippi start off in the mid-seventies, but given the high humidity, it doesn't take long to break a sweat. John Allen turned left on Greymont Street and breathed in the fresh morning air. The city had barely started waking up, and even the traffic on the nearby interstate was light. The only sound was the siren of an ambulance headed north.

As he jogged, John Allen's mind turned once again to Emma. He'd loved the way she'd been interested in what he had to say. It had been a long time since he'd enjoyed himself as much as he had last night. He wondered whether she liked to fish. He was curious as to what she thought of him. Could she be interested in him?

With approximately two miles done, John Allen made his way back to the hotel. His shirt was drenched in sweat, and he was hungry. There were two guys looking at his Porsche as he walked into the lobby. He shook his head and headed back to his room to get his day started. If his day went well, he might go fishing late that evening.

◆ ◆ ◆

The chief of the Choctaw tribe requested a briefing from Hoss at her office. She started her days early and worked late. It was not uncommon for her to be in before 6:00 a.m., and she expected everyone around her to be working as well. She didn't like an eight-to-five work ethic from her executive team. There was simply too much to do each day to pack it all into eight short hours.

Hoss arrived at seven, coffee in one hand and a box of doughnuts in the other. He entered her office and took a seat. He wished he had been earlier, but he'd overslept. He hoped the doughnuts would help make up for it.

"Have you heard from John Allen?" she asked, still looking at her computer.

"Yes, ma'am. He met with the FBI yesterday, and they're getting ready to set up a sting on Winston Walker. I think it may actually be a few days before they start, though. He indicated they had a problem."

"What kind of problem?" she asked as she removed her bifocals.

"I don't know, exactly."

"Keep me posted. I usually get a text update from him once every couple of days. He's good about keeping me informed. But I need you to help fill in the gaps." She rubbed the bridge of her nose where her glasses had perched. "Any luck finding any artifacts at Rosco's?"

"No, ma'am."

"When's the funeral?"

"Couple more days. You know how black funerals seem to take a little longer. I think they wait on all the relatives to arrive."

The chief sipped her coffee, then sat quietly for a moment before saying, "I would like to know where Winston Walker was the night Rosco Jones died."

"Yes, ma'am."

"Anything else? Any issues at the casino?"

"No, ma'am. It's all running smoothly."

"Keep me posted. That's all for now."

Hoss stood and started out of the office, relieved to be leaving. He could tell she was in a bad mood, and he wasn't helping. He was almost out the door when she stopped him.

"Hoss?"

"Yes, ma'am."

"Don't forget your doughnuts."

◆ ◆ ◆

John Allen arrived at his parents' house before 8:00 a.m. He didn't have a normal eight-to-five work schedule since he ended up working lots of nights and Saturdays to look for artifacts. Today was Saturday, and he pretended to have to work so he wouldn't have to spend all morning listening to his parents and sister.

The four of them drank coffee and caught up on one another's lives—well, everyone except John Allen, who still kept his secrets to himself. His sister complained about having a hard time finding a job, and his dad was enjoying his retirement. His mother was busy with planning a remodel of the kitchen cabinets and counters. Her biggest decision was whether to install granite or marble, and she couldn't make up her mind. John Allen voted for granite. He enjoyed his parents, but today, for some reason, he didn't want to hear about their issues. And he didn't want French toast like when he was a boy. He needed to drive and to listen to the radio like he had when he'd been in high school. John Allen needed to blow the cobwebs out of his mind, then get to work.

After he left his parents' house, he pointed the Porsche northeast toward Philadelphia. He planned to be there in time to eat lunch at Peggy's and enjoy some home-style cooking. Since working for the Choctaw Nation, he'd fallen in love with the restaurant, and not a week went by that he didn't eat there.

He'd been heading north along State Route 25 for fifteen minutes and listening to talk radio when his phone rang. He didn't recognize the number but still punched the green button.

"Hello?"

"Is this John Allen Harper, the artifact collector?" a well-spoken man's voice asked.

"Yes. How can I help you?"

"I have something that you may want. I'd love to bring it to you and talk."

"Sounds interesting," John Allen said. "Who is this?"

"Let's just say I am going to be your new best friend."

John Allen scowled at the phone. "I really need a few more details before I can set up a meeting."

"Would you be interested in a museum-quality seed-storage pot from the Tombigbee River Basin?" the voice asked.

John Allen's mind raced. It would be a great purchase. But who was this? "How did you get my number?"

"From you," the voice said, and laughed. "I have one of your business cards."

John Allen had given out cards all over the state to anybody who would take one. They generated inquiries weekly. "This pot, is it authentic?"

"Oh, yeah."

"Where do you want to meet? I can come to you."

"Why don't we do this at your place?" the man suggested cheerfully. "That may put your mind at ease."

John Allen tried to think. It wasn't like he could bring anyone to the Choctaw Nation office. That would not only blow his cover but also would be certain to jack everything up. People would be scared they were doing something illegal or see big dollar signs. He didn't really have a place other than his barn house, and he didn't intend to bring anyone there, either.

"Not a good idea. My place is kind of a mess right now. Where are you located?"

The man was quiet a moment, then sighed. "Well, let's keep you comfortable. I'm in Meridian. How about this afternoon, say four o'clock? Is that doable?"

John Allen looked at his watch. He could easily make four. He could even eat at Peggy's and make the meeting. Perfect. "Yeah, I can do that. Where do you want to meet?"

"Meet me at the Pop A Top bar. Do you know where it is?"

"No, but I can find it," John Allen said. "How will I know you?"

"You'll know. I'll stand out."

"So you're not going to tell me your name?"

"Do you really need to know?"

John Allen tried to think of a solid comeback, one that wouldn't just earn him another smart-ass comment from the guy. But nothing came to him. He could tell this man liked to play games.

"It would just be nice to know."

"All you need to know is I have a pot that you'll want to purchase, and you'll need to bring $10,000 in cash."

"Jeez! That's a lot of money."

"I thought you were—well, your card says you're a collector of high-value artifacts. Perhaps I misunderstood," the man said in a sarcastic tone. "Are you not interested?"

This wasn't a college kid selling Grandpa's old rocks. A tiny red flag went up in John Allen's mind, but it was clouded over by the thought of returning a perfect seed pot to the Choctaw Nation, where it belonged.

"Yes, I am interested, but I will need to examine it first. I'll be there at four."

"Whatever you need to do."

"And if I'm gonna give you anywhere close to that amount of money, I'll need a name."

The man laughed into John Allen's ear, giving him a creepy feeling about this call. The guy was way different from anyone he'd talked to before. He certainly didn't recall giving him his card.

"When the time comes," the guy said. "But you won't be sending me a 1099 form."

The line went dead, and John Allen looked at his phone, his heart pounding. This was what he'd been working toward. Finally, he had a big fish on the line.

◆ ◆ ◆

Federal agent Emma Haden sat in a government-issued black sedan with another agent and watched for a silver Toyota four-door. Their car was partially hidden in a giant cornfield, and the agents appreciated the fact that they could remain in the air-conditioning. It was much too hot to hide in the five-foot-tall corn that was just starting to tassel.

The agent paired with Emma Haden didn't talk much while on stakeout. He had three young kids at home and a wife who wasn't happy being married. Consequently, he didn't get much peace and quiet after work hours. He took advantage of any downtime while on surveillance to sleep. Emma didn't really mind except when he snored. She drew the line at snoring.

She punched him, and he grunted as he turned slightly to alter his breathing.

"You're probably a candidate for a sleep-apnea machine," she said as she studied the field in front of her for movement. A half mile in the distance, she could see the yellow crop-duster airplane where it sat on the tarmac. Their car was parked on a high spot in a cornfield that gave her a view of the small airport and its two points of access. If another car approached, she would see it in advance.

"I got one."

"Yeah?" she asked, checking the temperature gauge on the engine. She didn't want the car to overheat. "Does it work?"

"It's amazing, but it absolutely ruined my sex life."

Agent Haden laughed out loud at the thought of her partner wearing the mask with its long connected hose. "I'm pretty sure you're supposed to take it off first."

"Very funny," the agent replied without stirring. "Seriously, she changed the way she looked at me after I got the damn thing."

Emma doubted that had been the turning point, but she could agree that it probably contributed.

"Maybe you should lose a few pounds?"

The agent groaned. "Not you, too. I get this shit all night at home."

Agent Haden didn't try to hide her smile, and she didn't care, either. "Is it that bad?"

"It's freaking miserable."

Agent Haden laughed again. She enjoyed most stakeouts. The close proximity created a camaraderie that allowed the real person to come out. She got along with most of the guys and other female agents, though there were a few who made a stakeout more drudgery than usual.

"My wife goes on Facebook," her partner went on, "and sees all her friends going on vacations, with new houses and just generally better lives, and she gets depressed. If we plan anything, nine times outta ten I have to cancel and go do something like this shit. I miss more important events than I make, it seems. Last week I missed swimming-lesson graduation."

Emma looked at her phone and once again saw that it had no data service and only one bar of cell service that was hit-and-miss. She was interested in her partner's problems but couldn't solve them. In fact, you could insert the names of any of the twenty agents she worked with into the conversation. It fit all their lives. They were overworked and stressed to the max. It wasn't like they finished a project and went home. The job followed them everywhere they went.

"What are you gonna do?"

"If she ends up leaving me, I just hope she remarries soon so I don't have to pay alimony any longer than I have to," the agent said, almost snickering.

"That's your best option? It doesn't sound like a plan that's been well thought out."

"It feels like my only option. At this point I'm not thinking things through, I'm just reacting," he said, remaining in his relaxed position.

The handheld radio crackled. "Unit one to unit three, over."

Emma grabbed her radio. "Unit three, go."

"Any movement, over."

She laughed at the intensity of the agent on the other radio, who just couldn't help adding the annoying "over" to every transmission.

"Negative. No movement here." Agent Haden studied the terrain in front of her. Nothing had moved since they arrived. Two black ribbons of asphalt split the agricultural fields and ran by the grass airstrip. And so far no vehicles had approached the area.

"Ten-four. Over."

Chapter 22

Winston had forgotten that he had the old Indian seed pot. It had completely slipped his mind. A while back, he'd helped a friend hide his stolen artifacts for a few months, and the guy had given him some cash for his trouble. In Winston's mind it hadn't been enough, so he'd stolen one small pot for all his trouble. The guy would probably never miss it, or it would be a long time before he ever did. Now he dug the artifact out of his safe. It was wrapped up in his ex-wife's Victoria's Secret robe. He would take a chance and try to turn this chunk of clay into some cash.

The Moundville artifact heist had happened a long time ago, and the criminals had been forced to move the artifacts several times when circumstances required or law enforcement got too close. Originally, they'd been stored in an unsuspecting grandmother's storm cellar. It had been a perfect hiding place until she'd died unexpectedly and the family suddenly had buyers walking around uninvited.

The thieves had expected to unload the artifacts within the first year, but the small world of museum curators had made the stolen artifacts known to other museums and legal collectors. These items were very high profile in the artifact world.

As Winston unwrapped the pink robe, he saw that the pot was still intact. How could he have forgotten this gem? It would help solve some temporary cash problems, and if he could keep it along with John Allen Harper's money, that would be even better.

As he sat looking at the vessel, his phone dinged with the arrival of a text. Already feeling good, he grabbed his phone and saw that Runt's girlfriend needed him, which meant she needed his drugs. Runt was at the chicken plant right now, and she wanted to see Winston.

He had time. Today was going to be a good day. He wrapped the pot back up and set it in the corner of his office for later.

◆ ◆ ◆

John Allen drove straight to his office in the tribal admin building in Philadelphia. It was just a simple cubicle in a larger room. There were no photographs, plaques, or awards on the wall. On his small desk sat a half dozen books about Native American culture and artifacts. Outside his cubicle, the day seemed to be progressing normally. The office was busy with its usual functions. No one even noticed him. His in-box contained an interoffice e-mail announcing the funeral arrangements for Rosco Jones. He hadn't thought about Rosco lately. He wondered whether Hoss had learned anything new. Suicide was such a hard thing to accept.

John Allen tried to call Hoss, but he didn't answer. A quick check with his office staff revealed that he was at the casino working on a security-camera issue. John Allen's next call was to Emma. He hoped he wasn't interrupting something important, but the call went straight to voice mail. She had warned him that she didn't expect to have good cell service.

John Allen decided he would eat lunch, probably by himself, then prepare to meet the seller in Meridian. There really wasn't anything to plan for; however, he did wonder whether this seller and Winston Walker could be associated. Maybe even the same person. He hadn't forgotten that Meridian was the last-known whereabouts of the agent who'd disappeared. He would take precautions, but first he wanted some fried green tomatoes.

◆ ◆ ◆

Hoss was busy with a security nightmare at the casino. The previous night a trio of crazy Cajuns had been up from Louisiana for a gambling weekend. His team was sure one of them had been counting cards as they played blackjack. Another had gotten so drunk he couldn't sit on a stool and had ended up making a huge scene before security could get him out of the casino. The third, convinced that security had arrested his friend, had driven his pickup through the front doors in an effort to rescue him.

It was a miracle no one had been killed. There were destroyed furnishings and broken glass everywhere. The place was a mess. It wasn't until $40,000 in chips was discovered missing that Hoss and his team had realized it all may have been a diversion to cover up a bigger operation.

Now he was pissed and had everybody locked in separate rooms with the tribal police ready to take over. He couldn't get it out of his mind that of the three guys, two had been in no shape to evade capture. What kind of scheme was that? They had to have known they would get caught. One had been too drunk to stand up, and the driver of the truck had been pinned inside the vehicle, making his apprehension simple. The third, the card counter, was the one they were still trying to account for, and so far they hadn't seen video of him doing anything that resembled stealing chips.

Something else was amiss. There were forty seconds of video they couldn't see clearly. The impact of the vehicle had shorted out part of the electrical system, and in the darkness, the thief, or thieves, had grabbed the chips. Hoss had locked down the cages, and no one was to be given any large payouts without a floor supervisor's approval. But he couldn't just shut it all down; the honest patrons would get upset and might not return. They would call the chief, and she would call him. Nothing was ever easy.

The table with the missing chips had been manned by a dealer whom Hoss knew personally. He didn't think she would be part of a scam. He dreaded calling the chief. These sorts of events were always frustrating, and he had to fight hard to resist the urge to beat the truth out of someone. That was his style.

Hoss leaned against the dented Ford truck and tried to make sense of the situation. He realized it could have just been someone walking by at the time, an opportunist. The casino was full of those types of characters most nights. He needed an Advil.

◆ ◆ ◆

John Allen was unable to talk to Agent Haden or to Hoss before he left to go to Meridian, but he sent them detailed texts explaining where he was going, the purpose of the meeting, and the fact that he didn't know exactly whom he was meeting.

The road from Philadelphia to Meridian went by quickly in the Porsche until he was stopped by a Mississippi state trooper in Lauderdale County. The officer walked around the car and whistled. He wasted no time in writing a ticket to John Allen for traveling seventy-five in a fifty-five-mile-per-hour zone.

The Pop A Top bar address revealed itself through a Google search, and when John Allen pulled up, he instantly questioned the advisability of going into the place. The bar offered ample parking since there were only four other cars in the gravel lot. John Allen had a Filson briefcase containing $12,000, which the tribe had given to him to purchase artifacts. He quickly decided to leave it hidden in the car. Even though he was a law-enforcement officer when on tribal lands, that didn't carry any weight in the rest of the world. He couldn't legally carry his pistol into the bar but never considered leaving it behind. His sport coat would help conceal it. He hoped the bar had air-conditioning.

Before he got out of the car, he looked in the rearview mirror. He didn't know what he was getting into, but at least he was having fun doing it.

He checked his phone. He had no response from Emma to his text message, but Hoss had responded, telling him to be careful and to let Hoss know when he left the meeting. *Okay, good. Somebody knows where I am,* John Allen thought as he walked to the front door of the bar.

The place was exactly as he expected. It was a classic southern-roadhouse bar. You could drown your sorrows, drink away your pain, celebrate a victory, or get into trouble, all within the confines of its four cinder-block walls. The decor was mostly made up of signs donated by local beer distributors. There was a pool table and a couple of older deer-head mounts. There were a few patrons. One guy was watching the TV as if he were waiting to see himself on the screen, and another who looked like a Mississippi hippie was playing an antique pinball machine like his life depended on it.

John Allen was ten minutes early, and nobody in the joint paid him any attention, so he assumed the mystery seller hadn't arrived yet. He sat down at the bar and ordered a beer. The bartender set a cold bottle in front of him and slid over a bowl of peanuts. John Allen eyed the nuts suspiciously. He loved peanuts, but there was no way he was sticking his hand into that bowl. ESPN was on the television, and he was glad to have something to watch.

Within a minute or two, his phone rang. It was Emma, and she sounded pissed.

"Where are you?"

"I'm at this bar in Meridian, meeting a guy. I left you a text," John Allen said, knowing the bartender was listening.

"Dammit, John Allen, that's the bar where Winston Walker hangs out! You could be meeting with Walker!"

John Allen had considered this. He hadn't known the bar was Walker's hangout. But he had considered that Walker could be his seller, and he had a plan.

He had to be careful what he said. Everyone could hear him. The bar was not that big. "It will be fine. I have a plan."

"You're in the bar now?" she asked. Trying to think on the fly.

"Yes, that's right."

"John Allen, listen to me. You need to just get up and get out of there, and reschedule when we have backup and wireless mics."

"It's okay. Give me thirty minutes and I'll call you back."

"Is he there? Just say yes or no."

"No, not yet."

"Dammit, John Allen." She was pretty worked up. He could hear her breathing and thought he heard gravel crunching. He imagined her pacing in some parking lot. "Okay, okay. It'd take me an hour to get agents there to watch your back. That's worthless. If I call the Meridian police, there's no telling how they would handle the situation. They might even make it worse, might ruin whatever chance we have." She crunched and breathed for a few seconds. "There's also the chance that you could get some useful information."

"That's my hope, yeah."

She made a frustrated sound, then said, "John Allen, it's 3:55. You call me at 4:25, and do not leave that bar with him. Under any circumstances. Don't go anywhere alone with him. Do you hear me?"

"Yes, yes, I do. I'll call you," he said and hung up. Because the bartender was looking at him, for effect he added, "Women. Whatcha gonna do?"

The bartender smiled as if he knew, then both of them turned to watch Winston Walker and Runt stroll into the bar as if they owned it. Winston looked a little heavier than the photos John Allen had been shown, but clearly he wasn't into fitness.

John Allen faced the bar again. He tried to act calm and cool, but inside, his nerves were humming. The College World Series was being discussed on the TV over the bar, and it gave him something to look at.

A quick glance confirmed the skinny one was the guy he'd met at the Jackson gun show. No doubt about it. John Allen took a deep breath and exhaled. It was game time.

◆ ◆ ◆

The other agents had never seen Agent Haden this worked up. They'd endured a long day of surveillance with no success, and her shift was taking a break and planning for tomorrow. Some of the agents were stuffing themselves with truck-stop food, while others were drinking coffee. They all noticed her pacing in front, talking frantically on the phone to somebody.

When she came back in, she was unusually quiet, and Agent Garner asked her if the call had been personal or business.

"Business. Remember John Allen Harper, the Indiana Jones guy from the Choctaw Nation?"

"Yeah, I do," Agent Garner said. Then he sipped his coffee.

"He has a meeting going on right now with Winston Walker. He's trying to buy an artifact from him."

"This wasn't planned?"

"No, not at all. As you know, we were going to sting him soon, but we were assigned to this case. John Allen got a call out of the blue this morning, asking him to meet about this expensive artifact the guy has."

Everybody gave this some thought. Most knew at least the general outline of her work on the Winston Walker case. The coincidence that Winston would call was troubling to everyone. They dealt in coincidences all the time and didn't like them. Far too often, they turned out not to be coincidences at all.

"I'm gonna call the Meridian police and have a unit just hang out close to there," Agent Haden said, thinking out loud.

"Could spook the whole thing if Walker's nervous."

"Yeah, I know. I've thought of that, too."

"Can this guy take care of himself?" a young agent asked.

"To be honest, I just don't know."

"So are you worried that he's gonna booger up the case, or that something is going to happen to him?" Agent Garner asked, already knowing the answer.

She sighed. "He's smart, but I don't think he is criminal-savvy."

"That's not really an answer."

"Yeah, I am worried about him," she said. "So what?"

"It's okay. Just calm down. We haven't ever seen you care about anything except this job," he explained as he took out his cell phone. He pulled out his bifocals and searched for a name. "I know a man who's a detective with the Meridian police. I'll let you talk to him. He can do a drive-by and watch, and nobody will suspect anything. I hope he's working today and is close."

Agent Haden smiled and let out the breath she'd been holding since she got the text from John Allen. "Thank you."

Chapter 23

John Allen sat on his bar stool and acted as if he didn't have a care in the world. He watched Winston Walker take in the room as if he were looking for threats or opportunities. He didn't appear to be armed, though he could easily have a pistol on his ankle. He was wearing blue jeans and a Mountain Khakis short-sleeve shirt. Winston was about six feet tall and weighed at least 215 pounds, John Allen guessed. He looked like he hadn't done any hard work in his life. He had a goatee or a Vandyke—whatever facial hair is called when it's just mustache and chin hair. He could tell the man thought his shit didn't stink.

Taking a deep breath to calm himself, John Allen surreptitiously turned on the audio notes function of his iPhone, making it look like he was doing something like closing out Facebook, then slid the phone into his pocket.

The bartender handed Winston a bottle of beer even though he hadn't asked for one. He obviously had history here. The skinny one was ordering something from the bar while he checked his cell phone.

"Whose German race car is that outside?" Winston said as he took in the room, holding the beer bottle like a weapon. He knew exactly whose it was; he just wanted to jack with John Allen.

"That's mine," John Allen said and nodded his head.

"You overcompensating for something?"

John Allen chuckled. "Not at all. I just like the gas mileage."

"I bet you can get a lot of women with that ride," Runt said.

John Allen looked around the bar. There were no women to be seen. "Probably not here."

Runt was maybe five feet six and probably weighed 140 pounds soaking wet. His nickname fit him perfectly. He, too, tried to have some facial hair, but his genes were failing him miserably.

Winston waltzed closer, shifted his beer from weapon position to drinking position, and stuck out his hand to John Allen. "We talked on the phone," he said and squeezed, looking John Allen right in the eye.

"Yeah," John Allen said, and squeezed back.

"Fancy car. You must be selling a lot of something, or did your daddy give it to you?"

John Allen forced himself to laugh. "I quit talking about people's cars when I got outta high school."

Everyone in the bar laughed except for Winston, who cracked a slight smile.

"I came to buy a pot," John Allen said with a serious tone. "I trust you brought it."

Winston's smile broadened. "First things first. I'm just trying to decide who you are. Tell me about yourself. You look like a cop."

"You ever see a cop drive a Porsche?"

"No, but that doesn't prove anything. You wired?" He'd yet to break eye contact with John Allen.

"You've been watching too much television," John Allen said, and started wondering how he would explain his firearm if they found it.

"What do you do? Why are you interested in artifacts?" Winston asked as he sat down on the bar stool.

"I'm a certified public accountant by trade, and I have a client who loves artifacts. The best artifacts. And I help acquire them." John Allen thought his story sounded good. It helped that it was truthful.

"Who is he?"

"Who said it's a he? And I can't say."

Winston had been around stolen artifacts for a great deal of his life. He'd heard of a woman from Florence, Alabama, who had a massive collection. Could it be that this John Allen Harper worked for her? *Seems like she owned a car dealership,* he thought.

Runt sat down on the other side of John Allen. "Remember me?"

"Jackson gun show."

"That's right."

"What took you so long to call?"

"We were waiting until we had the right product, and we had to check you out."

"Just so you know," John Allen said as he opened his coat, "I am carrying. I don't go anywhere without it."

Winston wasn't smiling now. "That makes us even. But now I insist on Runt checking you for a wire."

John Allen held his arms up, and Runt patted his upper torso and checked each pocket of his sport coat. Then he patted him down from his ankles up. The others in the bar glanced their way for a second, then when Winston glared at them went right back to what they were doing. Finally, Runt looked in John Allen's wallet for a badge or anything that might indicate he was with law enforcement.

"I think he's clean," Runt said. "Unless it's so small I can't feel it."

"So what do you do?" John Allen asked Winston.

"I'm in the publishing business, and I dabble in artifact collections."

"You publish anything I may have heard of?"

"I doubt it, since we don't publish *Gentlemen's Quarterly.*"

John Allen laughed, and Winston saw him look at his watch.

"You got somewhere to be?"

"Look, I'm only here for the seed pot. That's it."

Winston looked hard at John Allen. He had navigated through life living on his senses, trusting his feelings, but he couldn't get a read on

John Allen. He looked like he could be a cop, but he didn't have the attitude that most cops gave off. Winston took a long pull from his beer.

John Allen couldn't tell whether Winston believed him—he was hard to read. His eyes were wild, and John Allen could tell he was a tormented soul.

He noticed the other patrons of the bar had quietly slipped out. The bartender was the only one left, and he was talking on the phone to someone. He didn't appear to be listening to their conversation at all. An idea suddenly floated through John Allen's mind, and he tried to hurriedly think it through. He decided to act on it.

"Listen, I'm here for the Indian pot that *you* called *me* about. I didn't set up this meeting."

Winston nodded in agreement, though his eyes were still narrowed as though his mind were racing, trying to make himself believe it was okay to talk business with John Allen.

John Allen decided to go all the way. "But while I'm here, do you know somebody that would be interested in buying an Indian skull?"

Winston was clearly caught by surprise. "You have a skull?"

"Yeah. My buyer doesn't like skulls and bones. Just arrowheads, spear points, pottery, and such."

"Where did you get it?"

"It was part of a bigger collection," John Allen said. He could tell that Winston was interested.

"It's authentic?"

"Oh, yeah. It's authentic."

Winston knew he could move a skull with one phone call or e-mail to his Japanese contact. The man loved Native American bones, and for the right quality, price was never an issue. He'd even buy the seed pot, but Winston knew he would beat him up over the price. He always did.

"Where is this thing?" Winston asked.

"It's out in the car."

Winston nodded at Runt, who went to the window to check the parking lot for surprises. A skull could fetch anywhere from $10,000 to $20,000, depending on the condition. When Runt nodded that the parking lot was clear, Winston looked at John Allen.

"Okay, let's see this thing."

"In here?"

"We're the only ones in here."

John Allen looked around the bar. It was just them and the bartender, who was still talking on the phone.

"I'll go get it," John Allen said, "but I wanna see your seed pot, too." John Allen figured he didn't have much to lose. If he could sell the skull to Winston, the FBI could arrest him later. If Winston were to steal the skull from him, he could still have the FBI arrest him. As long as John Allen didn't leave the premises with the man, he'd be safe. "I'll be right back."

"Runt, get ours," Winston said, grabbing a handful of peanuts.

As John Allen was leaving the bar, his eyes met the bartender's, and the man winked at him. That unnerved him. *What does that mean? Is he saying, "You're about to get screwed," or "I have your back"?*

John Allen walked outside, and the Mississippi heat and humidity settled around him. His heightened senses flooded him with data. The ever-present summer cicadas that most people didn't even notice were almost deafening. He checked the audio-notes app and saw that it was tallying up the minutes. He wondered how long it would last. The black Porsche was hot to the touch. Three cars away, Runt was digging in the back of a black Suburban with tinted windows. John Allen committed the tag number to memory. It could be useful to Emma. He grabbed the wicker box with the skull, but he didn't grab his money, which an inner voice told him to leave where it was.

On his way back inside, John Allen was shocked to see an owl sitting atop the shabby little bar's roof, watching the parking lot. You rarely saw an owl in daylight. This one seemed fearless and completely out of place. John Allen continued on toward the front door, with Runt falling into step right behind him, holding a package under his arm. Just before he opened the door, John Allen stepped back to see if the owl was really there or a figment of his imagination. Seeing it staring at him gave him a spooky feeling. He wondered if it was an Indian spirit overseeing the transaction of a sacred artifact.

"What you looking at?" Runt asked. "You haven't ever seen an owl?"

"Not in the daylight." John Allen said.

"I see 'em all the time."

John Allen thought if the owl was an Indian spirit, that comment made a lot of sense.

"Hawks, too?"

Runt looked at him like he was crazy. "All the time."

"I bet you do."

Back inside, Winston had started a second beer and was observing John Allen's every move as he approached him. The bartender was now busy organizing the cooler behind the bar and appeared oblivious to what was going on.

John Allen set the wicker box down in front of Winston. Runt set his package down as well, then checked his cell phone.

"There's your pot," Winston said calmly.

John Allen carefully withdrew the pot from its package and freed it from the pink, silky robe it was wrapped in. It was a gorgeous specimen. He had never seen a seed pot before. The Indians would use this vessel to store seed corn, or maize, as they called it, or any other valuable seeds they would save for the next year's crop. He knew that the Choctaw Nation would want this. He had to leave with it.

Winston smiled, pleased by John Allen's obvious appreciation of the pot, and opened the wicker lid and pulled back a velvet wrap revealing an orb of bone. Carefully he lifted the skull. He had no way of telling whether it was authentic, but he looked for obvious telltale signs. There were no fillings in the teeth that remained. That was good. There was no trauma to the skull, but it was obviously very old. Just how old he didn't know.

"Where did this come from?" he asked as he admired the object.

John Allen noticed that its presence did not have the same effect on Walker as it'd had on Emma and him. They'd both been creeped out by it, but if anything, Winston seemed to feed off the energy of the skull.

John Allen had already rehearsed a lie in his mind, a fiction that made sense to him. "Some artifact hunters along the Tennessee River in North Alabama found it. It was submerged in a mud bank near a known village that was flooded by the channelization of the river. The water and mud is thought to have preserved it."

Winston nodded. That made sense. North Alabama was a hotbed for artifacts along the river. He was now convinced that John Allen worked for the female collector he'd heard about. It made sense she would be spooked by the bones—they weren't for everyone. It took a special kind of collector to want human bones. Winston wanted the skull.

"How do I know it's an Indian skull?"

"How do I know this pot is for real?" John Allen parried.

It was an age-old problem for collectors. They could learn what to look for, but most weren't trained in identifying authentic artifacts. They acquired their patchy knowledge through comments they picked up along the way and a few books on the subject.

Winston slowly scrubbed his face with his right hand. He was clearly thinking. John Allen saw that Runt was texting, and the bartender was now polishing the far end of the bar.

"Do you want my seed pot?" Winston asked.

"How much?"

"Ten."

"I'll give you seven." John Allen loved to negotiate. "It's got a small crack, and it looks like somebody repaired it."

Winston hadn't studied it that closely. He had no idea whether it had been repaired or not. He didn't have any cash tied up in the vessel, so whatever he got was pure profit. Plus he was already ahead of what the Japanese would pay.

"It's a near-perfect specimen. Nine."

"I agree," John Allen said, "but nobody's paying that much for pots. I'll pay you eight in cash."

Winston smiled. He would take eight. "How much do you want for the skull?"

John Allen sipped his beer and noticed the clock read 4:21. He didn't need Emma calling him. "What are you offering?"

Winston had an idea. The previous night at the casino there'd been a flurry of excitement, and he'd stolen forty $1,000-denomination chips from a table. He couldn't believe his luck. He knew better than to try to cash the chips anytime soon; his plan had been to slowly cash them in, one at a time. The casino would no doubt be looking for the missing chips. He'd have to get several people to help him, and they would want a cut for the risk. If he could turn a portion of the chips into paying for this skull, though, then he'd be safe.

"I'd rather you tell me a price, and I'll tell you if it's fair."

John Allen didn't want to scare him off. He just wanted him to buy it. But to be believable, he had to act as if he knew it was valuable.

Winston figured the owner of the skull didn't want it. Like most folks, she was probably spooked by the idea of a skull, so she'd probably take any reasonable offer just to move it.

"This is your lucky day," Winston said as he reached for a cigarette. "That skull is probably worth ten, maybe eleven grand, but I'll pay you twelve if you'll take it in casino chips."

"Casino chips?"

"They're just like cash. They're from the Silver Star Casino in Philadelphia."

John Allen blinked his eyes, his mind racing. Could this be some kind of criminal loophole he hadn't anticipated? Could Winston squirm off the hook because he'd paid with chips instead of cash? The clock read 4:23. He needed to call Emma, and he needed this play to seem believable.

"If it's chips, make it fifteen grand."

Winston thought for a minute. It was all house money, and he was just turning chips into cash. This process would be faster for him. He nodded his agreement.

"I don't care what you tell your boss lady," Winston said. "Tell her you sold it for ten, and you keep five chips."

John Allen saw this as a chance to call Emma. He could explain to her what was occurring, and she could advise him. The clock now read 4:24. He nodded. "That's an interesting offer. I need to call my boss and make sure she's okay with the ten."

"Yeah, sure, go ahead. And get your money for my pot while you're out there."

John Allen nodded again. "Do you want to subtract what I owe you?"

"No. I need the cash."

John Allen stood to walk out into the parking lot. He liked the deal. It was all working out, and he was going to be able to call Emma on time. He pushed the door open, and once again the heat and the insect sounds overwhelmed him. He took out his iPhone and found it was still recording and had twenty-three minutes' worth. He pushed the red "Stop" button as he walked.

Inside the bar, Winston called Runt over. "When he comes back in here, you go out and tape this iPhone to the frame of his car. Tonight we'll use it to find out where he is, and we'll steal it all back."

◆ ◆ ◆

Agent Emma Haden was nervously pacing back and forth and checking her watch when her phone rang. She quickly hit the green "Accept" button.

"John Allen, are you okay?"

"Yes, I'm fine, but I can't talk long. I'm buying the pot from him, and he's buying the skull from me."

"Holy cow," she said. "Are his sidekicks with him? Can we get them, too?"

"The one called Runt is. He's been a part of the transaction for sure. Write this down. The vehicle they arrived in has a Mississippi tag number of NZK 297," John Allen said in a hushed voice as he walked away from the building.

"Got it," she replied. "Tell me more."

"I don't have time. There is one thing I gotta know before I go. If he pays me in casino chips, will that work as money for the bust?"

"Yes, we could prove their value. It should hold up."

"I thought so. I really need to go. I will call you back shortly. I don't want to say a time. This was nerve-racking."

"Just get it done and get out of there, John Allen. Oh, and if you get in trouble, the bartender is on your side. He's a plant from the Meridian police, who already had an operation going at that place. We just learned that, and he knows who you are."

John Allen pulled eight packs of cash from his briefcase as he listened to her. Each pack had a wrapper indicating it had been counted and was valued at a thousand dollars. "Good to know. I'll call you later."

John Allen took a deep breath, placed the cash in one pocket, then glanced around at the empty parking lot, which he imagined would be filling up soon as people got off work. He started a new audio recording and, after verifying that it was running, hurried toward the door to consummate their deal.

When he walked back in, he found a stack of bright yellow casino chips sitting next to his beer. He assumed there were fifteen of them. He saw that they were $1,000 chips and had the Silver Star logo on them. They looked official, although he'd never seen $1,000 chips before.

"And you can keep the robe," Winston said, pushing it toward him as John Allen counted out the packets of money. "Maybe your wife will like it."

Runt, who was talking on his phone, grabbed the skull and slipped outside while still talking. John Allen watched him leave and made eye contact with the bartender before turning to Winston.

"There's eight grand," he said to him, handing him the cash. "Don't spend it all in one place."

"You get some more bones, you call me."

"I don't even know your name."

"You have my number, though," Winston replied, then took a drag off his cigarette. He snapped his fingers at the bartender and pointed at John Allen. "Let me buy you a beer."

◆ ◆ ◆

Emma collapsed in the booth next to another agent. She picked a chicken wing off his plate and dipped it in ranch dressing while they all watched.

"You seem to be in a better mood," Agent Garner said.

"I think it's going to be okay," she said between bites, visibly relieved.

"So Indiana Jones did good?"

Emma smiled at the joke and tossed the chicken wing into the growing pile of bones.

"The best news is Winston Walker called him, so it helps us defend the case that we did not entrap him. He was predisposed to buy the skull and commit the crime. Our principal legal adviser will love that."

"I hope you can get him for more than that," Agent Garner said, sipping coffee.

"We will. We're getting at least one of his minions, and I think if we apply some pressure, he'll talk and we'll get what we need."

"You feel pretty confident."

"This case deserves a good break, and this may be it," she said.

As the group consumed coffee, Emma checked her phone for e-mails. The agents were talking about conducting surveillance again tomorrow when the crop duster prepared for his first flight. He planned to be in the air by 7:30, so he would start preflight checks at 6:30 and would be filling tanks by 7:00. They agreed that everybody had to be in position at 6:30 again in the morning.

"Does anybody think it's unusual that he wanted to pay for the skull with casino chips?" Emma suddenly blurted out.

"What casino?" Agent Garner asked.

"I don't know for sure. I assumed one of the Pearl River Resort casinos in Philadelphia."

"Golden Moon or Silver Star," an agent who liked to gamble commented.

"Uh-huh," Emma said. "I just thought that was a little odd."

Agent Garner had begun looking through his e-mails on his cell phone and found what he was looking for. "Listen to this, I got this alert a little while ago. The Silver Star Casino near Philadelphia, Mississippi, reported a theft of approximately $40,000 in chips today. The robbery occurred last night. Someone drove a pickup into the front lobby and knocked out power to part of the casino. In the darkness, someone grabbed the chips."

"How about that," Emma said.

"Would that fall under our jurisdiction?" someone asked.

"Not unless they ask for our assistance," Agent Garner said. "It would fall under the Bureau of Indian Affairs, and the tribal police would have the lead. It's all complicated up there, since the land is federal, but they are a sovereign nation. We can't just roll in there without being asked."

"Yeah," Emma said, "but you met the chief. You know she'd be all for our help if she thought she could get Winston Walker out of the population." She nodded to herself. "I need to talk to John Allen and that head-of-security guy," she said with a big sigh.

"You probably should go back to Jackson," Agent Garner said. "We can make this work up here." Everyone nodded. "And call us if you need some help."

◆ ◆ ◆

John Allen couldn't get out of the Pop A Top bar fast enough. He had the seed pot and was excited about getting it back to the Choctaws. He knew the chief would be proud of it.

As he backed up the car, he looked for the owl but didn't see it.

He thought the meeting had gone well. Winston had purchased the skull, which was exactly what Emma had wanted him to do. Without their assistance there wouldn't be an all-important recording of the event, but his testimony alone should carry the case. She briefly cussed his naïveté for not realizing how important that would be to the conviction.

As he pulled onto the paved road, he pointed his car toward Columbus and reminded himself not to get another speeding ticket. At the first stop sign, with no other vehicles in sight, he paused long enough to send Hoss and Emma a text saying he was out and that the meeting had gone well. They could call him if they needed him. After he hit "Send," he dropped the car into first gear and pulled away, leaving the underworld of Winston Walker in his rearview mirror.

He had traveled less than two miles when his phone rang, and Emma wanted a total recap. She was driving, also, and on her way back to Jackson. She listened to every detail and encouraged him to write it all down when he got home. She was pleased with the way the meeting had gone and promised to have Winston Walker arrested tomorrow.

Before she hung up, she asked John Allen to call her that night, and he gladly said he would.

The next call was from Hoss, who explained about the strange events at the casino the night before. He was certain that the chips John Allen had been paid with were the ones stolen from the casino, and that Winston or one of his crew probably had the remaining chips. They'd been reviewing footage and would know soon whether Winston had been in the casino that night.

John Allen promised to be at the tribal headquarters first thing in the morning and bring the seed pot for everyone to see. It would be a busy day.

◆ ◆ ◆

The bartender had watched Runt walk outside with the seed pot while he was talking on the phone, but he couldn't see Runt shimmy under John Allen's car and tape the iPhone to the frame.

While the bartender was helping a newly arrived customer, Winston informed Runt they were going to Columbus tonight. He didn't know exactly where, but Runt was to bring everything they might need to dispose of someone. Runt knew the plan and had the gear.

They finished their beer and were careful not to talk where anyone could overhear them. Winston gave Runt a $1,000 chip for motivation and said there would be another when they completed the job. When he had money, Winston was generous. When the money ran out, his generosity morphed into anxiety, and eventually, if more money wasn't handy before certain bills were due, desperation.

Runt texted his girlfriend and said he had to work tonight. She didn't immediately respond, and that aggravated him. It seemed that every interaction with her only deepened his certainty that she was seeing another guy.

Winston drained another beer and looked at Runt. "I need an alibi for tonight. You got any ideas?"

Runt looked around the bar. It was clear he was thinking. "Give me a few minutes."

Chapter 24

John Allen traveled back to his barn, feeling victorious. When he arrived home, there were still two hours of daylight left, and he was hungry. He carried the briefcase with the cash and casino chips into the house and left it next to the seed pot still wrapped in the pink robe. Seeing the robe wrapped tight around the pot gave him an idea of a prank he could pull on Hoss.

A quick look in the refrigerator revealed three bottles of Smartwater, four Coronas, five eggs, some cheese, and a jar of pickles. A check of the pantry revealed some Vienna sausages, a can of corned beef hash, a bag of Doritos, and a jar of roasted peanuts. As this was a hardly a supper fit for someone who had just successfully performed his first undercover operation, he decided to go to Harvey's and have a slab of prime rib.

After he hung up his sport coat, he considered changing shirts but decided against it since there was no one he needed to impress. He briefly paused at Sadie's picture and wished she were here to tell her the story of his day. She would have sat cross-legged on the couch and listened to every word he said. She would have asked more questions than he would have wanted to answer, but she would have been wide-eyed while listening to him. He realized again how much he still missed her. Every day got a little better, but moments like this were the worst.

After these deep thoughts, John Allen was no longer as excited as he had been earlier, but he was still hungry. He unclipped his pistol and laid it on the counter, grabbed his car keys, and punched his four-digit code into the alarm system's keypad by the door, then headed off for dinner.

As John Allen was eating an appetizer at the bar at Harvey's, he noticed Frank, the pain-in-the-ass accountant from his old office, walk in alone. Unsure why he was doing so, John Allen waved him over, and they ended up eating supper together.

Frank updated him with stories of the accounting world that made John Allen's skin crawl. He didn't miss it at all. Frank had achieved his dream of taking over John Allen's job, and the pressure of running the office was taking its toll on him. The owners of the firm would graciously allow him to work unpaid overtime, and Frank was gung ho enough to do it. Though Frank enjoyed being the boss, he was now facing the previously unseen challenges of motivating employees while also dealing with clients. The continual flow of new deadlines and constant complaining about the numbers was more than enough to make an accountant drink, and drink heavily. Or, in John Allen's case, get out.

John Allen enjoyed his night. He was so happy with the buzz from a top-shelf margarita, rare prime rib, and bread pudding that he didn't even mind spending an hour with Frank, who normally made him crazy. That never would have occurred when he'd worked at the firm. Walking out with him after their meal, Frank drooled over John Allen's Porsche. He ran his hands over the car's hood like it was a statue of a nude woman, and John Allen made a mental note to wash her tomorrow. The two men eventually ran out of things to talk about and shook hands.

On the drive home, John Allen was happier than he had been in a long while. He'd just been reminded of how lucky he was to be out of the accounting rat race, and he was proud of the role he'd just played in taking down suspected murderer and interstate criminal Winston Walker.

He was singing along with Neil Diamond when he remembered the audio recordings he'd made of his dealings with Winston and planned to listen to them when he got home. Afterward, he would call Emma. He wanted to talk to her about more than the case, but he didn't want to seem too interested.

This was bringing back how much he'd hated all the strategy of the early days of dating someone, and John Allen vowed to just put a stop to it. He promised himself to just do what he wanted and let things happen as they would.

◆ ◆ ◆

Runt and Winston used an iPad to track down the cell phone they'd attached to John Allen's car. They used a simple app called Find My iPhone. Winston was amazed by how well it worked.

By 10:00 p.m. the car had settled into a remote part of Lowndes County that was west of town and south of US Highway 82. Winston liked the fact that it was remote, as that meant fewer potential witnesses. An expert at the maps app, Runt quickly flipped to a satellite view in order to see the details about where they were going.

"Looks like it's an old barn," Runt said.

"Probably was when this picture was taken. I bet it's a house now."

"Yeah, you're probably right."

"Let's roll. We can be there by midnight. He should be wherever he's gonna spend the night by then, I would think," Winston pontificated.

"What's the plan, boss?"

"Let's go up there and see what the night gives us. It may be more than we expect, and it may be less."

◆ ◆ ◆

Emma hung up from an hour-long conversation with John Allen that seemed to last only ten minutes. It reminded her of how she'd felt in the ninth grade when a boy she was crazy about had called her. It was good to have her heart flutter again.

She'd explained that they planned to pick up Walker and Runt the next afternoon at the bar. The FBI felt they could utilize the bartender to tip them off as to when they arrived. She also fussed at John Allen for not immediately taking the pot and casino chips to the security office for safekeeping. They were evidence now, she explained, and they needed to do everything by the book to establish a clear chain of custody. Certainly he didn't have the training she'd thought he had.

There really wasn't much to worry about, though. They now had so many ways to charge Walker—buying and receiving illegal human remains; in possession of stolen chips from the casino; in possession of the seed pot, which was probably stolen; and probably, according to the bartender, in possession of meth rocks—that something had to stick. With any luck he'd have enough meth on him to be charged with intent to distribute, and there was still the whole Rosco mess to clear up. Emma felt good that she had Winston Walker and at least one of his crime partners.

All this combined was exactly the leverage she needed to make progress on solving the murder of Jim Hudson, which was her real goal. Tomorrow she would call his widow and bring her up to speed. It would be satisfying to have good news to give her.

Also, tomorrow she and John Allen had planned a dinner at a restaurant in Philadelphia, which she was looking forward to more than anything. She craved seeing and talking to him. Emma couldn't believe the way she was feeling. She hadn't thought she would ever feel this way again. John Allen had restored her faith in the male gender.

What should I wear? she thought.

Winston drove slowly, and Runt nervously twitched as the Suburban passed the gated entrance to where the iPad thought John Allen lived, or at least where the Porsche was parked. The dashboard clock of Winston's Suburban read 11:55 p.m., and the night was inky black. In the distance down the driveway they could see one security light on, and he thought they should give it one more hour to ensure John Allen was asleep. Some people were night owls, but shortly after midnight even they began to crash.

"Let's find us a construction site while we wait," Winston said. "I'd love to find one that's pouring concrete in the next few days."

"They're building that new golf course in West Point," Runt said. "It's called the Mossy Oak. I been hearing about it on ESPN radio."

"That's perfect. They're probably moving a lot of dirt and pouring some concrete somewhere. We have some time to kill, so let's go."

The two criminals drove toward the small town of West Point, Mississippi, which was only fifteen minutes from where the Porsche was parked. They saw a new Burger King under construction, but since it was on the highway, Winston was afraid someone would see them digging. They drove through Taco Bell and got some crunchy burritos off the dollar menu, then continued on toward the new golf course, which was across the street from the Old Waverly Golf Club.

Winston loved to golf and had played Old Waverly a number of times. He'd always wanted to own a condo on the property, for no other reason than to show the pricks he grew up with that he could. For a brief moment, Winston drifted into a trance. He'd grown up around the country-club set, and they'd never accepted him. Even when he had money, they blackballed him from Meridian's Northwood Country Club. He had spent half his life trying to be one of them, to get invited into their investment clubs and parties, but he'd never been successful.

He shook his head and came out of the trance, but the sour aftertaste it left lingered with him.

There was no one around when he drove into the construction entrance. He parked the Suburban, and they sat still with the lights off for five minutes by the clock. No one challenged them. There were two buildings already framed in, and bulldozers and front-end loaders parked randomly around the lot. There was a lot of work going on here, which only made the location more attractive as a dump site. Nobody would notice any digging, and it would be easy to conceal the grave because so much of the earth was already disturbed. Off to the side sat huge mounds of white sand that would soon be used to fill bunkers. When Winston saw the sand, he knew he'd found a good place to dispose of a body, and he knew something about hiding bodies.

Over the years he'd killed four men. He'd known the first one would never raise any concerns. He'd been a drug-addicted digger who'd hid a handful of ceremonial spear points from Winston. No one had ended up missing him.

The second had been an investigator for the Choctaw Nation who'd somehow gotten close to Winston and figured out what he was up to. For irony, Winston and Runt had buried his body on a very famous Indian mound, taking care to dig out the flora and fauna, then replace it perfectly. It was an unbeatable place to hide bodies. There was a fence around it to prevent anyone from walking on it, and nobody could legally disturb the mound. If law enforcement ever decided they wanted to dig, their efforts would be slowed, if not halted altogether, by the court system.

The third had been an employee who'd threatened to expose Winston's illegal and unethical magazine-publishing tactics to his client base. Winston had not only stopped him but also turned a profit on the deal because of the sympathy his death had created in his clients.

The fourth had been the janitor at the tribal-administration building. He was happy to make some extra cash by stealing a few artifacts that no one seemed to miss. But he'd gotten cold feet after taking a cache of treasures that Winston wanted. When he refused to sell them to

Winston and said he was going to return them, it got ugly for the man who had no idea how desperate Winston Walker was at that moment.

Breathing in the night air, Winston considered himself a criminal genius, and he determined that this new golf course, still under construction and with all its piles of fresh dirt, would be another great place to hide a body.

"Let's go," he said to Runt as he started up the Suburban. "We can make this work. We just gotta be out of here well before daylight. They'll probably start working at the crack of dawn to beat the heat."

Chapter 25

Hoss had been up late into the night, trying to make sure a construction crew had secured the front lobby of the casino. The construction workers themselves made Hoss nervous. They all looked like opportunists to him. Trusting people had never been his strong suit.

The chief hadn't said much that afternoon as he'd shown her the damage to the entrance of the beautiful structure. She'd been certain they could rebuild better and install barriers to prevent something like this from happening again. She was holding Hoss responsible for making sure none of the cashiers paid out on any suspicious $1,000 chips.

That night the female FBI agent had called him and asked for details. Upon learning the denomination of the chips, she was convinced Winston Walker was somehow involved. If they could match the casino's chips with the stolen ones, it would further cement a case against Walker. Hoss didn't like having extra law-enforcement agencies on his turf any more than necessary—but in this case, he knew he had to. He welcomed the FBI's help and said that she could consider their phone call a formal request for assistance.

Hoss knew the FBI had a lot more assets than the tribal police did to help make the case against Walker. His only request was that the FBI allow Hoss's team to participate as much as they could. It would be a good learning experience for them. Agent Haden agreed.

Chapter 26

At 1:13 a.m., Winston killed the Suburban's headlights and turned into the gravel driveway that was blocked thirty feet or so in by an old metal gate. Weeds were grown up next to either side of the entrance, making it look like it was seldom used. The iPad said the Porsche was parked at an old barn about a half mile across a field. Winston was convinced the map wasn't current and there was a home back there. He didn't trust the technology.

As he slowly pulled up to the gate, they were surprised when it opened automatically. Winston saw the motion sensor, then worried it might have a bell that would alert the house.

"Dammit," he said. "I wasn't expecting that."

"We going in anyway, aren't we?"

"Hell, yes."

With his pistol in his lap and Runt holding a second one, Winston crept down the gravel road. The river gravel popped under his tires, and he kept his speed as low as possible to minimize the noise. After about a quarter mile he saw the outline of a structure. It looked like an old barn. The security light they'd seen before was out. That was good.

"You think he has a dog?" Runt said.

"I don't know. Probably." Winston parked the vehicle and cut the engine. "This silencer will help with that."

"I hate killing dogs. They're just doing their job," Runt said, glad he didn't have the silencer.

"I don't mind," Winston said, opening the vehicle door quietly. "Get your stuff and let's go." He had rigged the overhead light to not turn on.

The night was dark, and stars filled the sky. Off to the east he could see the white glow of lights from Starkville, and back to the northwest, the lights of Columbus.

The building appeared to be just an ordinary old barn. No dog ran out to greet them or to alert anyone of their approach. Upon closer study, the Porsche could be seen in a side stall of the barn—new, clean German precision parked under an old, rusty barn built by people nowhere near as precise as the Germans.

A newer-model Jeep TJ sat under a large oak tree. *Maybe his wife's vehicle,* Winston thought.

"Get the phone from under the car," Winston whispered. "I'll wait." Runt scurried off to get it done. They couldn't leave that behind in case they didn't steal the car. When it came to crime, Winston was thorough and didn't like to leave loose ends.

When Runt returned with the phone, he found himself wishing they had a flash bomb like the police used. It would stun anyone in the room and render them defenseless for a brief period. He had experienced one a few years back, and they were very disorienting. Without it, they would just have to enter as silently as possible and hope for the element of surprise.

The barn was confusing. There were no windows and only one door. But the grass was cut, and a few bushes had been planted. He must have the inside fixed up, Runt determined, after they'd made a quick circuit around the place.

They shined a small light on the door locks. Standard doorknob, but above it was a heavy brass dead bolt.

"Can you unlock it?" Winston asked in a whisper.

"The doorknob lock, yes. The dead bolt? No, I don't think so," Runt whispered back. He could tell by the accelerated whistling of Winston's nose that he was pissed and added, "I'm just being honest."

Winston had never encountered a house without windows or at least a sliding glass door. Who in hell lived like this? If there was a fire between the man and his one door, he'd burn to a crisp. Winston was tempted to light one just to prove it to him, but that wouldn't get him what he wanted.

He forced himself to calm down and start thinking about a Plan B. If he could get John Allen out here, he'd have the advantage.

His eyes were adjusted to the darkness now, and he felt he owned the night. "Go see if you can break in to his car. It's okay if an alarm goes off. If it doesn't, see if you can crank it. He'll hear the engine and come running out here. I'll hide here in the shadows and jump him when he runs out."

"Got it," Runt said with enthusiasm. He had stolen lots of cars but never a Porsche. After two steps he stopped and softly added, "Do you think he has a wife in there?"

"He had on a wedding ring," Winston whispered, then formed a devilish smile. "We can hope."

Winston eased into position behind the door. John Allen wouldn't be able to see him until he stepped outside. The open door would block his view.

Runt had been gone about a minute. Winston had no idea what Runt was doing, but he expected to hear the car crank soon. He could be patient.

The car was locked. Runt didn't see any intermittently flashing light that would indicate an alarm was set, so he pulled a Slim Jim out of his bag and intended to slide it down the window, just like he'd done dozens of times on American-made cars. He slid the thin bar down, and as soon as it hit some interior structure, the alarm went off in a cacophony of blaring horn and flashing lights, sending Runt scrambling back away from it.

Winston shook his head and mumbled under his breath, "Well, that will do it."

He positioned himself to be ready.

John Allen thrashed awake from a deep sleep and struggled for a few seconds to make sense of the wild sounds. His car. Someone was trying steal it, or a cat had jumped on the hood again. Not taking any chances, he snapped on a light and ran for his pistol. At the door he slipped into his boots and jacked a shell into the chamber, then turned the dead-bolt lock and yanked open the door.

Standing there in his boxers and boots, he could see the lights flashing from his car at the end of the barn. He flipped on the outside security light. He didn't see anyone running and couldn't hear anything with the car horn blaring. There were no neighbors to worry about disturbing, so he let it continue to go off.

He started toward the car with his pistol ready, then the world went dark.

Winston had allowed John Allen to exit, and when he'd turned away, he'd knocked him unconscious with the butt of his pistol. He'd collapsed in a satisfying heap at Winston's feet, then sorted himself out on the gravel, so he looked for all the world like he was napping there on his side—but for the trickle of blood oozing down the side of his head.

After checking to make certain his victim was out cold, Winston rushed into the house and started flicking on lights, clearing each room in turn, expecting to hear a woman scream. His first pass revealed no other occupants, though, and he quickly found the key for the car and pressed the "Unlock" button to kill the alarm. The silence relieved him.

Runt came running into the room. "Secure him," Winston instructed him, and he instantly obeyed.

The barn was actually a house, or the house was a barn, depending on how you looked at it. Winston liked the simplicity of it. He took another tour of the place to make certain there wasn't a wife hiding under a bed or in a closet, then went back to the den to learn a bit about John Allen.

There was a briefcase with cash and the casino chips. The seed pot sat next to it, still wrapped in the same robe. *This is too easy,* Winston thought.

Outside, Runt had quickly zip-tied John Allen's hands behind his back and, once he was secure, placed two fingers on his throat to make certain he was still alive. He noticed the blood beginning to pool under his head, but he didn't care. He stood up and looked around to see whether anyone was approaching, and seeing nothing, he gazed about for something else to steal. The first thing he grabbed was John Allen's pistol.

Inside, Winston marveled at the barn's interior. It was like a brand-new house on the inside. There weren't any pictures on the wall, and the furniture was just placed for function. There was no woman's touch. Winston knew because he had lived in a female-influenced house, and he had also lived without.

He looked under the bed and in closets, searching for anything of value. There wasn't much. There was a heavy-duty gun safe. Winston tried to open it, but it was locked. He wondered what was inside but was smart enough to know better than to waste any time on it.

"Damn bachelor pad," he mumbled, realizing there wouldn't be any jewelry or silver. Grabbing John Allen's wallet and walking back into the den, he saw a pile of papers on the bar that separated the room from the kitchen area. Bills and a payroll stub. The stub interested him. He was curious about how much the man made being an accountant.

"Choctaw Tribal Nation?" he said out loud. That was a troubling coincidence.

Winston searched through more papers for clues to the identities of any of John Allen's other clients. He was about to give up when he found an insurance guidebook from the Choctaw Tribal Nation.

"I'll be damned," he said. The man was an *employee* of the tribe.

The implications of this discovery filtered into his brain. "Hey, Runt!" he hollered out the door. "This piece of shit works for the Choctaw Nation. I bet he's an Indian cop," Winston said with pure contempt.

"I knew he smelled like a pig!" Runt said as he walked in the door.

"Be careful not to leave any prints anywhere," Winston said. "I haven't found a badge, but look in his wallet." He tossed him the leather wallet.

Runt caught it, and before he opened it up, he looked around the den. "He sure ain't got much shit," he said with a laugh.

"More than you. I bet he just got a divorce," Winston said, pointing at a framed photo on the end table of a smiling woman at the beach. "And I bet she cleaned him out."

"He's got an expensive ride out there."

"That's his bait to catch his next woman, is all. That's just a monthly payment. They finance those cars for ten years. Trust me. That ain't shit."

Runt, who wasn't known for his superior intellect but did have a mind for police procedures, began to be puzzled by recent events. "So why didn't he bust us yesterday after you bought that skull?" he asked, already trying to distance himself from the crime.

Winston wondered about this, too. He couldn't understand why he hadn't been arrested yesterday, unless they were trying to sucker him into a bigger purchase. Would a more expensive artifact carry a stiffer penalty than the skull? He didn't know for sure, but he didn't think so. Hell, he wasn't a lawyer, but he knew he had committed enough of a crime to do some serious time—ten years, probably. Recently they'd started trying to make examples of artifact pillagers.

He had to think through the situation. He had the pot. He looked in the briefcase and put his hands on the casino chips and cash. *Good, good, good.*

Walking around, Winston's mind was racing. Now he knew the woman John Allen worked for was the Choctaw chief, the most powerful person in a very influential tribe.

"He didn't bust us yesterday 'cause he ain't a real cop," he said. "Maybe on the tribal lands, but not out here. He was just setting us up. That son of a bitch." He kicked over a chair.

Runt was busy pillaging the wallet. "No badge, sixty bucks in cash, a speeding ticket, and—wait, here it is, a photo ID for the Choctaw Nation. You're exactly right."

"I can't believe I was so stupid. I'm careful all these years, I drop my guard for a few minutes, and now this. This is all your fault, you know," Winston said, growing angrier and thinking about the seed pot. "All for a shitty $8,000!"

Runt knew what was coming now. Winston had a temper that would intimidate an MMA fighter when he got mad. He needed to manage him. "What do you want me to do, boss?"

"Shut up and let me think. Go load his ass into the back of the Suburban."

"I want his boots."

"I don't care and he don't need 'em," Winston said, exasperated.

Winston had dealt with a Choctaw agent before—he'd killed him and had hidden his body, and nobody had ever found it. Now he was going to have to do it again, but he didn't have much time to plan. One good thing about being a career criminal, though—he knew how to operate on the fly and cover all the critical bases. This was all second nature to him. But he couldn't overlook any details here or they'd bite him in the ass. He had to watch Runt, too. The man was no kind of thinker, and his mistakes could take them both down.

Winston stood looking at the inside of the barn, soaking in the scene. He slowly turned and looked outside. Runt had the Choctaw agent by the armpits and was struggling to drag him through the gravel toward the Suburban, rather than thinking to ask Winston to move the rig closer to the downed man. Yes, Winston would have to watch him like a hawk.

Or better yet, he could take the blame, he thought, and smiled.

Chapter 27

Winston and Runt took one more hurried look around the barn for any remaining traces of their visit and anything they might want. Runt took John Allen's guitar, a pair of Costa sunglasses, and the only beer left in the fridge. Winston took a Bertucci watch and, turning to leave, told Runt to put the wallet on the counter and grab the keys to the Porsche.

"Why can't I take the wallet?"

"Because your dumb ass will forget it, and some police officer will search your truck at some point and bust you," Winston said emphatically.

Once outside, Runt wanted to burn down the house, but Winston shot that down. "If we torch the place, someone will see the flames, and they'll start looking for John Boy. Right now we have a good twelve-hour head start before anyone should be looking for him."

Though Runt nodded his understanding, even in the darkness Winston could see he was disappointed. He couldn't tell whether that was because Runt wasn't going to get to burn the house, or whether he was frustrated that he hadn't himself reasoned through the risks. "That ain't much time, really," he pouted.

"It's plenty if we're smart," Winston said, looking at John Allen lying in the back of his Suburban. At least he had a plastic cargo tray that was catching all the blood. He would toss that out later, after they'd disposed of the body.

He checked his watch. Almost 2:00 a.m. "I tell you what," he said. "We don't know our way around that golf course well enough to navigate it in the darkness, and with all that construction going on, we might bury him someplace that they'd dig up in a few days. Let's stick with what we know and take him to the hunting camp. Nobody will be there, and we can get organized. We can dump the body in the same Indian mound as the other agent."

Runt thought about what needed to be done. Winston wouldn't be much help, if any. All the manual labor would be Runt's to do. They were almost two hours from that site. He'd have to carefully dig out and place the body, then pack it back with the same vegetation after removing the excess dirt. There was no way he could get all that done before daylight. He'd run a huge risk of being seen when the sun came up.

"You think we have time tonight?"

"I don't know," Winston said as he shut the back doors. "Maybe not."

Standing in the darkness, Winston looked around him. They could come after him tomorrow, but he had all the evidence with him. He opened the passenger-side door and placed the briefcase and the robe-wrapped pot on the front seat. Without the evidence, what kind of case would they have?

"Now, Runt, we'll have to play it cool when they ask us questions."

Runt nodded. "When do you think that will be?"

"Hell, it could be tomorrow. It all depends on who knew what he was doing," Winston explained in a quiet voice.

"How long did it take them to ask you questions about the other guy?"

"They never did," Winston said with a smile.

"Never?"

"Ever."

Winston opened the backseat door, took out the wicker box with the skull in it, and handed it to Runt. "We'll leave this here. It's probably not even real, and it may have a tracking device."

"Yeah, that's smart."

"Look, we'll tell them that we met with him at the bar, and he tried to sell us a skull, but we didn't buy it. They won't be able to prove anything now, and I have all the chips back, and—oh, yeah," he said, opening the passenger door and grabbing the briefcase. He quickly took the cash out and stuffed it in his pocket. "Put this on the counter inside." Since the briefcase was heavy canvas fabric, he didn't worry about fingerprints.

Winston had shut the door and was walking fast around the back of the truck when Runt emerged from the structure.

"Now what we need, Runt, my boy, is an alibi for tonight."

"You got any ideas?"

"Your girlfriend."

"My girlfriend?"

"We'll get her to lie for us."

Runt stared at the silhouette of Winston and blinked his eyes. He was unsure how this would work.

"You drive his car," Winston said. "We'll meet at the hunting camp. Check the gas gauge. We don't need any surprises." He calmly climbed into his Suburban as if he were leaving a party, and drove away.

Smiling at the thought of driving the Porsche, Runt tossed the keys up in the air and grabbed them as he jogged to the car.

◆ ◆ ◆

When John Allen awoke, he couldn't move. Worse, he had no idea where he was or why he couldn't move.

The back of his head was throbbing, and he could feel warm blood in his scalp. His hands and feet were bound, and he had a rag stuffed in his mouth. It tasted like a filthy sock. A bolt of fear shot through his body, and panic swept through his mind. His limbs ached, and the restraints cut painfully into his wrists when he tried to move them. They felt like plastic, and he assumed they were large zip ties that he knew would be impossible to break.

His mind finally processed that he was in the back of an SUV traveling at a high rate of speed. It was dark out. Turning his head to see out the back window, he could just see reflections from the dashboard. The radio was silent, and the only sound was road noise. Occasionally bright lights flashed through the vehicle.

The last thing he remembered was his car alarm going off. He recalled grabbing his pistol, opening the door, and seeing the reflections from his car's flashing lights.

He realized all he had on were boxer shorts, but modesty wasn't his concern. The desire to free his hands overwhelmed him, and he yanked and twisted until his shoulder felt like it was going to pull out of its socket. The effort left his chest heaving, his struggle for breath hindered by the awful-tasting material packed into his mouth. He tried to spit it out and gagged. He had to calm his breathing or he was going to have a panic attack. He strained once again, and this time his shoulder did pop, causing him to scream into the sock.

"Hey, calm down back there!" a sinister voice responded.

John Allen knew that voice. *Winston Walker!*

"Just relax and enjoy your last ride," Winston said, then laughed.

◆ ◆ ◆

At 2:33 a.m. Emma woke and couldn't go back to sleep. Her mind overflowed with thoughts of arresting Winston Walker and the satisfaction it would bring Jim Hudson's widow.

Annoyed by her restlessness, Billy Joel stretched his back into an arch, then jumped down to find a quieter spot to snooze.

Emma tossed in her bed and stared at the clock. Her mind drifted back to the crop duster, and she wondered how that case would play out. If the suspect didn't return while they had the surveillance going, they might never catch him. There were probably dozens of crop dusters in the delta. Ideally some vigilant citizen would jot down a tag number or snap a picture of him with their phone, but they couldn't count on that. Tomorrow she'd search the Internet and put together a list of crop dusters. And she'd get Louisiana and Arkansas involved, since they were also huge farming states.

Emma took a deep breath, then let it out. The pace of her job never slowed, and there was never any end in sight. Crimes were committed every day, faster than the Bureau could hope to clear cases. The work piled up. People wanted answers and justice. Her superiors wanted cases closed and convictions. Everybody wanted something, and the agents and other law-enforcement officers had lives as well. They had families and obligations, just like anybody working a traditional nine-to-five job. Only most in law enforcement couldn't leave their work at the office. The job was constantly bubbling up in their thoughts. Consequently, the divorce rate was high, especially for detectives and investigators. She herself had contributed to that statistic, though in her case it had clearly been his fault. The bastard couldn't keep it in his pants. But had she been emotionally unavailable for him? Had she been consumed with her work?

Emma stared into the darkness, mentally reliving those years. Sure, she'd been an aggressive agent. She'd always felt she had to work harder and smarter to earn the respect of her male counterparts and superiors. But she had been there for her husband, she decided. It was his wandering eye and lust for something different that had caused the downfall of their marriage. The Internet had just provided the means by introducing him to a busty Brazilian aerobics instructor named Roseanne. Emma wasn't upset or jealous anymore. In fact, she liked the way her life had turned out, except she did want a family. Although Billy Joel was great company, he wasn't quite enough.

After twenty more minutes of tossing and turning, she got up to take a sleeping pill. She needed rest for tomorrow, since it was going to be a red-letter day. Before she could make it to the bathroom, Billy Joel had slipped back into the room and reclaimed his place on the bed.

Her iPhone was plugged into the wall and charging, and as she was climbing back into bed, she grabbed it to see whether she had any e-mails from her boss. The phone glowed in her face as she checked her in-box. Thirteen e-mails awaited her, and as she browsed them, she noticed two from John Allen. She quickly opened the first.

"I forgot to tell you I recorded the meeting with my phone. I just listened to it, and you can hear most everything. Hope this helps. JA."

Emma was thrilled. She was impressed with his ingenuity. It was brilliant. Excitedly, she clicked the attachment, and it loaded to play. Clicking the arrow, the sounds of the Pop A Top could be heard, and she listened intently.

Annoyed at the noise, Billy Joel once again got up and strolled into the den, hoping for some peace and quiet.

◆ ◆ ◆

Runt was excited to be driving the Porsche. He hadn't driven a stick shift since grinding the gears on his daddy's Toyota pickup truck.

The headlights shined across an overgrown field as he fell in behind Winston. He turned the radio to a Sirius rock channel and cranked up the volume.

Their hunting club wasn't anything fancy, but they loved to hang out there on the weekends in the fall and winter. There were about twenty members who all paid $1,000 annually for access to a big chunk of timber-company land they leased. There were thousands of clubs just like it across the South. Some were nicer—much nicer—and probably some were rougher, though Runt hadn't seen any that were in worse shape. The clubhouse was an old dogtrot-style sharecropper's house they used to cook and eat. The ancient fireplace was a gathering spot for telling lies, and for drinking coffee in the morning and hard liquor at night. The house hadn't been dusted or cleaned since the club had been formed over twenty years ago, and it would surely freak out any female who saw it.

Through the years they had purchased two repossessed trailers and moved them next to the clubhouse for members who wanted to spend the night. The trailers didn't have good heat and had no air-conditioning. Red wasps had nests in the ceiling corners of every room, and each year they would find a skin from a chicken snake that hunted the resident mice. The trailers weren't hooked to a septic tank, and the members lived in fear that they would be fined for dumping raw sewerage into the creek. Years of use had combined to generate a steady stench so offensive in the hot summer months that it would gag a person.

No one visited the club during the summer, and they'd all long ago given up spending the night in the decaying trailers. The snakes, mosquitoes, and ticks were a constant threat, and with no air-conditioning, the July and August nights were too miserable to bear, even if the trailers had been habitable.

Regardless, the hunting club still represented heaven to Runt. He had grown up roaming its woods all year-round. On the weekends and nights when he wasn't digging for artifacts, he was hunting something in the woods. It was the one place where he truly understood what was happening around him. He knew the forest and its inhabitants; nature had a balance of give-and-take that he appreciated. The woods also fed him. Venison and flathead catfish from the creek provided meat for the year; and wild mushrooms, frog legs, muscadines, and wild plums added flavor. In the silence of the trees, he didn't have a supervisor making certain he cut the chicken correctly, or Winston making him do all the manual labor. If only he could have a relationship with his girlfriend that was as good as the one he had with the woods.

He loved where they were headed but wasn't looking forward to what he was going to have to do. Winston would pay him handsomely for the work, though, and that alone was sufficient motivation.

He texted his girlfriend, though he hoped she was asleep. A little dot-dot-dot text bubble popped up, though, and instead of blooming into a message, it vanished. This repeated every so often for a few miles, a pattern that he interpreted as an indication she was texting somebody else. Highly frustrated, Runt turned up the radio volume until it hurt his ears. The Allman Brothers Band was singing "Midnight Rider," which was at least fitting for him tonight.

◆ ◆ ◆

John Allen struggled with the sock in his mouth until he finally was able to spit it out, then lay on his side and tried to determine his next move. He had no idea where Winston was taking him, but he assumed it was somewhere near Meridian. He figured Winston had "made" him as an agent and would likely stay on familiar turf while trying to cover his tracks.

It was comforting to know that Emma and Hoss knew where he'd been and would immediately focus their attention on Winston, but that didn't help him at the moment. Winston was capable of anything, according to Emma. John Allen had to figure out a way to escape. Again he tried twisting his wrists and kept at it until the white-hot pain shooting through his messed-up shoulder forced him to stop.

He knew what he'd done—he'd reinjured the rotator cuff he'd torn playing college intramurals. He wasn't going to break the zip ties as long as they were behind his back. He was wedged in so tight he could barely move, but nonetheless he pushed and contorted himself until he could see the bastard's eyes in the rearview. They were smiling.

"Give it up, Pretty Boy. It's no use—you can't break those zip ties. The Memphis Zoo uses them to restrain their gorillas," Winston said with a laugh.

John Allen's head was pounding as his mind raced, trying to think of a way out. Talk—that's all he could do. Maybe he'd learn something that could help him.

"What's this all about, Winston?" he asked, his voice rough with anger.

The highway was deserted except for a few eighteen-wheelers. "Ah, I see you spit out Runt's sock," Winston said.

"This is no use. There'll be a lot of people looking for me in the morning."

"It won't matter, bud. They won't find anything."

John Allen sighed. "Why are you doing this?"

"Isn't it obvious? You tried to set me up to buy that skull. I know you work for the Choctaws. You people have been trying to bust me for selling artifacts for years, and it ain't ever gonna happen."

"How did you figure that out?" Anything to keep the conversation going.

"It doesn't matter. I have my ways."

It was a measure of the depth of his desperation that John Allen felt his best hope was to try to appeal to Winston's rationality. "You don't have to do this, you know. A violation of the Antiquities Act is not worth killing me over. If you let me go, we can just forget the whole thing. We can set something up so you can be sure I'll leave it be."

"You have no idea how much money I have made and will continue to make selling black-market Indian artifacts. It's going on all over the state, the South—hell, the country. So believe me, it's worth killing you to keep everyone off my trail."

"They'll figure it out. They knew I was talking to you, and this time the FBI is involved."

Winston didn't believe that for a minute. They had much bigger fish to fry than chasing the underground artifact market. They had proven their lack of interest through the years, and he knew that these days they had more than they could handle. Nope, he was safe from the feds. John Allen was bluffing.

"That's bullshit and you know it."

"I'm serious."

"Look, I'll agree you had a good cover. I believed you were a preppy accountant from Columbus, and the Porsche made me think you had access to cash, which I happen to need right now. I fell into your trap, but I know you're just an Indian cop or agent or whatever you want to call yourself. This ain't no federal issue."

"It is now that you've kidnapped me. Have you thought about that?"

Winston nodded. This much was true, but it didn't matter a bit. Kidnapping and killing John Allen was the only available means to end this mess. It was necessary for survival.

"Yeah, you may be right," he said, "but they can look at me and investigate all they want. They'll never figure it out. And without a body they won't have a case."

"Is this how you killed the last agent?"

Winston smiled. Maybe they knew—they had to know something for him to make that comment—but it didn't matter. They didn't have enough evidence. Feeling cocky, he looked in the rearview mirror and laughed.

"Yes, yes, it is."

The confirmation didn't shock John Allen, but the fact that he'd so brazenly taken ownership of it was sobering. All hope that Winston wouldn't kill him had just evaporated.

With nothing to lose, he shot right back at his captor. "What about Jim Hudson?"

Winston paused. Maybe they did know more than he realized. But again, there was no way to convict him of that murder. Still, and not that it mattered since he was talking to a dead man, he chose to lie about that one. "No," he said, "that was an unfortunate hunting accident."

"Yeah, I bet it was. People sure seem to die around you."

Winston continued to laugh. "Shit happens."

John Allen swallowed hard. He had to find a way out of this situation. Then he would beat Winston's brains in with whatever he could find that would work.

◆ ◆ ◆

When Winston pulled up to the rusted metal gate at the Foggy Bottom Hunting and Drinking Club, he hoped the key still worked. He was late paying the annual dues, but he was late almost every year. He hated the nasty old club. He wanted to be a part of a fancy hunting club, but he couldn't afford it right now. The club president didn't like Winston, but he didn't think he would go to the trouble of changing the lock on him and distributing new keys to everybody.

When he got out of the truck, the overhead light stayed dark. Winston had customized his vehicle for crime.

Soon headlights appeared in the back window, and John Allen recognized the sound of his Porsche's engine, along with music being played loudly. He tried to sit up and look out the back window, but he was wedged against a spare tire and couldn't get enough leverage. Without his arms and legs working together, it was impossible. Maybe if he had worked out more, like Sadie had wanted, and had done a few sit-ups . . .

Sadie was in his mind now, and he didn't want her there, didn't want to consider the pain she would have felt to receive the news that he'd met the kind of end he seemed likely to at the hands of Winston

Walker. She'd been spared that, at least. For the very first time, he found a positive reason for her accident.

He could hear Winston and Runt talking. After a few moments he heard the rattle of a heavy chain and the screech of an opening gate. Winston jumped back into the truck, and they proceeded on. The headlights behind the SUV followed for a few feet, then stopped. Runt must be closing the gate.

When they pulled up to the camp, John Allen didn't have a clue where they were. He didn't have his watch to time the drive. He'd listened, trying to learn whatever he could, but had learned exactly nothing. Now he was prepared to kick whoever opened the door.

Winston cut off his engine and slammed the truck door. Within thirty seconds, John Allen heard his Porsche pull up and saw the lights cut off.

"Runt, it's late," he heard Winston say. "I don't think we have time to dig it out proper tonight, do you?"

Runt replied, "Yeah, if I can get started tomorrow night about ten, I can get it done, boss."

"So here's what we do. Let's lock him in the back room of the trailer. Tomorrow is Sunday and you don't have to be at work, so you can stay with him. We'll go back to town after we get him settled, and you can drive back. That way you'll have your truck, and it's not suspiciously sitting at my house. I'll stay in town and act normal, and we'll figure out what to do with him."

"You wanna kill him tonight?" Runt asked, as casually as if he were asking whether Winston wanted him to run to the store. John Allen's blood ran cold.

There was a pause, then Winston said, "Hell, let's ask him," and threw open the back door.

John Allen kicked wildly, barely missing Winston with the first blow, causing him to step back and laugh. He shined a flashlight into John Allen's eyes and blinded him.

"So we're trying to decide whether to kill you tonight or tomorrow," Winston said in a spooky voice. "What do you think?" John Allen heard Runt laugh.

"Screw you, Winston!" John Allen screamed. "Untie me and let's settle this between me and you," he said with a grunt as he struggled to raise his throbbing head.

Winston laughed. "Thanks. Sounds like fun, but I need to be in good shape for the meetings you say I have coming tomorrow. And to be honest, I have never played fair. It's not my style."

"Untie me!"

"I'm enjoying seeing him struggling with the future," Winston said to Runt. "Let's do this later. See if his attitude improves after a day in the hot box."

"Sounds like a plan," Runt said.

"I'll help you get him in there, then we'll knock him out again. That'll buy you some time."

Runt reached out of the flashlight's glare to grab John Allen, who twisted to get away. "Hold still, you idiot," Runt said. "Unless you want us to cut your throat right where you lie."

"Surely you'd like to get your legs cut loose and stretched out, John Allen," Winston said. "Come on, now. But he's right about us cutting your throat. We can just hose out the liner when we're done."

John Allen finally stopped struggling and allowed Runt to cut the zip tie holding his legs together. Then Runt helped him to his very wobbly feet.

Winston was tempted to push him over, just because he could, but they needed to get going. "Tomorrow," he told Runt, "if he gives you any trouble, just kill him. Put a bullet between his eyes and one above his ear for insurance. You don't have to wait on me."

"I gotcha," Runt said. He had committed some awful criminal acts in his life, but he had yet to actually kill someone. Still, he would follow orders, and there always had to be a first time. "What about the car? It's a fine ride, boss."

"I've been thinking about it. I'd like to have it, too, but it'll be a dead giveaway, and it's too easy to spot. We're gonna have to sink it."

Runt nodded his head, but he was disappointed. His girlfriend would've loved the car.

"Let's walk him down to the skinning shed and get him locked up," Winston said. They'd be able to hose the blood out of that even more easily than they could've cleaned up the bed liner. The shed was made for such activities.

◆ ◆ ◆

Wrestling John Allen into the skinning shed had been harder than they'd expected. He somehow jumped, kicked Winston in the side of the knee, and knocked him to the ground. Once Winston got back on his feet, he was furious and beat John Allen unconscious.

Afterward Winston could barely stand, much less walk, and he was ready to kill John Allen. They only thing that saved him was Winston deciding he wanted to torture him the next day when he regained consciousness.

Winston popped three Advil for the pain while he watched Runt drag John Allen's limp body the rest of the way to the shed, tie his legs together again, and lock him in. When Runt was finished, he walked back to where Winston stood, his face beaded in sweat from the pain and exertion.

"You okay?" Runt asked him. "That looked like it hurt." He could tell Winston was in severe pain. He wasn't certain, but he thought he'd heard something pop or snap. It didn't sound good.

"Damn right it did. My knee's tore up. It ain't supposed to move in that direction. It's already swollen," he said with a grimace as he gingerly felt around it with both hands.

Runt wiped the sweat from his own face with his sleeve. He had never seen Winston injured. He'd always managed to avoid any hard labor or fights.

Winston set his jaw and looked up at him. "Go get in your race car, and let's go."

"Where we gonna do it? Lake Tiak-O'Khata is close. That would be my choice."

"Too many people around that would hear the splash, and I don't think the lake is deep enough right there by the road, anyway," Winston said as he winced in pain.

"Whatcha thinking, boss?" Runt asked, swatting a mosquito.

"Lake Pushmataha is perfect. Follow me," Winston said, then pulled his door shut and cranked the Suburban.

The two criminals drove to Philadelphia, Mississippi, then turned onto State Route 16, going west past the Choctaw school, administration, and health offices. Along the way they passed a tribal police officer on patrol. Winston noted they weren't speeding and didn't worry about it. After a few more miles, he turned right on Goat Ranch Road. The route was lined with giant pine trees and curved around until they came to a locked gate. Winston rolled down his window and waved at Runt to drive forward. When he arrived, Winston handed him a pair of bolt cutters, which made short work of the lock. Once inside and after a few more turns, a giant tree-lined lake appeared in the moonlight. When they parked and turned the lights off, the only sound was that of the cicadas. Runt had never been here before but had always heard of the beautiful body of water.

Lake Pushmataha had 285 acres of water that locals and tourists used for recreation. It was named after Chief Pushmataha of the Choctaw tribe, whom many considered the greatest of all their chiefs. He had been so revered as a diplomat that when he'd died, he'd been buried with full military honors in the Congressional Cemetery.

Winston parked the Suburban and cut the headlights, knowing it was too early for any fishermen to be on the lake. He emerged from the truck feeling a bit better since the Advil had kicked in, but he was still hurting.

"You see that levee there? That's the deepest water. It's plenty deep to hide the car. Cut the lights, pull out on the levee, and point the car downhill. Roll the windows down, put her in neutral, and let gravity do the rest."

Runt started grabbing some of the stuff he'd stolen from John Allen's house and wanted to put it in Winston's truck.

"Are you crazy?" Winston snapped at him. "Leave that shit in the car, man!"

Runt left the guitar in the Porsche but put John Allen's sunglasses in his pocket. He parked the car and looked down the levee at the still water. He loved the car and hated to do it, but he gave it one big push, and she rolled down the hill and splashed into the water. The car floated for a few minutes, then drifted out farther from the bank. Eventually $89,000 worth of fine German engineering disappeared beneath the surface.

Swinging open the passenger door of Winston's Suburban, Runt looked again at the car's watery grave and moaned his disappointment in losing it.

"It's the only way, Runt. We have to make it look like John Allen has driven off somewhere."

"I wish we could have just hidden it for a while," Runt said with remorse for the car. Then he remembered something he stole. "Damn, I forgot the boots!"

Winston grimaced in his pain. "Too risky. Get your ass in the truck. I'll buy you some boots. We need to go."

Chapter 28

John Allen opened his eyes slowly, adjusting to the semidarkness. Had this all been a bad dream? His wishful thinking lasted only seconds before the reality of the warm blood on his face hit him. He could also feel blood caked in the back of his hair. He was sore all over from the beating Winston had given him, but he remembered crushing Winston's knee. The beating had been worth it.

The rough concrete he was lying on was cool to his skin. It must be early morning. His head was pounding, and his shoulder burned, then was pierced by a succession of sharp, molar-grinding pains as he eased himself over onto his back. He could see sunshine filtering in through the cracks around a metal door. The warm rays illuminated the room enough for him to make out heavy wood beams above him and walls that looked like wood frames covered in tin. There was a rough-looking sink on one side and a counter next to it that looked like what somebody with only the most rudimentary carpentry skills had slapped together. Two heavy ropes spanned the room and dangled down to two rusty, hand-cranked boat-trailer winches. He was in a homemade skinning shed used to butcher white-tailed deer.

Various tools were stuck in crevices and could prove useful if he could somehow get to them before Runt came back. The sight of the tools inspired him as he fought his way to a sitting position to take inventory of the situation.

If he could free his hands, he felt sure he could bust out of this shabby building. He just had to break the zip ties. When he tried again, though, his shoulder ignited with a spasm that stopped him cold and left him fighting to calm his breathing and manage the pain, which had now settled into a constant, powerfully aching throb.

John Allen wondered what time it was, and whether Emma had realized he was missing yet. She would start calling or texting him at eight, probably, but she wouldn't likely be worried or concerned for a few hours, maybe not even until noon—and if there was a new development with the terrorist surveillance, possibly even later.

Hoss would be expecting him, though. He would want to see the pot John Allen had purchased. Thank God he'd stuck it in his gun safe. He still wasn't sure why he'd done that, beyond a general fear it would somehow get broken if it were just left around. As a prank, he'd wrapped up an extralarge ceramic coffee mug in the robe to give to Hoss. Some prank, he thought now. Locked away in that safe, how would the pot ever find its way back to the Choctaw Nation if he didn't find a way out of this?

Well, then, find a way out, he instructed himself.

◆ ◆ ◆

Agent Emma Haden had finally fallen back to sleep after listening to the recordings John Allen had made of his dealings with Winston Walker. She could hear everything clear as day and knew it would help with a conviction. It was an unorthodox way of doing things, but the prosecuting attorney would be pleased to have the recordings. And she was completely satisfied that it wasn't entrapment, for two reasons: The first was that Winston already had been known to engage in the trafficking of illegal artifacts. And the second was even better still—Winston himself had contacted John Allen about selling the pot.

Now up and exercising, she had her hair pulled back in a ponytail and was sipping pomegranate juice as she put in her two miles on the treadmill before going into the office. It was Sunday, but that didn't matter. Crime didn't take a day off. She had on tight biker shorts and a ratty, loose-fitting Anytime Fitness T-shirt, which didn't matter at all since no one could see her. Her view of the sunrise over the Barnett Reservoir made her feel it was worth it to have risen at such an early hour.

Once at the office, Emma planned to let the Meridian police know of her intentions to pick up Winston Walker and his sidekick, Runt. She'd found it was better to work *with* the locals than against them. She didn't like tipping her hand to someone else about her plans, but she was always one to follow protocol. It kept her out of trouble with her superiors.

Several other agents would be at the office, as she had alerted everyone to her plans last night. She hated to pull them away from their families on a Sunday morning, but she wasn't going to miss a chance to place cuffs on Walker's wrists.

She glanced at the wall clock, which read 6:22 a.m. Still too early to call John Allen, even though she badly wanted to.

Emma upped her speed and added more incline as she started her second mile. She could see a few fishermen beginning their morning across the lake. She wondered what they were fishing for and whether they were catching any. She hadn't been fishing since she was a little girl and had spent Saturday afternoons with her dad. They would fish and eat Vienna sausages. Those were precious memories. So why hadn't she fished since? Because no one she'd seriously dated—and least of all her ex-husband—had ever asked her to go fishing.

Maybe that should've told her something about them. Maybe that was a quality to judge a man by.

She wondered whether John Allen liked to fish.

◆ ◆ ◆

Winston drove home from the reservoir, worrying about the events of the night and about Runt. He pounded the steering wheel several times and cursed himself for having ever met up with John Allen. He readily admitted that it had been a stupid move. He was smarter than that. The situation had forced him to kidnap John Allen in an effort to clean up the mess. Pride made him think he'd done nothing that could link him to the crime, but because it had happened so fast, he knew there was a chance he'd miscalculated somewhere. The fact that he needed fast money was causing him to make some rash decisions.

It wasn't lost on him that his life and future depended on Runt. He could be trusted as much as any meth head could, but even when he was straight, Runt couldn't make good decisions. Winston had to do all the thinking, as Runt could only consider the moment and not the future, and certainly not the potential consequences.

The future had always mattered to Winston. He'd grown up watching other kids get all the accolades and awards. His dad had worked as a maintenance man for a wealthy, local owner of a construction company. In addition to maintenance duties, the man had used Winston's dad for every job he didn't want to do himself, from school science projects to teaching his children to drive. Mr. Walker had just been trying to provide for his family, but Winston was always embarrassed by what his dad did for a living. His dad's boss had a son and daughter close to Winston's age, and they had everything, while Winston, who attended the same school, had nothing. The rich man had paid for Winston to attend a private school, to make it easier for his dad to be there to help out with tasks like mowing the football field before games. Instead of donating his own time to the Booster Club like every other parent, the rich man had donated his dad's time. The daughter had been two years younger and wouldn't even look at Winston, even though his dad washed her dad's car, cleaned her pool, set up her parties, and most days, picked her up from school. It was Winston's first experience with not being who he wanted to be and not having what he wanted.

He had still been in junior high school when he'd decided he would change his name. He'd wanted to be influential, powerful, and someone people admired, but the problem was he hadn't known how to go about it correctly. All he'd ever known was how to cut corners and to cheat. He'd started by stealing Ralph Lauren shirts and stylish shoes like the other kids wore, and it had gradually escalated. While other kids were proficient in certain subjects or athletics, Winston came to realize he was good at conning and conniving people out of things he wanted. It was much easier than working for them.

Though his house wasn't much now, it had once been really nice. Years ago when the money had been flowing, he'd overextended himself and purchased it. Very quickly, though, he couldn't even afford regular, basic maintenance on it. If—or more likely, when—the bank repossessed it, it would bring about half what Winston had paid for it, due to his neglect and drunken, drug-fueled abuse. The pool house, or what was left of it, was so contaminated from cooking meth you couldn't stand to be in it. The pool itself was only half-full and hadn't been cleaned in so long it was greener than a golf-course pond.

After he parked the Suburban, Winston cussed his knee and limped into his house with help from Runt. On the drive home it had swelled up and stiffened. He needed some serious pain medication, and fortunately he had some. If the Indian police came to talk to him tomorrow, he would need an excuse for his knee that wouldn't arouse suspicion.

After he set the seed pot on the counter, Winston grabbed a beer from the fridge and two OxyContin pills from his stash. Runt helped him to the couch, and he crashed onto it in a cussing fit.

It wasn't daylight yet, but Winston had a list of things for Runt to do. Winston needed him to pull the plastic liner from the rear of his Suburban and clean John Allen's blood off it at the car wash. Winston also needed him to hide the artifacts, the drugs, and the two pistols that were in the house in case a search warrant was somehow issued.

"Can I count on you?" Winston asked as he handed his phone to Runt to plug in to recharge.

"You know you can," Runt answered.

Winston grabbed a knife and pointed it at Runt. "You don't tell anyone what we've done," he said, then dipped the knife's point and used it to split his pants from the thigh down to expose his bruised and swollen knee.

Runt stared at the swelling and felt squeamish. The knee was almost twice its normal size. There was no discernible kneecap visible, and the bruising was horrific.

Winston didn't seem surprised or concerned. He'd grunted when he first saw it and now touched the swelling here and there as he went on talking.

"They'll try and split us up and tell you that Winston said this and Winston said that. But trust me, I ain't saying shit."

"I ain't, either, boss," Runt said, turning his head from the injury.

"They'll get frustrated and threaten you and try to scare you into telling them what they want to know."

"They can't."

"Good. I'm counting on you. Now just do what I asked, and we'll be good. Tomorrow we'll make a plan to deal with John Allen. I'm hoping my knee is better by then."

Runt shook his head doubtfully. "Yeah, I'm betting it's not going to be. My daddy blew out his new knee jumping off a ladder, and he had to have surgery. His knee didn't look as bad as yours."

"Shit, that's the last thing I need right now," Winston said. "That pissant John Allen will pay for this." He grunted in pain as he lay back against the pillows.

"I'm just saying it looks bad, dude."

Winston grunted again as he retrieved two $1,000 chips from his pocket and tossed them to Runt. "That's for you. Just go, and keep your phone close. I may need you. But look here, don't text about any of this shit. I don't know for sure, but I bet they can retrieve our texts if they want to."

Winston then closed his eyes to let the meds take the edge off his pain. He was tired, and he had a lot on his mind. He'd begun to wonder whether he'd been set up by Rosco. As he'd feared, the man had gotten cold feet about selling him any more artifacts, and Winston had been forced to silence him. He'd known he couldn't trust him to stay quiet, and he'd been right to put a bullet in his head. It had been easy to make it look like a suicide. What he didn't know was whether Rosco had already turned him in before Winston had gotten to him.

◆ ◆ ◆

Sunday morning started as it always did for Hoss: he read reports and checked in on the front lines to learn what had occurred the night before. Saturday nights were always busy in the casino, and Friday nights weren't bad, either. He sipped coffee and thought about all the work-related problems he had and how he planned to deal with them.

Tomorrow was Rosco Jones's funeral, and so far the county detective had found no reason to believe it wasn't suicide. Hoss had already been through Rosco's locker before the detective had arrived and asked to do the same. Hoss knew it was clean. He'd hoped to find artifacts, but he hadn't. It had contained only a worn Bible, an apple, a can of sardines, and a box of crackers.

Hoss had already briefed the chief on the security situation and the progress to repair the eyesore the truck had created at the entrance of their beautiful casino. She wasn't happy and wanted the forty chips back without having any of them redeemed by a cashier paying more attention to Snapchat than her job. She let Hoss know she expected him to handle the situation, and he was depending on others. That always made him nervous.

The casino was a huge source of revenue for the tribe. It attracted all sorts across the entire socioeconomic spectrum. There were a number of wealthy gamblers and many people who didn't have any business gambling with their paychecks. In between were middle-class men and women who enjoyed the art of gambling. Sometimes they won and sometimes they lost. They had systems to win and dreams of what they would do if they hit it big. The casino allowed people to forget their problems and gave them a chance, however remote, to score a financial win that they could immediately realize. They drank beer and booze and dreamed their nights away at various gaming tables. The casino had programs to help people with gambling addictions and had been known to turn away people they knew shouldn't be there. It was a business, but they did care about their community. The chief reminded Hoss of the importance of keeping the business running smoothly.

Soon his phone would start ringing, and more problems would arise. He spent his days handling issues that popped up faster than they could be solved, but he enjoyed both the challenge and his role. He never lost sight of his commitment to protect the tribe's assets—a subject that now brought John Allen to mind.

Hoss had agreed that the tribe needed someone who would travel and acquire the spiritual artifacts that had been located. It was an important job. He hadn't wanted to hire John Allen, but he did think the tribe could trust him. That was no small thing. They had every reason to fear being taken advantage of, and earning their trust could be a slow and difficult process. Hoss just didn't think John Allen would have a passion for the job and stick with it. He saw him being more of a businessman who after a year would crave returning to the helm of an accounting firm.

The chief had listened to him but asked that Hoss trust her. She'd had a feeling about John Allen, a trust that he would empathize with their plight and be a good face in the communities to represent them. He was Caucasian, and she felt it would help other white people understand the plight of the Choctaw spiritual artifacts and also help the tribe recover as many as possible. John Allen was more than just an agent scouring the countryside for artifacts to purchase. At times he was a PR representative for the tribe, and the chief hoped he could bring more community awareness to their situation.

Hoss also didn't like the tribe leasing the Porsche for John Allen. He did understand the reasoning, and he could see how it might help with the front John Allen was presenting at times. When you boiled it down, Hoss resented driving a three-year-old leased Buick LeSabre, while new employee John Allen was tooling around in a shiny black Porsche 911.

Being the focused security expert he was, Hoss had attached a GPS tracker to the car and spot-checked John Allen the first few months of his employment. He'd always found him to be exactly where he said he'd be. Hoss did this not because he didn't trust John Allen but out of the extreme guilt he felt about losing their first agent. The man's fate haunted him. He and his car had simply vanished, and Hoss couldn't get past it.

He didn't expect to see John Allen today. Tomorrow, though, he would be here and tell the story of his role in the apprehension of Winston Walker with the enthusiasm of a rookie cop announcing his first arrest. Hoss wouldn't begrudge him that, but getting his hands on the artifact John Allen had purchased was what had him charged up. He couldn't wait to see it, and make sure it was returned to his people.

◆ ◆ ◆

By ten o'clock Emma was furious with John Allen. He wasn't answering his phone or texts. *Maybe he's in church.* This was the South, smack-dab in the middle of the Bible Belt, and she could see him turning his phone off during Sunday school, and especially during church. She remembered him saying the blessing before their meal. She couldn't be mad at him for going to church, but he could have touched base with her. Their operation was still ongoing even though it was Sunday.

She listened again to the recording and was amazed by his presence of mind. She knew federal agents with way more training who'd lost their nerve in undercover situations. He'd done well.

She tried to call once more, and the phone rang until the voice mail picked up. She didn't think she needed to leave another message. If he got the first one, he would know to call. If he listened to the second one before he called, he would know she was pissed.

Before Agent Garner left to go back home, he'd suggested they wait one more day to arrest Winston Walker. Emma hadn't wanted to wait, saying she didn't really need to talk to John Allen since she had his voice-recorded evidence of the sale. But Garner was right: protocol dictated a formal debriefing before they would roll out an arrest team. She had reluctantly agreed and realized she was only growing madder at John Allen as more time was lost.

Fueled by frustration, she shuffled through her business cards like a librarian going through an old card-catalog system until she found the one she wanted. The head of security might have talked to John Allen, or at least might have some insight. She quickly dialed his cell phone and hoped he wasn't a deacon.

Hoss answered on the third ring. "Hello."

"This is Special Agent Emma Haden," she said. "I hate to bother you on a Sunday morning."

"That's okay," Hoss responded. "I'm working."

Agent Haden was glad someone else was. "Have you spoken to John Allen today?"

"No, I haven't. Is something wrong?"

"It's just that we talked last night about picking up the subject he sold an illegal artifact to, Winston Walker, and I haven't heard from him this morning."

"John Allen usually doesn't work on Sundays. I think he works a lot of Saturdays but not Sundays."

"I get that, but this was a big deal. Do you think he's in church?"

"I don't have any idea," Hoss answered. "You say you talked to him last night?"

"Yes, we talked for about an hour. It was late," she said, suddenly aware of just how odd that sounded.

"I can try to call him if you like."

"Yes, please, and if you talk to him, tell him to call my cell as soon as he can."

Hoss was holding her card, which had been on top of his pile. "I have your number. If I hear from him, I'll let you know."

"Thanks."

They hung up, and Hoss flipped her card onto his desk. He couldn't imagine John Allen not calling Emma back. He could sense John Allen liked her. However, it was Sunday, and Sunday mornings in the South are easy, just like Lionel Richie sang in his song. People sleep late, but it was true that many others go to church. He checked the wall clock. It was almost 10:00 a.m. Most church services started at 11:00 and hoped to get out by noon, or at least 12:15, if the preacher wasn't too long-winded. But there was Sunday school prior to that, if John Allen was a Baptist or a Methodist.

Hoss realized he didn't know anything about John Allen's private life. He was probably golfing and didn't want to be bothered.

He dialed John Allen's number and after a few rings got a message, to which he responded with one of his own asking him to call him as soon as he could.

Leaning back in his chair, he didn't have time to think about the situation, as his cell phone immediately rang. The casino had a female trying to cash in a $1,000 chip and wanted to know what to do.

"Stall them, don't let 'em leave the premises, and I'll be right there!" he said as he scrambled out of his chair.

◆ ◆ ◆

John Allen finally found the strength to sit on his knees. Every bit of movement hurt. Excited to be up, he tried to force his hands under his rear in an effort to pull them in front of him. It would make it easier to break the zip tie if it was in front. He strained, drooping his shoulders to allow his hands to pass, but they wouldn't.

He grunted, then screamed in frustration. Surely there had to be a way out of here. He looked around. If there was an exposed nail he could back up to and scrape the zip tie across, he could break it.

The sunlight drifted softly into the gory shed through small cracks. Inside this room a deer would be hung up, then gutted, skinned, and butchered. Venison was a healthy red-meat choice, and normally John Allen loved it. Grilled tenderloin was his favorite. But right now the smell and stains of dried blood only served to remind him of his mortal peril. He knew Winston and Runt were coming back to kill him. He wasn't certain why they hadn't already. Winston was capable of anything imaginable. Runt, though, seemed to be someone who simply did what he was told. If John Allen could get Runt alone, maybe he could talk some sense into him.

After several excruciating tumbles, he managed to hop his way to the edge of the skinning shed on his battered knees and peer outside through a crack. The sun was visible as it rose in the sky. He marked the direction as east for future reference. He could also see the trashiest trailer he'd ever seen in his life. It wasn't level, and it was stained from years of mold caused by the hot, humid summers. He could see tires stacked all across the roof, placed there to weigh it down and prevent it from popping at night as the temperature changed. John Allen laughed that he knew that. He had no idea where he'd picked it up.

There appeared to be another structure past the trailer, but he could only see the chimney. It looked old. The area was overgrown; weeds and small trees were growing everywhere that couldn't hold a parked vehicle. The grass probably got cut once a year in preparation for hunting season. Some member's twelve-year-old son was probably forced to do it and was happy to be at the hunting club.

Looking around inside the shed, he was surprised he didn't see any knives stuck in cracks between the boards. He knew there had to be some somewhere, waiting to be found. Wearing nothing but his plaid Ralph Lauren boxers, he carefully hopped to the darkest side of the shed in search of something that could be useful. As he hobbled forward, he said a silent prayer.

◆ ◆ ◆

Runt had spent the predawn hours doing exactly what he'd been told except for one thing: he forgot to take the plastic liner that John Allen had bled on out of the back of Winston's Suburban and pressure-wash it.

He'd gathered up all the illegal drugs—some homemade and some stolen prescriptions, the seed pot still wrapped in the robe, and finally, the two hot burner pistols. He considered hiding them in his trailer, but he didn't want to take that chance. He lived in a trailer park, and there was always a curious face at a window or someone loitering around the street. So concealing something outside was a gamble. He had a few good hiding spots inside the trailer, but if the cops served a search warrant, none would pass that kind of scrutiny.

He wrapped the drugs and guns in a black plastic garbage bag and thought about tossing them into the bottom of Winston's pool. After further consideration, he figured someone would probably drag a skimming net across the bottom just out of curiosity. In a moment of clarity, he realized where he could hide everything: the house had a crawl space. With a flashlight in one hand and the illegal gear in the other, he crawled under until he found the dryer-vent tube. He used a pocketknife to slice the foil lining and peel it back, revealing a dark hole eight or ten inches in diameter. He picked a spot close to where the tube made contact with a PVC pipe, so the silver duct tape he would use to seal it back would not stand out, and hurriedly inserted the drugs, then the pistols. The pot wouldn't fit in while covered in the robe, so he carefully unwrapped it.

When he discovered it was a coffee mug, he stared at it in shock for a brief few seconds. He didn't know what to think. Either Winston or John Allen was behind this, and he figured it had to be John Allen. With no time to waste, he taped up the foil and rubbed dirt on it to make it look weathered. Satisfied, he crawled back out and went inside to tell Winston.

Winston was feeling little pain from the drugs, which also made him drowsy. When Runt explained about the seed pot, though, he recovered some energy. His eyes narrowed with anger.

"You're shitting me," Winston said, as more of a statement than a question.

Runt held up the coffee mug. It was huge, big enough to hold two cups of coffee, more than anyone would need—the kind of thing someone would give as a gag gift. It was very similar in size to the seed pot but not quite as wide, now that Winston really looked at it.

"He'll pay for that shit," Winston pledged, grimacing as he adjusted his position on the couch. Anger and desperation flashed in his eyes.

Runt explained where he hid the guns, and Winston, who always seemed to remember details, reminded him to clean the back of his truck.

"Right," Runt said, ready to go. When he was finished at the car wash, he wanted to go see his girlfriend, even if it was the crack of dawn. She lived two streets over from him in the same trailer park, and he wanted to make certain no one had spent the night with her. There was a high probability someone had.

Chapter 29

When Hoss arrived at the casino, he was told that the female who wanted to cash the chip was enjoying the free breakfast they'd offered her while they collected the money for her. They'd explained the delay by claiming the tellers were changing shifts. They'd just asked for a few minutes, and she'd obliged.

With a tribal police officer in tow, he walked over and sat down with her. When she saw the officer, her eyes widened, and she tried with difficulty to swallow a mouthful of scrambled eggs.

"Good morning, Miss . . . ?" Hoss asked.

"Gina," she said nervously. "Gina Goodson."

Hoss didn't even bother to introduce himself. He summed her up quickly. She wore dirty blue-jean cutoff shorts, flip-flops, and a free T-shirt from Verizon. The track marks on her arms were evident until she became self-conscious and folded them. Probably only twenty-five years old, she looked forty. The dark circles under her eyes made her look exhausted. Hoss had seen it many times before. She used meth and probably heroin. Her purse, a Michael Kors, stood out—it was either stolen or a fake.

"Can I see your chip?"

Gina pulled it out and handed it to him.

Hoss studied it. The hard clay chip was theirs, all right.

"Where did you get this chip?" he asked calmly.

"I won it."

"Miss Goodson, we've reviewed footage of you walking straight in to cash the chip. We know you were *not* gaming here tonight."

Gina was fast on her feet. "I won it a while back," she said with a straight face.

"When?"

"I don't remember."

"You don't remember winning a thousand bucks?"

Gina looked around the restaurant. There were a dozen people eating brunch. She was hungry, but she was also suddenly nervous. She didn't have a good track record with the police, and these two were looking at her like she was guilty of something.

"Did someone give it to you?" Hoss asked.

Gina mentally cursed her boyfriend, Runt. She should have known something was up with him, giving her a thousand freakin' dollars.

Gina didn't respond; she was thinking about her answer, trying to decide her next move in this chess game she couldn't afford to lose.

Hoss shook his head. He didn't want a scene in the casino. "Miss Goodson, we need you to come with us. We have an issue we need to discuss."

"I don't want to."

"I'm afraid you don't have a choice," Hoss said emphatically.

"We'd prefer not to handcuff you in front of all these folks," the tribal officer added.

"I really don't give a shit," she said with spite.

Hoss didn't like the wild look in her eyes. He exhaled and peered straight at her while speaking to the officer. "Cuff Miss Goodson and read her rights."

Gina stood up fast, but Hoss was faster and caught her before she could run. She screamed and shouted obscenities, but the officers had little trouble quickly leading her out of the restaurant.

Once she was secured in the back of the police car, Hoss wiped sweat from his brow and leaned against the unit. The officer lit a cigarette. Every arrest caused a bit of stress.

"We do everything right?" Hoss asked.

"Yep."

"Do me a favor and call for a female officer to come and be with you through the whole process. This princess might scream that the two male officers took advantage of her," Hoss said, trying to get in front of a problem.

After the officer radioed in the request, he leaned against the car with Hoss, who also heard the response and estimated the arrival time of the female officer.

"I'll wait until she gets here," he said. "I wanna interview her as soon as we get to the jail."

"No problem."

Hoss looked at Gina sitting in the backseat. She was giving him a go-to-hell look.

"You know," he said, "if she had gone in and gambled, had that chip busted into smaller chips, we might not have gotten a call."

"You think it's one of the stolen chips?"

"Yes, I do."

"That's good. Only thirty-nine more to go. Hey, I saw your boy and his Porsche this morning."

Hoss was deep in thought and answered without thinking about it. "Oh, really?"

"Yeah, he was up late or early. I saw him about 4:30 a.m., driving past the offices. I love that damn car he has."

Hoss was focused now on the officer's comments. "Where and when did you see him?"

"He was coming from Philadelphia, headed east," the officer said, sensing something was amiss. "Like I said, I saw him drive past the offices about 4:30."

"You're sure it was John Allen?"

"I'm positive. I'd recognize that car anywhere. We don't see many around here."

Hoss was deep in thought once again, now wondering what John Allen could have been doing. Maybe he'd been at the casino all night and was headed somewhere. John Allen didn't really seem like an all-night gambler, but Hoss knew you couldn't always pick them out, either. He needed to interview Gina. After that, if he hadn't heard from him, he would go and check out his GPS location.

◆ ◆ ◆

Runt drove back toward the hunting camp to execute and dispose of John Allen. It was almost noon.

He'd showered, then taken a $1,000 chip and given it to Gina just to watch her eyes light up. She'd been excited, and he knew Gina needed the money. She was a cashier at a convenience store and was struggling with her finances. Any extra money went toward continuing the tattoo sequence she'd started a year ago. *That ought to keep her happy for a month or so,* he'd thought.

Then he'd pulled into a gas station and bought a box of fried chicken breasts and a Mountain Dew, a Sunday tradition for him. He knew two guys who were sitting in the shade, and they talked for a few minutes. Runt made an effort to tell them a fabricated story about what he'd done the previous night. He was trying to build an alibi in case he needed it.

When the chicken was consumed and the bones were picked clean, he'd wanted one more chicken leg but settled for a Reese's Peanut Butter Cup. He had much to do, but since he needed the cover of darkness, he wasn't in a big rush. Winston tried to hurry him, but Runt knew what he had to do and the proper sequence of events to pull it off. He'd prefer to walk John Allen to the mound and kill him there, rather than carry him.

Now as he drove north, he wondered what Winston was going to do. When he'd checked with him before he left, he'd been talking out of his mind, yammering about leaving town. Runt had never heard Winston want to run from anything. He wasn't a fighter, exactly—he had others fight for him—but he never ran. He always figured out a way to approach everything head-on, or at least have someone do so on his behalf. When Runt had promised to kill John Allen and cover everything up, Winston had seemed relieved.

◆ ◆ ◆

Agent Emma Haden was still furious with John Allen; however, the fury was slowly turning to concern. It was almost 2:00 p.m., and he couldn't still be in church. She didn't know what he normally did on a Sunday, but based on the excitement of their call last night, she felt he would've talked to her by now.

She was thinking there had to be a way to find him without driving all the way to Columbus when she remembered: she was a freaking federal agent. She would call the local sheriff and have an officer ride out and take a look at his house.

After she hung up, she was satisfied she would have some news within the hour. The deputies had located John Allen's residence in their database and promised to call her back when a deputy was on-site. In the meantime, Emma made a tuna sandwich in the office kitchen and waited for her phone to ring. She used the extra time to shop online, looking at shoes and summer dresses. It hadn't mattered last week, but suddenly everything in her closet looked ten years old. An ad for a new perfume popped up, and she realized she hadn't worn any in so long she didn't know the name of the latest popular scent. In college she'd worn Obsession, and she wondered whether it was even available anymore.

When her phone rang, she jumped and answered it immediately. "Agent Haden."

A young male voice responded, "Yes, ma'am. I'm at John Allen Harper's address, and no one's home. There's no Porsche here. I see a late-model Jeep. It doesn't appear to have been driven lately."

Agent Haden sighed. "Can you look in a window and see anything out of the ordinary?"

"No, ma'am," the deputy responded.

"You can't see anything?"

"There are no windows. Apparently he lives in a barn."

"What?"

"Yes, ma'am."

"A barn? Like a red barn?"

"No, ma'am. Like an old rusty tin barn."

An old rusty tin barn was hard for her to visualize as a place to live, especially for John Allen. He was educated. He always dressed well. It didn't make sense that he lived in a barn.

"Is the door unlocked?"

"Stand by, ma'am," the deputy responded.

It evidently was unlocked, as she heard some doorknob rattling, then heard him holler, "Sheriff's department! Mr. Harper? Are you home?"

A few moments passed, then he again called, "Sheriff's department!"

"Officer, what are you seeing?"

The officer laughed. "You sure can't judge a book by its cover. From the outside this place looks abandoned, but the inside is really nice. It's nice and smells new. It's plain, like maybe he just moved in."

"Do a quick search of the premises, please. Be careful."

"Yes, ma'am."

Seven minutes later the deputy called and said he saw nothing suspicious. There were a few drawers open, but then nothing out of the ordinary, at least given the state of his own apartment, he admitted.

After Agent Haden thanked the deputy, he shut the door and walked away. As he sat down in his cruiser, John Allen's cell phone began to ring inside the barn, but the officer couldn't hear it.

◆ ◆ ◆

Winston Walker was in pain and had been a guest in the emergency room for an hour. He'd waited until almost noon before he had to accept the fact that his knee needed some medical attention. The ER doctor was young, and Winston didn't like her at all. Her name had almost all vowels, and he couldn't understand what she was saying. She also didn't respond to any of his flirts, and that bothered him the most. Accepting rejection was not something he was good at, even though he'd had lots of practice.

The MRI revealed he hadn't torn the ligaments, which she explained was good news. He wouldn't need surgery, but a brace and crutches were in his immediate future. She preferred he stay off the knee for the next few days and suggested that when the swelling went down, he would need to see a rehab therapist.

Winston didn't have insurance and didn't have the cash to pay for the visit. But through the magic of the health-care system, he got all the attention he needed, including more pain meds. The doctor warned him they were addictive and to not take them unless absolutely necessary, and he laughed in her face.

Once he was discharged, he limped his way back to his vehicle and winced his way back home. As he arrived, he was half expecting the police to be waiting for him, maybe already searching his house, and he was glad he didn't see them. He wanted to go and help Runt, or at least supervise him to make sure he didn't mess things up or fail to ensure John Allen suffered sufficiently, but his knee was having none of it.

◆ ◆ ◆

The interview didn't go well for Hoss. Gina proved to be a tough nut to crack and wouldn't give him any details about how she'd come to possess the chip. Hoss pushed hard, as he needed her to talk since the chip didn't have a serial number. He knew she hadn't won it, but he couldn't prove that she hadn't or that some sugar daddy hadn't given it to her. A good lawyer could argue her out of the charge with ease. He was trying to keep lawyers out of this.

She seemed to sense his nervous tension, and that just made her quieter. She knew how the game worked and was waiting to see what they would offer her. Gina was good at frustrating men, and she would play the game as long as she could. In the end, if she had to give up Runt, she'd do it. He didn't mean that much to her.

Hoss needed a break but couldn't see one on the horizon. His mind circled back to the officer's comments about seeing John Allen before daylight. That made no sense to him. He decided to let Gina cool her heels in a cell while he went back to his office computer and traced John Allen's location.

Hoss had more than twenty vehicles equipped with GPS location transmitters. He double-checked John Allen's PIN number and carefully entered it into his computer program. The map only took a few seconds to activate, and within fifteen seconds it showed John Allen's location as Lake Pushmataha. *That's interesting,* he thought, having expected to find the Porsche parked at a country club somewhere. He dialed John Allen's phone number once more, and again it rang and went to voice mail. His next call was to the tribal officer who'd recently seen him.

"I need a favor," Hoss said.

"Anything."

"Go ride out to Lake Pushmataha and see if you see John Allen parked near the levee."

"Roger that."

"I'll wait on your call."

Hoss leaned back in his chair. John Allen could be fishing or sunbathing, though the latter would be surprising. He probably had a woman with him and didn't want Agent Emma Haden to know. That thought made Hoss smile.

◆ ◆ ◆

Sweat was beading all over John Allen as he continued to struggle with the restraints. The stress of the kidnapping and the increasing heat inside the skinning shed were quickly dehydrating him. He had, at least, managed to position a plastic bucket where he could sit on it, which took some strain off his knees.

He needed to find a way out of here before they returned. If he didn't, this would be where he died. He wasn't afraid of dying, not after all he'd been through losing Sadie and their unborn child. He'd often felt like dying over the past couple of years. But with the reality of his death hitting home, he realized he didn't want to die, especially not at the hands of Winston Walker and his partner. But it wasn't just his current, dire circumstances that had triggered this reversal. He hadn't thought about dying in some time. What had changed his feelings, and when had they changed? He didn't recall a specific moment when he'd felt the shift. All he knew for certain, sitting in the dark skinning shed, hands and feet bound by giant zip ties, was that he wanted to live.

Suddenly John Allen was overwhelmed by all the things he hadn't done. He wanted a child to show the world to—to teach to fish and to skip rocks, to coach their baseball or soccer teams. He wanted a wife to love and to share experiences with. He wanted a love like he'd had with Sadie. And along with that thought came the utter certainty that she would want him to move on. That was hard to accept, but he knew in his heart it was the truth. If the situation were reversed, he would want her to be happy and to live a fulfilled life. John Allen bowed his head and said a prayer for strength and courage. The act of praying calmed his mind.

A few minutes later, John Allen sighed. None of this mattered if he didn't get out of here today. Right here, right now, it was time to man up.

His mind slid to Emma. Was she looking for him by now? He knew she'd be trying to call him, at the very least. Just the idea of Emma gave him strength. He didn't even know her that well, but the image of whom he thought Emma was flowed through the channels of his mind like clear, refreshing river water.

◆ ◆ ◆

Hoss answered his phone, expecting to finally hear some news about John Allen's whereabouts. "Did you find him?"

"No, sir. I drove all the way around the lake, and I didn't see his Porsche. I even asked a few people, and they haven't seen the car."

Hoss was confused, as the GPS trackers were usually very accurate. They might be off a few hundred feet at most. "Where are you now?"

"I'm in the field beside the levee. Right where you said he'd be parked."

Hoss scratched his head. "Okay, thanks. I'm sorry to have sent you on a wild-goose chase."

"Not the first time, boss," the officer said with a laugh.

"Yeah, and it probably won't be the last. I'll see you back at the jail," Hoss said, appreciating the officer's attitude.

Hoss stared out the window. Maybe John Allen had found the tracker and had thrown it into the lake. Now that made some sense. It had been two months since Hoss had checked up on him. That thing could have been at the lake for weeks. Hell, he would do the same thing if the chief put one on his vehicle. In fact, he checked his car frequently. He didn't want anyone to know where he was all the time.

He thought about calling Agent Haden and letting her know he'd struck out, but he decided that would be implied if he didn't call back. Hoss needed to get back to the jail and take another run at Gina before she got smart and lawyered up.

◆ ◆ ◆

Emma was mad, concerned, and just downright frustrated. Normally on a Sunday afternoon when she didn't *have* to work, she had plenty to do at home. There was that long bed of daylilies in her yard that needed to be divided. Sometimes in the spring and summer, she would lie in her happy chair and soak up the sun. Her car needed washing, and the house needed cleaning. She'd also promised herself a six-mile run on part of the Natchez Trace. Emma had options—some she needed to do, and some she just wanted to do—yet what she did was enter John Allen's address in the GPS of her BMW X1 and start driving toward Columbus, Mississippi.

She had to see for herself that he was okay. And if he was just hanging out or playing golf, she was going to let him have a piece of her mind. In a way she hoped he *was* playing golf. It was better than the image her worst fears formed in her mind.

As she drove, Emma called Agent Garner and asked him to call his contact at the Meridian police and have him check with the bartender to see if he'd seen Winston lately. He grunted but agreed because he knew Emma had good hunches, and he'd seen them pay off too many times.

She then worried about whether Winston had a snitch in the police department. It had happened before. The FBI often withheld information from local police departments for that very reason. You never knew.

Chapter 30

Winston positioned a chair where he could see down the driveway and watched for anyone to approach. He figured that somehow John Allen had to have been wired when they were in the bar, and the police should be swarming him soon. He couldn't understand why they hadn't already. He thought he had a grasp on police procedures, but this one was confusing to him.

The knee injury forced him to really sit and think, something he couldn't recall doing in years and years—if ever. He bounced between moments of paranoia and moments of profound audacity until suddenly he realized he was tired of his life. He was exhausted from trying to stay one step ahead of everybody. The bank wanted to foreclose on his house, and he owed more than it was worth. The magazine-publishing business was a disaster. He owed two printers money and didn't have any hope of printing another issue. The situation was so bad it had forced him to kill a key employee to keep him from talking. The artifact business was lucrative, but it was getting complicated. He now believed Rosco, the janitor at the Choctaw offices, had set him up, so Winston was glad he'd killed the man. He took stock of his situation and realized he had no wife, no girlfriend, no business, and no real reason to stay in Meridian, Mississippi. Plus, if he stayed, there was a good chance he was going to be locked up.

Depressed and guzzling a cold beer, Winston thought about leaving—just packing up whatever he wanted to keep and driving off to start over. He could start over someplace where the locals didn't know his reputation. Suddenly he was excited in a way he hadn't been since before the magazine started tanking several years ago. Looking around the room, he saw that he didn't have much. The furniture was cheap and worn. Picking up his iPhone, Winston dialed another misguided individual who would always help him if there was a promise of cash or drugs. Knowing exactly what to say, he made a promise, and help was on the way. The worker was used to odd requests at odd hours. Since he wasn't doing anything, he was happy to come help. In return, Winston promised him the accessories to make him the hit of the club later that night.

With a little luck, Winston Walker would roll out of Meridian before sunset. He planned to drive south and stay in Mobile or Fairhope for the night. He could sleep in his Suburban and work his way down to the Keys. That's where he'd always wanted to live. That's where he'd start over. There, in the sunshine and surrounded by water, would be an unlimited number of young women aspiring to be models. They would be ripe to take advantage of in more ways than one. He could nurture their careers with advice and specialized photography that he could learn about on the web. He'd make a fake Wikipedia page documenting his prowess and be in business. He'd start over as a photographer for aspiring models. *Maybe there's a digital magazine idea in there,* he thought. Digital was the future. He wouldn't have to pay a printer or postage. *The Girls of South Florida.* The more he thought about it, the more he loved it. He'd stop at the first Hooters he came to in Florida, pretend he was a well-known photographer, and start working on his con. By the time he arrived in Key West, the ruse would be perfected.

Winston never thought about Runt again.

◆ ◆ ◆

Silent Approach

Runt picked the remnants of his chicken meal from his teeth as he drove. He'd never once considered not doing what Winston asked of him. He always did what Winston asked.

They'd met after Runt had moved back to Meridian to get away from an ex-wife and mother-in-law. He'd grown up near there, but after dropping out of high school in tenth grade, he'd moved to Pascagoula and had started working on the local fishing fleet. He'd been a bait boy and had cleaned fish, working his way up to his dream job on a shrimp boat. There had never been enough money to make it to the next week, but the salt air and the roar of the diesel engines were reward enough. On the water, he hadn't had bill collectors chasing him or known where to spend the money he hadn't had. It was perfect. Friday had been payday, and Runt had been broke by Monday.

By the time he was eighteen, though, he'd gotten a local girl pregnant. After a shotgun wedding, he went to work for her father, sanding and painting boats. The money was better, but he was expected to spend it in ways he didn't enjoy. They had a single-wide trailer he hated going home to, since his mother-in-law was always there. From day one, they'd despised each other. She knew he was worthless and rarely missed a chance to point it out. All he wanted to do was stay in the bars and drink. He had no idea how to be a daddy to the little boy. He basically looked at the kid and only saw the thing that had ruined his life.

One Friday night there was rumored to be a Jubilee occurring on the beach near the Alabama line. Everyone in the trailer park left with nets and coolers to go scoop up the bounty of fish and crabs that floated in during this rare event, which only happens along the Alabama and Mississippi coast. Runt was as excited as everyone else about a chance for free food. After packing every cooler he could steal with crabs and flounder, he made a determination that he wasn't going home to the trailer. He couldn't take the torturous lifestyle any longer. With a freshly cashed paycheck in his pocket and stolen Yeti coolers packed with seafood, he started driving and ended up back in Meridian, the only other place he knew. He sold seafood and even traded some for a place to live for a week. Happy and homeless, he met Winston Walker, who promised him opportunities to make quick cash and a chance to put his past behind him. Runt admired Winston. He had things, and he knew how to talk to people and get them to do what he wanted. He viewed Winston as a big brother looking out for him.

Runt started out doing odd jobs and lived in Winston's pool house until he found a place of his own. He was fearless and would do whatever was asked of him. Winston knew Indians and was like an encyclopedia of knowledge. He knew where they lived and where they should dig to find artifacts. Fascinated, Runt soaked in all this historical information that he'd never heard. The more they dug and found, the more Runt loved it, and soon he was addicted to digging for artifacts. Within a few months, he was Winston's main digger, capable of finding the locations Winston pointed out on a map and never getting caught by the landowners.

Runt's only problem was that he didn't like sharing all the artifacts. Winston sold everything they found within a few days, but the more Runt learned and understood about the Indians, the harder it was to part with his findings. Careful not to let Winston suspect anything, he'd held a few back each time to slowly build his own collection that he promised himself he would never sell.

He searched the messy dash for his Skoal as he turned his old Toyota truck into the gate of their hunting club. It would be dark soon, and he had a job to do.

◆ ◆ ◆

The digital thermometer on Emma's car read ninety-five degrees as she followed the GPS that led her to John Allen's house. When she pulled into the gravel drive, she couldn't see a barn anywhere, but the GPS was telling her she'd arrived. The gate wasn't fancy—it was just a rusty farm gate. The road inside the gate crested over a hill, and she wondered whether the barn lay over the horizon. It was the only option that made sense.

She looked for cows. If she climbed over the gate, Emma did not want to be chased by a bull. She'd done that in college when she and some sorority sisters tried to tip a cow. She hadn't thought of that in years, and the memory made her smile.

The gate didn't turn out to be a problem. As she pulled closer to park her car out of the road, it sprang open. *That's nice,* she thought, and drove forward.

When she topped the hill, she saw the barn and the Jeep parked off to the side. She parked in the gravel and looked around. There was no landscaping around the barn or the only door, though to the south there was a beautiful pond that had two adult Canada geese and several goslings swimming in the center. The nervous parents were eyeing her suspiciously while the youngsters swam in a tight ball that prevented her from counting them.

Taking in the whole scene, she noticed the grass had been recently cut. The FBI agent touched her pistol to remind herself she was working and needed to be careful.

Knowing the sheriff's deputy had touched the doorknob, she went ahead and did the same. The new knob turned effortlessly, and she pushed open the door.

"Is anyone home?" she called, and added a quick "Hello?"

Silence greeted her, so she was convinced John Allen wasn't home. She flipped on a light and surveyed the room. The furniture looked like it had been purchased recently at a chain furniture store. There were no pictures hanging on the walls, but she wasn't there to judge John Allen's tastes in decor. She looked for signs of a struggle or for a clue that would indicate where he might be.

On the floor was a slip of paper that turned out to be John Allen's pay stub from Choctaw Nation. She couldn't help but look at the amount but didn't compute his salary from it. She thought that was a bit odd. That's not something someone leaves lying on the floor, especially someone as neat as John Allen appeared to be.

Moving into the bedroom, she saw a few drawers open, just like the deputy had said. Although it looked like a teenage boy's room, something seemed out of place. Studying the room more carefully, she noticed a leather change holder beside the bed. It didn't have any change in it, but tucked in the corner was John Allen's wedding ring. Now that seemed odd. She hadn't seen him yet without his wedding ring on. She doubted he'd gone anywhere without it unless he was playing golf. She figured some guys probably took off their wedding rings to play.

She backed out of the room and went down the main hall. The next room was a catchall. In the corner were fishing rods and tackle boxes, a deer stand, camo waders, and a bag of mallard-duck decoys. There were several hunting jackets thrown on top of a mounted deer head, and a treadmill that looked like it hadn't been used in years. It all looked like he'd just moved in and hadn't arranged anything. The agent saw everything but a set of golf clubs, and again thought—hopefully, now—that he might just be out golfing after all.

The gun safe was the largest item in the room. It was the size of a refrigerator, and purely for investigative reasons, she tried the handle and found it locked.

Emma felt strange looking around the house of the man she had a personal interest in, but she was doing it as Agent Emma Haden in search of answers to a nagging hunch.

As she walked back to the living area, her cell phone rang. The caller ID indicated it was Agent Garner.

"What did you find out from the bartender?" she asked, getting right to the point.

"Not much. He hasn't seen Walker today. He was there until about ten last night."

"Shit, I was hoping he would say he closed the place down."

"But he said that they rarely see him on Sundays, for whatever that's worth."

"There are other places he could go."

"Emma, what are you thinking?" Agent Garner asked.

"I don't know. I'm at John Allen's house, which is a barn, and he's not here, and it just doesn't feel right."

"You have good hunches."

"I just think it's really odd that I can't find him today. He was so excited about the artifact sale to Winston Walker. I really feel like he would have called me this morning to be a part of arresting Walker."

"He's still not answering his phone?"

"Nope. And I just can't believe he's out playing golf or something."

"Okay, let me think. If his phone is on, we can have it triangulated and at least get an idea where he is. That's if his phone is on."

Emma snapped upright where she stood. "That's a great idea! Can you do that today?"

Garner laughed. "Well, I'm enjoying a lazy Sunday afternoon watching my Cardinals play the Royals, but for you, yes. I'll get with the technical guys and see if I can pull some strings."

"Thank you. I owe you one."

"No problem, but I hope you're wrong, because I know you're thinking the worst."

"He's a good guy. He's just pretty green at this law-enforcement business."

"I get it," he said. "Stay by your phone, and I'll let you know what I find. Oh, text me his phone number."

"Will do. Thanks again," Emma said as she sat on the couch in John Allen's den.

She immediately texted John Allen's number to Agent Garner, then leaned back and looked around. She decided she might as well try and call John Allen again. "Hey, I'm at your house" would be awkward to explain as a potential girlfriend, but it would be easy as an agent.

The phone rang twice in her ear before she heard another phone ringing in the room. She stood and heard it again, then hurriedly walked to the counter in the kitchen and saw it lying there with her name on the caller ID. Her heart leaped into her throat. *His phone is here! No one, no one, goes anywhere without their phone these days.*

Setting John Allen's phone down, Emma noticed a fancy wooden box at the end of the counter that looked out of place. She opened the top and saw the skull. Her mind raced. She knew she'd heard the tape of John Allen selling it to Winston.

Winston had determined the skull was a setup and somehow had come back to get John Allen to prevent him from exposing him. *That has to be it!*

Emma dialed Agent Garner as fast as she could and explained her find. He agreed it was unusual.

Hurrying to the door, she said, "Let's pick up Winston Walker!"

"It's the weekend," Agent Garner said. "Maybe John Allen just left his phone?"

"No way!"

"Just because he left his wedding ring and phone at his house—on the weekend, mind you—doesn't mean he's in some kinda trouble."

"Mack, I gotta feeling."

"Do you even have your gear?" She knew he was just trying to buy some time and calm her down.

"It's all in my trunk."

Garner laughed. "You're always prepared." He sighed. "Let me get the boys together, and we'll meet you in Meridian in a couple of hours. I'll be in touch with details."

"I'll be there," she said. As she walked with purpose to her car, Emma realized she still had John Allen's ring in her hand. She immediately went back inside and placed it on his nightstand, then took one more look her around and soaked in John Allen's world.

◆ ◆ ◆

John Allen hadn't been able to find anything jagged and exposed to rub the zip ties against in hopes of breaking them. It was like somebody had purposely removed anything that might be used. When he hopped into a stream of sunshine, he could see his feet were swelling and turning darker. The ties were constricting his blood flow, and he could only assume his hands were suffering the same fate.

Frustrated and rapidly becoming dehydrated, he stared at the handles on the boat winches used to raise deer up to be gutted and skinned. If the handles were two feet lower, they would be useful to help him break his zip ties.

He'd been in the skinning shed for hours upon hours, and throughout most of them it had been baking in the hot Mississippi sun. He had no idea how long he'd been inside, but he could tell the sun was starting to fall from the sky. His boxer shorts were soaking wet. He knew he needed water. A green water hose lay curled on the floor like a long serpent but wasn't connected to an outlet. It aggravated him that he couldn't find an outlet and finally guessed it must be outside. Leaning against a wall, he closed his eyes and worked to take shallower breaths as he tried to rest and conserve his energy.

John Allen was growing delirious and had to force his mind to focus. Left unattended, it raced with memories of Sadie and the life they'd been trying to build before tragedy struck. The lights of the fire truck right before the crash were vivid in his mind. He replayed the accident over and over, flinching each time. His mind drifted to a scene of his parents standing at the fence while he played center field in a Little League baseball game. They'd never missed a game, all the way through high school. The next scene was Sadie walking down the aisle toward him on their wedding day. She was so beautiful. Memories flooded him as he fought to hang on to consciousness.

◆ ◆ ◆

After an hour of directing his helper, Winston's Suburban was loaded with the only things he cared about. He'd packed little from inside the house. There was the television, a laptop computer, and a wireless router that only worked half the time. The Internet was his connection to the artifact underworld, which he intended to keep an eye on, and it would be critical in his new career as a model photographer as well. He packed the clothes he liked best, a pillow he bought off a TV infomercial, a small strongbox that contained what little cash he had left, and a small pistol he'd acquired in a bad trade.

His helper carelessly tossed a set of golf clubs in the back that rattled like metallic bones. The idiot had no idea how expensive they were. He was trying to squeeze a fake leather recliner into the back when Winston hobbled out and told him about the pistols under the house. The big guy pushed, and the recliner popped inside.

"Under the house?" he asked dubiously.

"Yeah, Runt put 'em there this morning. I need you to crawl under and get 'em."

"Are there spiders under there?"

"I don't know. Here's a flashlight. You can have the rocks," he said, referring to the meth Runt had stowed. "I just need the pistols."

"How big are the rocks?"

"You'll be happy," Winston said with a knowing look on his face.

The big guy remained hesitant, but Winston knew the thought of the meth rocks would motivate him. Squatting down, the light illuminated the darkness and damp dirt under the house. It was a prime spot for spiders and snakes, and the guy knew it.

Winston struggled back inside to make certain he had his Square card reader for his iPhone, another piece of business equipment he needed. It was critical for his scams, and he envisioned it being useful in the near future.

When he arrived back outside, his helper was crawling out with pistols in one hand and the rocks tightly squeezed in the other. The flashlight was in his mouth. Winston generously made a gift of the flashlight, though he never thought about helping him brush the dirt off his sweaty shoulders and back.

"Where you going?" the big guy asked as he admired his prize.

Winston knew better than to tell the truth, as somebody would eventually question him. He even considered killing the big guy just so he couldn't talk, but quickly decided he might be more useful to help create a diversion.

Hobbling to the back of his Suburban, Winston finally said, "I think I'm gonna head to California. I have a big publishing opportunity out there."

He looked around at the place he'd tried to make into a similar version of the compound his father had maintained for the wealthy family. It had never been anything grand, but he'd always thought he would add on as his businesses flourished. He had almost five acres. He'd planned to build a four-car garage and a workout area. One night while high on cocaine and watching the US Open, he'd decided he needed tennis courts, even though he'd never played the game. That never got past the idea stage, though. He'd also planned to redo the whole house, but that, too, had just never happened. He'd had a few good years, but he'd spent the money. After more bad years than good, it was falling apart. Everything needed maintenance, and it was time to move on and let the bank have it. He was tired of his life and needed a new start. He'd never be accepted in the crowd he wanted to be in, not in Meridian. *To hell with 'em,* he thought.

"Am I gonna see you again?" the big guy asked as Winston closed the back hatch.

"Who knows? But I tell ya what. You're welcome to stay here in the house until I get back."

Chapter 31

Hoss had spent two agonizing hours trying to get Gina to give up how she'd come into her $1,000 chip. She'd dug her heels in and wouldn't talk until Hoss explained that if she had stolen the whole forty grand's worth, she'd be on the hook for a federal crime. Then he convinced her that as far as he was concerned, she *had* stolen all of it, and he planned to prosecute.

As this reality set in, Gina sobered and finally told him that her boyfriend had given her the chip. With tears welling up in her eyes, she went on to say that she hadn't stolen anything in her life.

"Do I need a lawyer?" she asked.

"Not if you just tell me the truth," Hoss assured her. "That's all I want. I'm really not out to pin this on you. I just want to find out how your boyfriend came into possession of that chip."

Gina took a deep breath and further loosened her resolve. "He really ain't my boyfriend. I mean, we ain't serious. I just wanted a new tattoo, that's why I was cashing it in," she admitted.

Hoss wanted details, names, and times. Gina hung her head and reluctantly told him what she knew. There really wasn't much to tell. Her boyfriend had dropped by this morning and had given her the chip. She knew he had at least one more chip because he'd shown it to her, and basically that was all she had for him.

Sliding a notepad across the table, Hoss looked pleased and smiled for the first time since they'd been locked in the bare room. "Write his name and address down for me."

She picked up a pen. "After this, can I go?"

"Soon. We need to verify your story. If it checks out, you're free to go."

"I'm telling you the truth."

"I believe you, but it's like Ronald Reagan said, 'Trust, but verify,'" Hoss replied as he stood up to leave the room. He was mentally tired from the interview and needed a Coke. He figured she did as well.

As he was walking down the hall to the break room, his officer friend rounded the corner.

"Hey, Hoss, we just had a call from a concerned fisherman. He says there's an oil slick bubbling up in Lake Pushmataha near the levee, and a guitar floated up while he was watching it."

Hoss rubbed his face with both hands. He didn't like what he was thinking. "You know anybody with some scuba gear?"

"Yeah, we got a man that's trained."

"Get him and meet me at the levee as fast as you can."

In another couple of minutes, Hoss was cranking over his car's engine while a knot of dread was building in his stomach. He really liked John Allen. He could have been a lot nicer to him. He hoped this wasn't what he thought it was. He decided to try John Allen's cell one more time, and he prayed he would answer.

One the third ring, he heard a female voice.

"Hello, this is John Allen's phone."

"Agent Haden?"

"Yeah, it's me. I'm at his house. There's no sign of him, and his phone was lying on the counter."

Hoss shifted the car into drive and grunted. "Is there any sign of foul play?"

"Negative. Have you heard anything from him?"

"No, not a word. I'm on my way to a lake a few miles from here. An officer saw John Allen's car in the area early this morning before daylight, and we just got a report of some oil on the water at the lake."

Stunned, Agent Haden placed her hand over her mouth, then took it away. "Where is this lake?"

"It's a few miles west of Philadelphia. Look, it's unlikely it's related. I mean, thousands of people drive down this road every day, and the oil could be from a boat that sank. But I'm going to check it out with a diver." He didn't tell her his GPS had pinpointed the car to this location.

Agent Haden was torn between joining in the arrest of Walker and going to the site where John Allen could be lying at the bottom of the lake.

"I'll call you as soon as I know something," Hoss said.

Making up her mind, she replied, "I'm on my way. Can you drop me a pin where you are? If you can do that, I can find it."

Hoss was familiar with the technology and agreed to do it.

"I'll be there as fast as I can."

◆ ◆ ◆

Emma was deeply concerned for John Allen as she pointed her BMW southeast toward Philadelphia with no concern for the speed limit. She hated when she couldn't understand things, but that's what made her good at her job. She was able to think from different perspectives and piece together plausible scenarios out of chaos. In this situation, she could only think of one. She felt that Winston had come after John Allen, and she prayed to God she was wrong.

When the pin landed in her inbox she slowed down long enough to determine where she was going, then floored the gas pedal once again.

Agent Garner was gathering up some troops to descend on Winston's home and arrest him. They could do that without her, he explained. He encouraged her to get to Philadelphia and let him know what she found.

◆ ◆ ◆

The lake looked normal to Hoss. He didn't come out here very often, especially in the hot summer. He enjoyed the peacefulness of the water, but his job demanded so much of him he didn't have time to enjoy it.

From the edge of the levee he could see a small oil slick on the water's surface. As he moved closer, a bubble rose to the surface. However, there was no guitar floating anywhere.

Walking farther down the levee, he could see an impression that tire tracks had made in the recently mown grass. They went straight to the water's edge and had to lead to the source of the oil slick.

"Dammit!" he mumbled under his breath, then called the tribal police office on his cell phone. He requested two units and asked for the ETA on the diver. He also wanted to know whether anyone had a boat with a sonar display.

"10–4, units and diver en route," was the response.

Knowing the FBI would be on the scene, he wanted to make certain he handled the situation properly. There could be evidence here that could help make the case, he thought as he looked around. He needed to call the chief and let her know what was happening. John Allen was her golden boy. She would want to know.

Within three minutes the diver pulled up. Hoss instantly recognized him. He was a young officer, a full-blooded Indian who'd been a football star for the local Choctaw high school until a concussion in a playoff game ended his career. The kid was fearless, a great example of the spirit of the tribe.

The diver and the officer Hoss had first sent up here joined him at the lake's edge where they could see the oil slick on the water. It was about fifteen feet in diameter.

"What ya thinking, Hoss?" the officer asked.

"Clear enough. That's gas, oil, or antifreeze, or something from a car. Over there are tracks leading down to it," he said, pointing with his cell phone.

"That's the deepest part of the lake right there," the diver offered.

"That's right. It's close to forty feet. Can you dive down and check it out?"

"Yes, sir," he quickly replied, then started back to his car to grab his gear.

"Hang on," Hoss said. The young diver stopped and turned back to him. "Just so you boys know. I'm worried that might be John Allen down there. Let's not waste any time, but please be safe."

The young diver was visibly affected by the news but just nodded and headed off for his gear, his resolve to make the dive clearly fortified. They had all met John Allen, and while they were jealous of his car, they also appreciated what he was trying to do for the tribe. The mood instantly became solemn, and word spread as other officers arrived.

Hoss had them start by blocking the only road into the lake to keep any rubberneckers from gawking. He worried about boat traffic. There were several out there, enjoying the sunshine.

He decided to call the sheriff for assistance. They kept a boat ready for rescues and recoveries on the Pearl River. He exhaled and dialed.

◆ ◆ ◆

Runt loved this part of Mississippi. He had grown up here, hunting with his dad. They had been members of the club for as long as he could remember. He'd even gotten Winston a membership, though he was always slow to pay his dues. None of the members really liked him, but he always brought plenty of beer and liquor, which made them tolerate him.

The club was close to the Nanih Waiya Cave Mound. The rectangular mound measured twenty-five feet high, 140 feet wide, and 280 feet long. The mound had become sacred to the tribe because legend had it that the mound had given birth to the tribe. A small cave not too far from the mound was where Choctaw lore said the tribe's people emerged from the underworld and rested on the mound's slopes before populating the surrounding region.

The mound had a fence around it with steps up to an enclosed platform that offered the only view of it. In the past, before the tribe installed these security measures, people climbed all over the mound and dug at night, though they didn't find much since it was thought to be a ceremonial rather than burial mound. Whatever it lacked as a potential dig site, the giant, earthen mound made up for as the perfect place to hide a body. The tribe, which had jurisdiction over the mound, wouldn't allow any digging or unauthorized activity. So no one except another illegal digger would ever find anything, and no illegal digger would betray his own activities. Runt had buried the last Indian agent here, and nobody had ever noticed. He'd taken great care to preserve the existing vegetation and to haul off the excess dirt.

Runt was infatuated with the place. The mound was huge and had a surreal appearance, especially when one considered the work that had gone into building it. Mounds were located all over the state—and the South, for that matter—but few were as impressive as this one. During his nighttime visits over the years, Runt had found many projectile points and red jasper beads, as well as a few pipe stems, only a few hundred yards away in a small mound that most folks didn't know about. Like so many smaller mounds located in fields, time and tractor plows had eroded it, but Runt, being trained by Winston, knew where to look.

Tonight when it got good and dark, he would drive John Allen close to the mound, cut the zip ties on his legs, and walk him to his grave, as it would be too far to carry his corpse.

Runt parked his old Toyota truck in the camp and took notice of the skinning shed. The door was closed, just as he'd left it. Before he left the truck, he texted Gina to see what she was doing, but of course he received no speedy reply. He hoped she would be waiting on him when he returned later, but she was so unpredictable.

Finally tired of waiting for her, he left the keys in his truck, stuck a pistol in his back pocket, and made his way to the shed. He enjoyed the intensity of these moments.

◆ ◆ ◆

During her drive to the lake, Emma allowed herself to admit that she cared for John Allen, and cried as she worried about what had happened to him. She knew how savage and violent the criminal world could be, how easily people took others' lives for the stupidest reasons. As an FBI agent, she shuddered when she thought about just how close the average person came to real criminals each day. You could encounter a serial criminal standing in line at a fast-food restaurant, sitting at a red light, or walking through the mall and never know it. There were more criminals than jail cells to hold them, and rarely did convicts stay locked up for their full prison terms.

When she pulled into the area that Hoss had pinned, she saw that it was taped off, and her heart jumped back into her throat. After flashing her badge to gain access, she shot her car into a parking spot and ran toward the scene.

As she neared the water, the diver was adjusting his mouthpiece before wading in. They had a red rope tied to him, which she figured was to pull him back up. Or maybe to pull a body up. She shuddered at the thought. She'd been around numerous scenes like this in her career, but this was a whole new magnitude. She needed to pull herself together and act professional. Her training needed to take over, but it was so hard to push her personal feelings aside.

She slowed down as she approached Hoss, who was standing at the water's edge. He turned as he heard her approach. There were four boats anchored about a hundred yards away, with the passengers watching the scene unfold.

"What have you found?" she asked, fighting to catch her breath.

Hoss shook her hand, then pointed. "We have tire tracks leading into the water, and you can see the slick that we assume is from some automotive fluids. The diver's just now going down."

She stood stone-faced. The recent run in the heat had lifted a sheen of perspiration on her forehead. "Do you think it's John Allen?"

"I don't know, but I don't feel good about it." Hoss wiped sweat off his face. "It could be some drunk teenagers who lost control of a car. They like to come up here and park. I haven't seen it, but supposedly a guitar floated up."

A guitar? Her hands were trembling. "That's unusual."

While they waited, she explained to Hoss that there were agents en route to pick up Winston Walker. He nodded his head at the news.

Time crawled as they watched the red rope coiled on the bank slither slowly into the water. While they waited, the sheriff's boat that had launched at the other end of the lake arrived. The officers held them off about forty yards from the bank until the diver surfaced.

Bubbles marked the diver's location, permeating the surface in a rhythm all their own. Agent Haden squatted down and crossed her arms. Hoss glanced down at her but didn't stare. Watching these sorts of events, much less participating in them in any way, was difficult on everybody. Police officers often needed counseling just to cope with what they saw and experienced.

After ten minutes of watching the bubbles, Emma decided they seemed to be coming up faster. She looked up at Hoss, who shrugged his shoulders.

Another few minutes went by, and the officer holding the tether indicated he was coming up. When he surfaced, the sheriff's boat steered alongside him, and they pulled him into their boat. Once he had his mask off and caught his breath, he stood as the boat motored to the bank.

"It's his car, all right," the diver said.

Emma wanted to scream.

Hoss sighed.

"But he's not in it," the diver added. "The driver's-side window is down."

Hoss and Emma looked at each other. They knew they didn't have a solid answer. He could be alive and somewhere else, or his body might've just floated out of the car.

"Did you feel around the car and in the backseat?" Hoss asked.

"Yes, sir. Nothing," the diver responded. "Nothing close, anyway."

Emma was taking deep breaths, trying to think clearly. "Does that car have a trunk?"

"Hell, I don't know," Hoss answered in a low voice, knowing what she was thinking. "Stay ready to dive again," he said. "There's a wrecker on the way, and you can help them hook up to the car. The sheriff's team will want to drag the area, and they may need some help."

Emma and Hoss both turned away. They both wanted to see the car. It could give them clues. Emma would call Agent Garner and fill him in, after which she intended to issue a missing person bulletin on John Allen. Before she could lift her phone, though, Hoss said, "While we wait, let me tell you what we learned about one of Winston's running buddies today."

◆ ◆ ◆

Agent Garner and three other agents were approaching Winston's house as darkness began to fall. Two agents had night-vision goggles, and all of them were armed for a worst-case scenario. Agent Garner had also decided not to tip off the local police for fear there might be an informant. It was completely his call, since the FBI was handling the case.

They had worked out the details before leaving their office by studying the layout of the property with the aid of satellite imagery. They planned to split into two groups, one going around to the front, the other around back. None of their intelligence suggested they were walking into a dangerous situation, but they were prepared for one.

The night-vision goggles didn't reveal anything other than a raccoon in the backyard. With constant radio contact, each group moved into position. The group at the rear of the house could see flashing lights inside that they assumed was the television.

"No vehicle, Captain. Over," the rear group leader whispered into his radio.

"He may not be here. Over," the captain whispered back.

"See if you guys can get a look at whoever is inside," Agent Garner whispered in an aggravated voice. "It would be helpful to know what we're looking at. Over."

"Yes, sir. Over."

When the FBI agent peered around the edge of the sliding glass door, he saw an overweight male who appeared to be asleep on the couch, watching a *Game of Thrones* episode. He observed him for a few minutes, but he never moved. And there was no other activity in the house. On the floor next to him was a beer can that appeared to have been modified to smoke meth.

"I have a white male on the couch; he doesn't appear to be our target. He is taller and built heavier. I believe he's been doing drugs. Over."

"Okay, get ready," Agent Garner said. "I'm going to ring the doorbell. Watch what he does. Over."

"Roger, over."

Agent Garner crept to the front door. He didn't expect the doorbell to work, based on the appearance of the place. Before he tried it, he looked for security cameras and listened for movement inside the house, but he neither saw nor heard anything. He pressed the doorbell and heard it ring.

The two agents in the back reported they'd witnessed no movement inside the house. The guy on the couch must be passed out.

They decided to breach the front and back doors at the same time. On the count of three, they were inside, the front-door crew clearing rooms while the back-door crew tried to wake up Winston Walker's guest.

Chapter 32

Emma leaned against a black-and-white police cruiser while she talked to Agent Garner. Winston Walker hadn't been at his residence, and the person who had been there was so high that they didn't put much stock in his story that Walker had gone to California and left him to house-sit. They'd finally asked for assistance from the police, and when they hadn't been able to turn him up at any of his usual haunts, Agent Garner issued an all-points bulletin for Walker and his black Suburban.

"We need to have somebody check flights out of all the airports within a three-hour radius," Emma said.

"Good idea. I'll have the office get right on it. Let me know what the situation is after the wrecker pulls the car out."

Everybody at the lake was watching the wrecker. The diver had just surfaced, and they were about to begin pulling the car up. The sheriff's department was dragging the area near the car and hoping to not find a body.

Through force of will, Emma kept turning her mind back to the investigation, trying to think of what they were missing. Suddenly, she looked at Hoss, who was leaning against the other end of the police cruiser.

"Is the girlfriend still in custody?" she asked.

"Yes, she should be."

"I need to talk to her, right now."

Her urgency and confidence had Hoss straightening away from the cruiser. "Go get in your car," he said. "I'll have an officer lead you over there with lights. I'll stay here and let you know what we find."

◆ ◆ ◆

The wrecker slowly dragged the Porsche free of the lake. Water poured from every crack and crevice. Hoss instructed the wrecker driver to pull the vehicle up to flat ground away from the water's edge.

When they opened the driver's door, water poured out and soaked the officers' shoes.

The waterlogged vehicle still looked as if it were in mint condition. It was sad to see such a beautiful car drowned by lake water. It appeared as if it just needed to be dried out, but everyone knew it was ruined.

Hoss had hoped there would be something in the car that would at least point them in a useful direction, but there was nothing inside the passenger compartment that offered a single clue as to what may have occurred, except a pair of boots.

It took the officers a while to open the trunk, only to discover the engine was in the back. This triggered a brief moment of levity that helped relieve some of their anxiety. Moving to the front, it took another five minutes to pop the hood. Before the young officer who'd made the dive raised it, he paused, and he and everyone present looked at Hoss. The young officer didn't want to open the hood only to see John Allen, and everyone knew it. Hoss nodded at him, and the young officer stepped back to allow Hoss to lift the hood himself. A sigh of relief went up as everyone saw the compartment was empty.

Hoss actually smiled, but his smile quickly faded as he turned and looked at the lake. John Allen could still be out there. Probably was, if he had to guess. And with the elevated water temperature, it would only take a day for his body to float up.

He took out his phone to inform Agent Haden of the latest.

◆ ◆ ◆

Emma arrived at the tribal police station and was escorted quickly to an interrogation room. As a result of Hoss calling ahead, within three minutes they had Gina sitting in front of her. Her orange outfit didn't fit her, and Gina wasn't happy to still be incarcerated.

"Who are you?" she asked in a hateful voice.

"I'm Agent Emma Haden with the Federal Bureau of Investigation." She didn't bother to show her badge.

Gina was a bit confused. "I told them all I know. They said I could go home."

"If I have all the facts, that's true."

"I'd rather go tonight. I don't want to spend the night in jail."

During the course of Emma's career, she had interviewed hundreds of people. Everyone was a snowflake, each person unique. Some would talk immediately, some were slow to talk, and some never would. She didn't have time to waste right now.

"You help me, and I'll do what I can to help you."

Gina looked her up and down. "What do you need?"

"I don't have time to play games. I need answers. Do you know Winston Walker?"

Gina nodded. "I know him. Everybody knows him."

"Have you heard any talk of Winston and maybe your boyfriend kidnapping somebody?"

Gina immediately backed up. "No!"

"There's a man missing, and we think that Winston Walker is involved. We need to find Winston."

Gina was struck by the look in Emma's eyes. These weren't regular police eyes. She could see the intense concern there. It was a look no one had ever directed her way. Not her parents or any boyfriends, ever.

"Have you tried the Pop A Top or the J & J?"

"Yes, they've looked in all his usual places. Has he ever mentioned going to California?"

Gina furrowed her brow. "Nah. Not to me, anyway."

"What's your boyfriend's name?"

"You mean Runt? His real name is Billy, but he ain't really my boyfriend. I mean, he thinks he is, but he really ain't. Sometimes when it's convenient, I refer to him as my boyfriend. It's complicated."

"Where is he?"

"I don't know."

"Gina, a man's life may be at stake. If you don't help me . . . let's just say you'll regret it. This is way bigger than you and the casino chips."

Gina was thinking. Her DNA was not programmed to help the police, but this lady seemed different and might help her. Gina was wanting out of jail and to be free of the worry of the casino chips. Runt really didn't mean much to her. She used him just like every other man to get what she wanted until a better offer came her way.

She cut her eyes at Emma. "You'll help me get outta here?"

"I will." Emma was careful to not make a definitive promise that she would get her out. She had promised to help. That she could do and not undermine another agency's case.

"They got this huntin' club. I been there a few times on Saturday nights when they had football parties. It ain't nothing fancy. Do you know where the Nanih Waiya Indian mounds are?"

Emma shook her head no. She had never heard of such a place.

"It ain't too far from here. Coming from the south, from Meridian, it's"—she closed her eyes and thought for a few seconds—"the second gravel road on the left past the mound. The road goes straight back to their hunting camp. It's a buncha trailers. They go hang out there a lot. It's quiet, and nobody knows they're there."

"You think they both could be there?"

"That's where I'd look."

"Winston drives a black Suburban, right? What about your—What about Runt?"

"A piece o' shit, rust-colored, some kinda truck," Gina mumbled with disgust.

Emma's heart jumped, and she winked at her. "Thank you. I'll help you. Just hang on. We may need you again."

In the hall was a map of the tribal lands and the surrounding area. Emma asked an officer to point out where the Nanih Waiya mounds were. She memorized the directions, then as she was about to leave, she took a picture of the map, just in case.

◆ ◆ ◆

John Allen had heard the vehicle drive up and forced himself to stand and look out the crack. He saw Runt pull up in his old truck and park. There was no sign of Winston. Judging by the angle of the sun, it would be dark soon. He looked at the sunlight being diffused through the pine limbs and knew he didn't want to die. He had lost strength but needed to summon what he could to fight for his life.

The sweating had stopped about an hour ago. John Allen was still covered in it, but he could tell his body wasn't producing more. His skin had goose bumps and was tingling. John Allen recognized this as a sign of serious dehydration. The skinning shed was so hot it was putting him in danger of heat exhaustion or a heat stroke.

He leaned his forehead against the hot tin and watched Runt walk toward him until he passed out of sight near the door. He heard Runt fumble with the lock and chains, then the door swung open.

Careful to check for John Allen's position in the shed before he walked straight in, Runt saw him leaning against the side and could tell he wasn't in good shape. His feet were purple from the zip ties.

"How we doing, sport?" Runt asked with a laugh.

John Allen glared at him. He could see a cold beer in Runt's hand and imagined how good it would taste.

"I hope you've enjoyed our hospitality," Runt said as he pulled out a pocketknife. "I'm gonna cut the ties on your ankles. Don't you go doing something crazy like you did to Winston, now."

"Why are you doing this?" John Allen asked in a wrecked voice.

"We're just protecting our way of life. You tribal guys come around and want to stop us from selling artifacts that you don't own. Nobody owns them. We got as much right to 'em as anybody."

Runt stood silhouetted in the doorway as he opened the knife. He was wearing a worn-out Saints tank top, cut-off jean shorts, and nasty sneakers that looked as if he'd had them for years. John Allen could also see a semiautomatic pistol on his hip. It looked big. He guessed it to be a .45.

"You don't have to do this," John Allen said, trying to stand up straight. "I can pay you. You can have my car."

"Yeah, well, I wished you had offered that last night before we saw if it could float," Runt said with a laugh. "Guess what? It don't float. Did you know that?"

"Seriously, just think about it. We can work this out."

"Nah, there ain't nothing to talk about." Runt stepped close and bent down to cut the zip ties around John Allen's ankles. "There you go. I need you to be able to walk. We got a boat ride and hike ahead of us."

"How much money do you want?"

"Winston said you would try and trick me. I ain't stupid, mister."

"I'm not trying to trick you," John Allen said as he stared at his feet. They looked awful. They were the color of an uncooked steak that had spoiled.

"Can you walk?"

"I don't know."

Runt peered out the door at the sky. "Well, you got about thirty minutes to get yourself together; then we're going on a boat ride."

So that's how he's going to kill me, John Allen thought. *Even if I were strong enough to swim, with my hands tied there's no way I could hope to.*

"Just sit right down," Runt said, eyeing him carefully. "I'll turn on the water, and you can have a drink from the hose."

John Allen sat down and thought about Runt. He looked like he only weighed about 150 pounds, but he was wiry like the guys on *American Ninja*. John Allen probably weighed 185, and he was six inches taller than his captor. If he wasn't debilitated from the zip ties, he could take him. But with his feet, hands, and shoulder injured, it wouldn't be easy.

When the water first flowed from the hose, it was scalding hot. John Allen let it run until it was cool, then drank until he almost threw up. He wanted more, but Runt cut the water off.

◆ ◆ ◆

The BMW was hugging County Road 21 as Emma pushed the accelerator harder, crossing a solid yellow line and passing two log trucks.

She'd seen the thunderstorm brewing in her rearview mirror moments before as she'd told Agent Garner where she was headed. Garner and crew were at least an hour out, and he'd begged her to wait for them to arrive. She imagined he knew she wouldn't.

Before she'd left the building, she'd learned that they hadn't found John Allen's body in the car and had wanted to shout for joy. But she hadn't. What she really wanted was to find Winston Walker and put a pistol to his head.

Once she was on the road, she'd called Agent Garner, then Hoss. She'd told him what she'd learned, and Hoss had informed her that because the land around the mound wasn't tribal, he would be calling the Neshoba County sheriff to ask him to send deputies to assist her. If for some reason she ended up at the mound itself or at the cave, then that was indeed tribal land. He'd be on his way there as soon as they hung up, he said.

Emma guessed she'd arrive in fifteen or twenty minutes. She drove hard and looked for 393, the number for the county road she remembered she'd need to make a hard left onto.

During the drive, she went through a mental checklist: she had a bulletproof vest and a twelve-gauge pump shotgun in her trunk, a small pistol in an ankle holster, plus her duty piece on her hip.

She also went over the possible scenarios she might encounter, and she didn't like any of them. That thought only made her more determined.

◆ ◆ ◆

Runt stood over John Allen and was enjoying imposing his dominance. John Allen was the kind of guy he and Winston hated. Not because he was a cop, but because he was clean-cut and had an honest job. He was everything they weren't, and they hated him.

"You rich or something?" Runt asked, then took a pull of cold beer. He knew from Winston that this type of guy either was mortgaged to his eyeballs or was spending his daddy's money.

John Allen tried to sit up. "No, not by normal standards."

"What's that mean? You being a smart-ass?"

"Well, what does rich mean?"

"It means you gotta shitloada money. Enough to burn a wet cow," Runt said with a laugh.

"No, I don't. I'm just a working stiff."

"That's a fancy barn you live in. That was pretty cool, and that car was sweet. Man, I woulda loved to have had that thing."

"I would have given it to you."

Runt laughed again. "What did it cost?"

John Allen was encouraged that they were talking. He figured this was the best thing he could do at the moment.

"About ninety grand."

"Holy shit, man. What's the payments on that cost you?"

"I honestly don't know; it belongs to the Choctaw Nation. They lease it for me."

Runt laughed out loud. He was enjoying himself immensely. "I hope they got insurance on it."

John Allen shook his head. "So, tell me, did you guys kill the Choctaw agent who disappeared about two years ago?"

"He sat right here, just like you," Runt said with little care and no emotion. The thought sent chills down John Allen's spine. "He was trying to stop us from digging, just like you."

"I never realized. I don't guess any of us realize how serious you guys are."

"Shit, we dead serious, man, and it ain't just us. There's folks all over the country chasing artifacts and will kill you to protect what they're doing. You ever been up there in North Alabama along the Tennessee River?"

John Allen grunted and nodded. He'd been on the river several times, fishing for smallmouth bass.

"All those divers you see—the ones that claim they're diving for zebra mussels? Most of 'em ain't. They're diving the bottom for artifacts. They find lots of stuff along the river bottom where the bank erodes. They tie 'em up in a bag under the bottom of the boat in case the Man comes along."

"All I know is the Choctaw people want their artifacts back. They're spiritual to them," John Allen said.

"We don't give a shit." Runt gave his hip a small kick. "Come on, it's time to get up. We gotta walk down to the creek and go for a boat ride."

John Allen was feeling better now that he'd gotten some water. He was going to take a shot at Runt. He'd wait for the best time, and he hoped he'd know it when he saw it. As he struggled to his feet, Emma flashed through his mind. Was she looking for him yet? He knew she'd be worried that he hadn't been available today. Worried, or just plain mad.

"So as long as you gonna kill me, tell me: did Winston murder Jim Hudson on that quail hunt?"

Runt backed up a step and laughed. "You heard about that?"

John Allen nodded. He'd made it to his feet now and leaned back against the shed wall.

Runt smiled while he shook his head in admiration. "Shit! That was genius, and all Winston's idea. He told me that there was no way to prove it wasn't a hunting accident, and guess what?"

"They couldn't prove it."

"That's right. And they had everybody looking at it. They wanted like crazy to pin it on him, and after all that police work, they couldn't."

John Allen's spirit sank a little deeper. He thought about the effort it must take to get away with murder. Winston was no doubt as evil as Emma had warned. He decided to push for one more answer.

"What about Rosco Jones?"

Runt cocked his head. "Who?"

"Rosco Jones. He was a janitor at the Choctaw offices."

"What happened to him?"

"He either was murdered or committed suicide."

Runt thought and half smiled. It sounded to him like Rosco had crossed Winston.

"I ain't got no idea." Fumbling with his holster, Runt growled, "Come on, let's get going." Then he pointed his pistol at John Allen.

Chapter 33

Winston drove south on US Route 45, heading toward Mobile. His leg was stiffening up, and he took another pain pill. He decided he wasn't going to sleep in his truck tonight. He needed to stretch his leg out, maybe even prop it up. He had the credit card from the organic-fertilizer hippie folks. If he could keep the desk jockey from asking for an ID, he'd get a room at a Hampton Inn or someplace like that in Fairhope. It was a nice place, and he wouldn't have to worry about getting robbed. And there was a Hooters right close at hand.

He had a little cash in his emergency getaway bag. He'd actually prepared, figuring this day would eventually come. He could make it to Key West without using his own credit cards—they would be watching those. He'd have to get a new identity and cards. But he knew that could be done and guessed it would be even easier in South Florida.

◆ ◆ ◆

Emma perked up when she passed over a creek named Nanih Waiya, and within a few hundred yards she saw the famous mound on the right. It was much larger than she'd imagined it would be, but she didn't give it another thought as she drove on. "Second gravel road on the left," she kept saying to herself, looking for the turn.

Just past the mound she saw an open field, then the first gravel road, marked by a sign reading **BRIDGE OUT**. Emma slowed even more after she'd left that behind, not wanting to miss the upcoming turn, but ended up traveling two more miles before she found the second road just as she came into a turn.

Stopping even with it, she saw an old metal gate that was much older than the one at John Allen's. *This has to be it.* She pulled in up tight to the locked gate. With the engine still running, she got out to see what would be involved in unlocking the gate. Too much, she quickly realized. There was a heavy lock that held two thick, rusted pieces of chain together. There'd be no way to unlock it without a bolt cutter or a blowtorch.

Standing at the gate, Emma looked down the road. The edges were overgrown with brush, and thick pine trees lined either side. Studying the ground, she could see fresh tire tracks in the disturbed gravel and a fresh cigarette butt tossed at the base of the metal pole that held up the gate. *This has to be it,* she thought again. This gate was clearly meant to keep people from driving up to the hunting camp.

Hurrying back to her car, she opened the trunk and pulled on her protective vest. Then she picked up her Benelli M4 Tactical twelve-gauge shotgun and loaded it methodically as she stared down the road ahead. When she'd finished, she placed the shotgun atop the car and pulled her ponytail through the back of a black FBI-logo cap, then settled it onto her head. She reached in, turned the car off, and locked the doors.

Pulling out her cell phone, she saw she barely had enough bars to do what she wanted. Navigating to her mapping app, she dropped a pin at her location, then satisfied it was correct, texted the image to Agent Garner and replaced the phone in her pocket.

Preparations complete, she exhaled and looked left, then right, hoping to see help coming. She saw and heard nothing, however, except the threatening rumble of a Mississippi thunderstorm. She was alone, and the sun was almost down. She knew her fellow agents were coming, and Hoss had called the local sheriff. But waiting didn't feel like an option. Not knowing how far away the camp was, she grabbed the shotgun and a flashlight and climbed over the gate. Agent Emma Haden had a job to do.

◆ ◆ ◆

Off to the southwest, Hoss could hear a thunderstorm building in the sky and turned to see the ominous clouds. Storms like this were very typical this time of year and all throughout the summer. He hoped the sheriff's department would have time to drag the corner of the lake before the threat of lightning forced them off the water.

There wasn't much left to do here. He had already requested that the wrecker driver haul the soaked car to the Tribal Law and Order Building and not let anyone disturb it.

His mind kept returning to Agent Haden. The thought of her heading to a remote hunting camp by herself was unsettling. After calling a tribal officer over and making him promise to contact him immediately if they found anything related to John Allen, Hoss climbed into his unmarked car and left so he could determine the exact location of the hunting camp that had intrigued the FBI agent.

◆ ◆ ◆

Fifty miles southeast, Garner and the three other agents were already driving toward the area that Agent Haden had described, every one of them deeply concerned about her safety.

Agent Garner cussed the way this was going down. He was riding shotgun and trying to understand the pin she'd dropped. He'd never been to this remote area before and was struggling to map the fastest way to get there.

They'd left Walker's home more confused about the man's whereabouts than before they'd arrived. If they hadn't been called away, they would have taken him to a federal interrogation facility. But the thought of their colleague facing Walker on her own easily trumped questioning a simpleminded drug addict.

With even a little luck, the all-points bulletin on Walker would yield results. If he was driving around anywhere, somebody in law enforcement would see him. The Meridian police especially knew what to look for, and where. They were Agent Garner's ace in the hole.

◆ ◆ ◆

The skinning shed was stiflingly hot inside. Runt wiped the sweat from his face with his left hand and held the pistol on John Allen with his right. It was getting darker, and he heard thunder rumbling in the distance, so he was ready to get moving. He stepped over behind John Allen and kicked him in the butt.

"Come on, get going," he said.

John Allen tried to take a step and caught himself on the door as a crippling spike of pain shot up his leg. His feet were a mess. After hours of constriction, his blood flow wasn't back anywhere close to normal. But he knew Runt was determined to get him moving, even if it meant stumping all the way to where they were headed, so he ground his molars against the pain and kept at it, leaving the shed behind for the first time in God knew how many hours. The air outside the skinning shed was remarkably clear and fresh even though it was hot. John Allen breathed deeply, filling his lungs.

"Where we going?" he asked, hoping to distract Runt from how slow he was moving.

"You see that boat down there on the creek?"

John Allen saw it. The aluminum johnboat pulled up on the bank was in rough shape from years of running the creek. Very little of the dark-green paint remained, and John Allen could see dents from his distance.

As if reading his thoughts, Runt said, "Don't look like much, but I love that old boat. That little twenty-horsepower Mercury never doesn't start." Something hard shoved against John Allen's shoulder—the back of the blade of a shovel Runt had picked up. "Not like *you*," he said with a chuckle. "Get moving."

"My feet feel like they're on fire," John Allen complained, looking for something to use as a weapon even though he didn't know how he'd grab it.

"I don't care. Move your ass."

"You don't have to do this," John Allen said again. The gravel on his ravaged bare feet was making it even more difficult to walk.

"I done told you we protect what's ours."

"Just let me go. I won't say anything to anybody, and I'll turn a blind eye to what you're doing."

"I don't trust you, and Winston would never agree to it, so shut up and walk." This time it was the pistol Runt pushed into his back.

"You do everything he tells you?"

"What's it to you?" Runt asked.

John Allen stumbled and fell on one knee. A clap of thunder shook the woods around them, and the wind began to blow a cool breeze.

"Believe me, Winston knows what he's doing," Runt said as he studied the storm. He didn't mind getting wet, and it would provide him even better cover. Nobody would be out at the mound tonight in a thunderstorm. *This is perfect,* he thought.

Pushing himself back to his feet with the help of a pine tree he backed against, John Allen started walking again. "Yeah, I'll say he does. I don't see him here. He's got you doing the dirty work. I promise you when the shit hits the fan, he'll have an alibi for where he was. He's setting you up."

"That ain't true. He's not here because you jacked up his knee."

John Allen was in too much pain to smile, but the thought of Winston's knee offered a small bit of consolation. "And because he needs an alibi."

"Just shut up."

The two men finally arrived at the boat. John Allen's boxers were freshly soaked in sweat. As he stood there panting, he watched Runt pull a set of keys from his pocket. John Allen's mind raced as he realized the boat was locked to a tree. John Allen knew this was his chance, maybe his only chance. He had to get Runt off his feet, then . . . then he didn't know what he would do.

When Runt bent to unlock the boat, John Allen called on all his strength and jump-kicked him, driving one heel into the small of Runt's back and knocking him onto the ground. Then John Allen, lacking any better ideas, screamed at the top of his lungs and threw himself on top of Runt in an effort to pin him down. Runt thrashed under him, cursing, but was able to push John Allen off without much trouble and get to his knees, since John Allen couldn't use his arms. John Allen lunged at him again, but this time Runt punched him in the face, then jumped to his feet.

Once he was standing over John Allen again, Runt kicked him in the stomach as hard as he could. "That was stupid!" he yelled down at him. "You can't fight me!"

"Untie me!" John Allen screamed.

Runt unlocked the boat and pushed it off the bank into the dark water of the creek. A two-and-a-half-foot water moccasin that had been under the boat slithered into the water and floated, staring at the men, as if it were made of Styrofoam.

"Now get your ass in the boat," Runt commanded as he tossed the shovel into it, "or I'll shoot you in the back of the head right now."

Convinced he meant it, John Allen crawled on his knees to the edge the boat and fell over the bow into it. The small boat heaved and shook from his weight, and the aluminum was warm to his skin. With his weight driving the bow into the water, the stagnant rainwater that had gathered in the boat flowed around and underneath him. He didn't care about anything but trying to find a way out of the situation.

As Runt stepped into the rear of the boat, a flash of lightning illuminated the woods. The clap of thunder was immediate, and a few sprinkles began to fall. The weight change forced some of the stagnant water to return to Runt's end.

John Allen prayed for the fresh rainwater to fall on him. The sky was now dark. He lay on his back, looking up and wondering how he'd gotten himself into this situation. *I've got to be more careful,* he thought, then laughed out loud.

Runt was busy priming the motor by squeezing the bulb in the fuel line. "What's so damn funny?"

John Allen could see him standing and wished for the strength to stand up and attack him again, but he didn't have it in him. He smiled at Runt and managed to say, "You wouldn't understand."

On the third pull, the motor started, and Runt revved the engine for no good reason. Smoke from the engine boiled up, and Runt looked eerily happy. He gunned the motor one more time, then twisted the handle and engaged the motor into forward gear.

The boat motor was so loud that neither man could hear the frantic female voice just over a hundred yards away, yelling at them to stop.

Chapter 34

The Neshoba County Sheriff's dispatcher's phone was ringing wildly. The thunderstorm carried straight-line winds and was causing damage in the western half of the county. AccuWeather Doppler radar promised it was moving east rapidly, with more of the county about to be covered in green, yellow, and red.

During all this weather-related churn, the dispatcher was trying to juggle the few deputies she had to cover everything when she took a call from the head of security of the Choctaw Nation about an FBI agent headed to a hunting club near the Nanih Waiya mounds who needed support. She'd just said she'd do what she could when an Agent Garner from the FBI called and said they were en route to the mound area and requested that a pair of deputies join them. She started to panic. It was rare that the FBI called. In fact, she couldn't remember the last time, and now that they had, there wasn't enough manpower to cover everything. The sheriff himself was helping a family whose roof had blown off, and a child was missing. Two other deputies were directing traffic where a chicken house had been destroyed by winds and freed three thousand future KFC two-piece meals to run across a busy road. The rest of her officers were at Lake Pushmataha. They should be able to help but were just too far away to have any immediate impact.

The mound was in the northeast corner of Neshoba County, near the county line. She tried getting the neighboring Winston County sheriff to help her, but they had their own storm-related problems. The winds had blown down trees, and power was out in the heart of the county. They were assisting homeowners and trying to make certain no looting occurred.

The dispatcher told her sheriff what was occurring, and he promptly encouraged her to light a fire under the deputies who were loading the boat. He would break free as soon as he could.

The Neshoba County Sheriff's dispatcher didn't have to be told anything twice.

◆ ◆ ◆

When Emma heard the first screams, she wasn't certain what she was hearing, but she headed in that direction anyway. The falling darkness had allowed her to move fast without worrying about calling attention to herself. Still, thunder and wind had made it hard to hear, and her training had forced her to approach the trailers with caution.

When she'd heard the screams again, she was seventy-five yards from the trailers, and she took off running. Then the screaming had cut out again. Not knowing exactly where the sound had come from, all she could do was begin clearing the trailers as she'd been trained to do. With a flashlight held under the shotgun forearm, she fearlessly kicked in the door to the first trailer.

Methodically she cleared each old trailer, then the skinning shed. Her mind was processing what she was seeing, but she was solely focused on finding John Allen. Her breathing was labored from the recent sprint down the road, and her brain was frazzled from trying to anticipate what was in the darkness before her. The longer it took to find John Allen and Walker or whoever had him, the more intense her adrenaline rush became. Emma tried to suppress the growing anxiety that she was walking into a trap.

She stood looking back at the old trailers she'd cleared. Next to them was Runt's worn-out truck. The door to a shed was barely open, and she carefully cleared the structure. Giant pine trees swayed back and forth in the wind, and drops of rain began to fall. She'd relied upon the proven tactic of the silent approach as she'd advanced on the camp, but now she was past wanting to be silent. She didn't know where they were, and she didn't care whether they knew she was here.

Where the hell are they? They've got to be here somewhere!

With her flashlight she searched every crevice and dark corner. They had to be hiding, was the only thing she could deduce. Nothing made sense until she heard the outboard motor crank. Lightning flashed, and turning toward the sound, she could see a man in an old boat, pulling away from the creek bank.

Another flash, and she saw a foot hanging over the side of the boat. Someone else was in the boat. It had to be John Allen!

Running down the hill, she identified herself and hollered for them to halt. There was no telling whether she was being ignored, or whether they could even hear her over the boat's motor. As the boat started down the creek, she clearly saw John Allen lying in the front. It was too far for a shot with her pistol, and if she tried to use her shotgun, John Allen was lined up behind the target and could be hit. Besides, this wasn't the Wild West. Even if she had a clear shot, she couldn't just open fire unannounced. She had training, and there were protocols she needed to follow. She had to fight to keep her feelings for John Allen from changing how she handled the situation.

She stood in the wind and rain and watched the boat leaving. The man driving the boat had never given any indication he'd noticed her or heard her shouting at him.

"Dammit!" she yelled to no one but herself.

Her analytical mind started processing the situation. The man in the boat didn't look anything like Winston Walker. Where was Walker and his vehicle? Where could the man be taking John Allen?

Suddenly she remembered the "Bridge Out" sign. There was access to the creek down the road a few miles in the direction the boat was headed. She took off running.

She had three-quarters of a mile to run back to her vehicle, then those miles to drive to that bridge. There was every chance she might not make it in time to intercept them.

She stopped and pulled out her cell phone. Once it was ringing, she took off running again.

◆ ◆ ◆

The wind and rain in Runt's face only served to excite him. The nasty weather ensured that no one would see him as he worked his magic to build John Allen's grave in the mound. He didn't mind working in the mud at all. It just made his job easier.

He relished the irony of hiding an agent for the Indians in the mound that was so spiritually sacred to the Choctaw Nation. The idea that their own rules, beliefs, and laws would prevent this guy from ever being found made him laugh.

No light was needed to navigate the winding creek since he knew the run like the back of his hand. The water shined in the darkness, and it was easy to follow its path. Runt throttled the old outboard but was careful not to run too fast and run aground or into a stump. The creek was about twenty yards wide and growing slightly wider as they traveled south. There were giant oak and cypress trees lining the bank and leaning over the water. They were the only witnesses to what was occurring, and they would never talk.

Runt smiled at the setting. Winston had taught him that *Nanih Waiya* meant "leaning tree." They were in the Nanih Waiya Creek and headed to the Nanih Waiya Mound. Runt exhaled and enjoyed the beautiful boat ride in the darkness. The leaning trees seemed to be reaching out and protecting him.

John Allen stared at the sky and watched the lightning flash. Every part of him was sore, and without his hands to help him sit up, he was forced to just lie in the position where he'd landed. Runt had kicked him in the ribs, and he was sure something was broken, but that was the least of his worries. He knew Runt intended to kill him. The water scared John Allen since he realized that if he fell in, he wouldn't be strong enough to swim even if he had the use of his arms. He was running out of time and was out of ideas. He dropped his head back onto the bottom of the wet boat and did the only thing he could. He prayed.

Runt was passing landmarks and expertly steered the boat down the creek. He had about two miles of winding creek to navigate and took the time to think about his plans. They were straightforward and all but foolproof. He would beach the boat close to the mound and make John Allen walk to the grave. Then he would kill him and bury him in the mound. He would take meticulous care to return the mound to its original state. After that he would navigate back to the camp and clean up there before returning home.

◆ ◆ ◆

When Agent Garner received Agent Haden's phone call, she was out of breath and running. He placed the call on speaker so everyone in the car could listen. The group hung on every word, hearing her rapid footsteps and the anxiety in her voice as she explained the situation.

One agent frantically worked his iPad's satellite map to locate the scene so he could offer her advice, while the rest could only sit there. They all knew they were at least twenty-five minutes away.

"Got it," said the agent with the iPad, pinching out its screen to zoom in. "Emma, you're right; there's an old bridge that goes across that creek. It's hard to say how far, the creek winds back and forth. You're sure they're headed south?"

"I'm positive!"

"If you get lucky and beat them, they'll have to pass right under you."

"What's your ETA?"

"Emma, we're twenty minutes out, but we're burning up the road!" Agent Garner said.

"Dammit," Emma said under her breath.

"Be careful, that bridge looks really old," the agent with the iPad said as he zoomed in closer. "It's one of those old metal ones that has overhead beams."

"Where could they be going?" Agent Garner asked, and no one knew the answer.

"I don't see anything that looks like it could be a destination," the agent with the iPad said. "If she misses them at that bridge, there's one more a mile farther down, right before that Indian mound. It's on the main road."

Agent Garner nodded. "Emma, did you copy that? There are two bridges. The second is a mile or so farther down the creek."

"Roger!"

"Emma, listen to me. Use a silent approach. Set up in the shadows and observe. We'll have other agencies help us surround them. I want you to be careful. We don't know what's going on, and I don't want you to get into a dangerous situation alone. We're on the way. I'll call the locals and see if they can get there faster!"

Emma was approaching her vehicle, running on pure adrenaline. With one quick step up, she was over the rusted fence and scrambling for her car keys.

"Emma, do you copy? Set up and observe!"

"Copy that!" she said. She understood her instructions, but that didn't mean she'd follow them.

Silent Approach

At the car she paused to catch her breath and listen. She couldn't hear any vehicles approaching, but the wind and rain and her heavy breathing would've made it almost impossible for her to do so. She opened the door and tossed her shotgun muzzle first onto the passenger floorboard. The engine roared to life, and gravel flew as she reversed away from the gate.

◆ ◆ ◆

All over Neshoba and Winston Counties, deputies were being advised of the situation developing on Nanih Waiya Creek. The dispatchers didn't know many details, but they understood an FBI agent was requesting backup for a possible kidnapping scenario. As their counties were being ravaged by the storm's straight-line winds, everybody had their hands full and had to make decisions. Officers engaged in serious situations were forced to stay where they were, while others made beelines to assist. The radio chatter was constant as they tried to determine what assets were needed where.

Chapter 35

Once Emma got settled on the gravel road, she punched the gas again. The windshield wipers slapped rain out of her view and revealed the orange, reflective **Bridge Out** sign she'd glimpsed earlier. Within just a few bends in the road, the skeleton of the bridge appeared in her headlights, and she slid to a stop in the gravel.

If she were in a government-issued car, she would have taken a few seconds and radioed in her position. But she was in her personal car and did not have that luxury. Besides, though she was alone, she knew the cavalry was on its way.

Normally protocol saves lives, adding clarity to murky situations, and she had always followed the imprinting her training had left on her. Tonight, though, her feelings for John Allen and her fear that she was already too late to save him were flooding her mind. Protocol didn't stand a chance. She cut the headlights and engine, grabbed her shotgun, and ran toward the bridge with all her senses highly focused. She hoped to hear the boat motor. She hoped her eyes adjusted to the darkness, and she would be able to see the wake of the outboard as it approached.

Once on the bridge, she would figure out her next option.

As she approached, she heard or sensed a movement in the brush and quickly pointed her shotgun at the silhouette of a deer that appeared as startled as she was and bounded on across the road. It stopped, and she imagined it was looking back at her before it made one more leap and disappeared.

The bridge must have been built eighty years ago. It was a one-lane, metal, truss-style structure that at one time had wooden slats for cars to ride over. This bridge had been out for a good long time. Emma stood in the darkness and peered across it. Most of the boards were gone, and the rain would certainly make the remaining skeletal boards slicker than usual. She would not have wanted to attempt to cross the bridge in the daylight, much less at night in the rain. Now it was all she could do not to sprint out onto it.

She needed to traverse about forty yards to reach the center, and that was her goal. Like a gymnast on a balance beam, she picked a path and began placing one foot in front of the other. Under her breath she cussed the nighttime but was at least proud of her choice of shoes for the day.

The shotgun made balance difficult until she put both hands on it and held it out in front of her. She saw weeds and small trees growing on the structure. How many years had it been since it had been condemned?

Ten yards in, she'd gained some familiarity with the boards. The key was to always have a beam of the metal frame under them, as she knew many had to be rotten. She was able to pick up the pace for several strides, then encountered a nearly board-free stretch that required her to balance along her beam. Looking down as she moved, she could see the outline of vegetation and the blackness of water, and she knew she was over the creek's edge.

As Emma arrived at the center of the bridge, she estimated it was at least thirty feet down to the water. Presuming the water had some depth to it at midstream—and it appeared to, as no white water showed itself in darkness below her—she could jump if she had to. As a kid visiting relatives at Lake Martin in Alabama, she'd been a daredevil and had jumped off Chimney Rock multiple times. That was much higher than this, but the depth was tested there, and she was much older now. She hadn't jumped off anything since she was a teenage tomboy.

The continuing silence of the night made her wonder whether she had missed them, or whether perhaps they'd stopped someplace before reaching this point. Now she doubted every move she'd made and was second-guessing each decision. Grabbing her phone and taking care to conceal it behind a metal post, she texted **On bridge waiting** to Agent Garner. So up to this point, anyway, she was obeying his instructions.

She wiped the raindrops off her screen and placed the phone back in her pocket, then squatted next to the post. Lightning flashed in the distance, and she considered what would happen if it struck the old bridge. This did not bear thinking about. Her shotgun and pistol gave her confidence against bad guys, but not against Mother Nature.

A thunderclap coincided with Agent Garner's return text—**Which bridge?**—and she didn't hear the ping.

◆ ◆ ◆

Runt rounded a corner, idling quietly to navigate around some stumps that were known to tear up boat props if you weren't careful. As he turned onto the straight run to the bridge, he saw a dim light on the skeletal structure.

This had no place in a rainstorm. On a normal night it could've been someone lighting a cigarette or baiting a hook, but not tonight.

Runt took the engine out of gear while he studied the light. It wasn't shining out; it was illuminating a face.

Runt had no idea whom it could be. He didn't have a reason to feel threatened, but he had enough paranoia in him to be concerned.

"Hey, rich boy," he whispered to John Allen, "get back here."

John Allen raised his head but had no intention of moving beyond that.

"If you want to live another ten seconds, get back here," Runt said darkly. He pulled his pistol and pointed it at John Allen's head.

Ribs shrieking at him, John Allen raised himself up. With a great deal of effort, he pushed his stomach up onto the middle bench seat of the johnboat; then Runt grabbed him under his arms and dragged him to the backseat. John Allen nearly passed out from the combined pain of his ravaged ribs and his rotator cuff.

"Sit right here and don't move," Runt ordered, positioning himself right behind John Allen with the motor tiller in his left hand and the pistol in his right. With a twist, the motor engaged, and he started toward the bridge.

The light had disappeared. Maybe he'd imagined it. The night could sometimes play tricks on his mind. Oftentimes he would be at a dig and think he saw lights approaching. It was always just his paranoid imagination.

As he approached the bridge, its bleak skeleton looked normal except for a bulge at the base of the center beam. Was that something or not? The closer he got, the more certain he was that it was somebody.

"Don't move, and don't you say a word or I'll kill you immediately. Do you understand me?" Runt said to John Allen in a menacing whisper.

Runt was worried about something, and John Allen struggled to comprehend what. He couldn't see anything in the darkness but the outline of an old bridge. At first he hoped the structure might help him figure out where he was, but there must be hundreds of them in Mississippi, tired old antique structures that had served their communities for generations. Though this one looked like it had been bombed or something.

What did Runt see?

As they got closer, Runt twisted the throttle, picking up speed. The boat was traveling fast now, dangerously fast for a small creek in the night, but this was Runt's world. When the bridge was less than thirty yards away, the form he'd been tracking moved. The movement was unmistakable, and Runt flew into high alert. He sensed there was trouble on the bridge and the boat would be passing right under it.

John Allen saw the form move, also, then a spooky, thin, red-laser light surgically penetrated the darkness above it. Whoever it was had a pistol with a laser sight. The thread of red light appeared to go on forever into the sky.

Just as fast, a bright white beam of light flooded the darkness and pointed straight at the boat. Then, each drop of rain falling could be seen, outlined. Barely audible above the sound of the outboard motor, a voice called out to them, "FBI! Stop the boat!"

Runt yanked John Allen in front of him as a shield and opened the throttle wide, intent on shooting past his foe rather than laboring to turn the boat around. With his right hand, he aimed his pistol at the light source.

"Stop the boat! FBI!"

Recognizing Emma's voice, John Allen's heart leaped, then immediately seized up in fear for her. "He's got a gun!" he screamed as they approached the bridge.

Runt squeezed off two shots before the red laser started dancing around his head, driving him low behind John Allen.

He couldn't understand why a single FBI agent was on the bridge. The red laser freaked him out. He'd seen them on television but not in person, and certainly not pointed at his head. The only thing he knew to do was duck behind John Allen and get the hell past this bridge.

◆ ◆ ◆

A dull metallic thump had finally given away the boat's approach to Emma. She could just see the outline of the craft when she heard the motor.

As it approached, she'd eased into position and decided to hit it with her flashlight and order them ashore. This seemed a far better option than merely observing them, which would accomplish precisely nothing.

After clicking on her Glock pistol's laser sight and shooting its red beam out into the night, she'd bathed the boat in white light and felt a flush of relief to see John Allen, then quickly observed that his hands were tied. And he looked traumatized. *But he's alive!* Then came two bursts of light and the sound of shots fired ringing in her ears, and she'd been driven back behind the metal pole.

When she'd peered around it, she saw John Allen's captor scurrying behind him like a sand crab retreating into a hole. She'd tried to draw a bead on the man's head as the boat approached the bridge, but the laser sight spent most of its time dancing all over John Allen's torso. Seeing how close he held John Allen, she knew she wouldn't get a clear shot from the other side of the bridge as the boat traveled away, either.

Now the boat had accelerated and was almost under the bridge. Her mind raced to process the situation, calculating boat speed, the bridge's height, and her assessment of the threat to John Allen. She could think of only one solution.

As the boat passed under the bridge, Agent Emma Haden recalled being fourteen and fearless. Without another thought, she took off, and with three quick steps and a jump, launched herself over the far side.

◆ ◆ ◆

The local radio chatter continued as officers reported their progress. No one was closer than ten minutes out. Agent Garner listened to the locals and cussed aloud. Their vehicle was moving so fast it felt like it was airborne as it topped each rise. The agent driving was the finest high-speed driver in their office, and each agent sat buckled in tight, mentally preparing for their arrival.

Their vehicle was a mini office, complete with Wi-Fi, and radios that could monitor the surrounding counties and municipalities. The agent with the iPad was tracking the path of the storm and keeping everyone informed.

Agent Garner was even more anxious than the others. He had texted Agent Haden twice more, asking for her location, and hadn't gotten a response. He didn't want to call her for fear that she was hidden someplace and the phone's ringing would betray her location.

He contemplated calling his supervisor, but he didn't think he had enough information to prevent more questions for which he didn't have answers.

Agent Garner had plenty of experience worrying about his fellow agents. He sighed and, directing his thoughts to Emma, said, "Please be careful."

◆ ◆ ◆

Runt had panicked when the white light illuminated his boat. He'd pointed his pistol in the general direction of its source and fired off two shots to buy time to get under the bridge.

Now, as fast as he dared, Runt guided the boat beneath the bridge span and worked frantically to pull John Allen around to protect his backside, which was about to be exposed to the shooter.

He was still yanking John Allen into position when a falling movement in front of him flashed through his peripheral vision, followed immediately by a crash that almost submerged the bow of the boat and nearly catapulted him down after it. He just managed to keep his feet as the stern heaved back down, then fought his way to an understanding of what had happened. The shooter had launched herself into the damn boat. The spinning light that had accompanied her landing was her flashlight flying off into the creek at impact. Her weapon's laser sight waved around and finally pointed straight up in the air.

Still fighting to balance the boat, Runt pointed his pistol at the shooter and grabbed the tiller to steer away from the bank they were about to crash into. Then he let off the gas and shoved John Allen aside and to the floor of the boat as he moved to the middle seat and pointed his pistol right at the shooter's head.

"Who the hell are you?" he asked, standing in the darkness. The boat glided in the dark water as the motor idled.

Emma had hit awkwardly on the bottom of the boat. Her legs had shot out from under her on the wet surface, and she'd landed on her back on a homemade metal anchor. She had a death grip on her pistol, but the nerves in her arm were on fire, and she couldn't move it to aim.

Finally sorting the situation out, John Allen knew he had to help. He rolled over and kicked Runt in the knee as hard as he could. The flimsy boat tipped, and Runt grunted as he went over the side. As soon as he splashed, John Allen pushed himself over the middle seat, his arms still tied tight behind him.

"Emma! Emma! Are you okay?" he screamed as he tried and failed to get up.

Emma's mind told her to stay calm, but she wanted to scream. She could see John Allen's silhouette and hear his voice, but she couldn't speak. The anchor had knocked the breath out of her and has also affected the nerves on the right side of her body.

The rain continued to fall, and the night was darker than ever. The only light was the red laser that was like a pointer leading right to the barrel of the pistol in front of John Allen's face. It was only eighteen inches away, but his arms wouldn't move. He strained mightily against the restraints, but they didn't budge.

Emma was slowly getting her wits back. The drop from the bridge had been farther than she'd expected, and the landing a whole lot rougher. But, then, she didn't know what she'd expected. She'd just jumped.

Water thrashed outside the boat, and John Allen felt the boat being pulled, then its side dipped steeply down as Runt groaned and pulled himself back on board as he'd done a hundred times before. There was nothing John Allen could do about it.

As soon as Runt was in the boat, he snatched Emma's pistol from her and stood dripping above them both while he thought about what to do. When no clear next move occurred to him, he simply sat on top of John Allen to pin him down and stared at his new captive. He could see her outline, and the white FBI letters on her hat seemed to glow.

"Who are you?" he said, pointing the agent's pistol at her, and his own at the top of John Allen's head.

Emma had begun to catch her breath and realized she was in a bad situation. At this moment it seemed hopeless. The outboard motor continued to idle, and the boat drifted down the creek. She ignored Runt and looked at the man she'd been worrying about. "At least I found you, John Allen," she said with a sigh.

John Allen managed a smile that no one could see. "Yes, you did. Are you okay?"

"I don't know yet."

Runt waved his arms wildly and asked more loudly, "I *said*, who are you?"

Emma took a deep, painful breath. "I'm Special Agent Emma Haden of the FBI, and you're under arrest," she explained with much effort.

Runt laughed as if this were the funniest thing he'd ever heard. "Is this about the Indian rocks?"

"Not really," she said, trying to think of what to do and say. "It's much more serious than that."

"How about that! I'm wanted by the FBI?" Runt said, and laughed again.

He sat in the darkness on the Nanih Waiya Creek and enjoyed the moment. His nerves had settled down, and he was back in charge. Runt liked being in charge, and the pistols fueled his ego.

Emma twisted to get off the anchor and exhaled in pain. Without his arms for leverage, John Allen was helpless against the weight of Runt. He could hear Emma's voice just a few feet from him, and it sounded better than anything he'd ever heard. She'd tracked him down. That amazed him. How had she figured it out?

"Why are you here in this godforsaken place to arrest me?" Runt asked.

Emma's arm was getting its feeling back. It had gone from burning to tingling.

"Don't get too excited," she said. "I'm really just here for John Allen."

Runt was cocking his head sideways like a dog that's confused by something.

"Give him to me and we'll let you go," she said, recalling some of her negotiation classes. *Promise anything.*

"Yeah, I don't think so."

"I know you're just the guy Winston makes do all the dirty work. Just let us out on the bank, and you're free to go."

"You got balls, lady," he said with another laugh, then added, "Looks to me like I gotta dig two graves tonight."

Again John Allen tried to move but couldn't. So he said, "In a few minutes there'll be a dozen FBI agents here, Runt. Just give it up."

"Here in this swamp?"

"I found you," Emma pointed out. "They know where I am."

Runt stood up, kept one pistol on her, and pushed one into John Allen's temple. He realized she'd made a good point. They probably would have an idea where she was. He needed to get out of the area. He looked around and didn't see any movement on the bridge, or any lights anywhere. The silence was comforting, but he believed what she said. And he was smart enough to fear the FBI. Knowing he had more creek to travel, which meant adding more distance from the bridge, he felt he could still complete his task. That's what Winston would want. He wished Winston were here to help, but when had he ever been there for him? He realized she was right: he *was* just the guy always doing Winston's dirty work.

Runt looked her over. His eyes were well adjusted to the night. The FBI agent looked injured. Maybe she broke her back on his anchor? He needed to be in the back to operate the motor and steer. He had her pistol, but he wished he had more zip ties to bind her hands.

Pointing the pistols at each captive's face, he advised them, "Okay, I'm going to the back of the boat, and I don't want either of you to move a muscle. We're going for a boat ride."

The agent nodded. With that communicated, Runt stepped over the middle seat and sat down on the rear. The boat was only fifteen feet long, so everybody was within arm's reach of one another.

While he paused to orient himself on the creek, he held the agent's fancy laser-sighted pistol on her with his right hand and revved the engine with his left. Runt sat, trying to decide what to do. This was more than he'd bargained for, but he knew better than to just let them out of the boat. They would hunt him down. His survival instinct said he should bury them somewhere and get the hell out of here. The fact that no one was approaching made him decide to keep to his original plan and just expand it by one grave. It was still early in the night, and he had plenty of time before daylight. The stormy night played right into his hands.

Emma pushed with her legs so she could see John Allen, who'd fallen back from the middle seat onto his knees and was staring at her. He was in bad shape, and seeing it tore at her in a way nothing ever had.

Chapter 36

The FBI agents had homed in on Emma's last reported location. Agent Garner had talked to the Neshoba dispatcher, and she'd assured him that two deputies would be there at any moment.

He took a deep breath, hoping that they'd find her immediately and that the situation would be under control.

"How far out are we from that bridge?" he asked the driver.

"Four, maybe five minutes," the driver guessed.

Agent Garner had never been in this part of the county in his life, but the GPS was usually accurate. His cell phone rang, and he didn't recognize the "251" area code displayed on the screen but quickly answered.

"Agent Garner."

The caller identified himself as an Alabama state trooper and explained that one of his men had just apprehended Winston Walker at the Hooters on the eastern shore of Mobile Bay. He quickly hit the high points of the arrest and confirmed again that the fugitive, Winston Walker, was in custody. Agent Garner was energized, thanking the trooper and promising to call him back.

"One down," he said as he tossed the phone in the cup holder, but then his elation vanished. *Who was in the boat with John Allen, then?*

◆ ◆ ◆

Agent Haden purposefully stretched her legs while she studied Runt as he drove the boat. He was a fool, she realized. But if she wasn't careful, she knew this fool would kill her.

She didn't waste any time trying to think of how she could have handled the situation better. Her entire focus was on trying to keep both of them alive.

John Allen couldn't move, and he felt useless. He could see that Emma was in pain, and he knew she was injured because of him. *Hell, she's going to die because of me,* he thought.

He wanted to say something but couldn't think of the right words. "Sorry about all this," he said finally, in a voice just loud enough for Emma to hear over the motor. "They came for me in the night."

"Yeah, that's what I figured when I found your phone at your house, or whatever it is."

"It's a barn," he said with a soft laugh. It felt odd to be laughing, but he did.

"Yeah, I noticed," she said, almost giggling as well. Emma knew he was hurting, but his sense of humor was a good sign that he wasn't mentally broken and panic-stricken. Many people would be, and terror wouldn't help the situation at all.

"You got a plan?" she asked as she stretched again, trying to feel her left ankle. Her arm strength was returning, and she pressed her leg into the aluminum bench seat and could feel it flex. *No broken bones.*

"I was just about to arrest him myself when you dropped in on us," John Allen joked.

"You looked like you needed a little help," she said with a small smile. "So, do you know where we're going?"

"No idea. I sure need my arms untied."

"Just hang on, I have a plan," she said to him as she studied Runt.

"That fast, you have a plan?"

"You'd be surprised."

Silent Approach

John Allen could barely hold his head up. His body had been strained and stressed for almost twenty hours. The thought that she'd formulated a plan reassured him. Prior to Emma dropping from the bridge, his plan had been to jump out of the boat and stay submerged as long as he could, then hopefully swim away underwater. The plan made him nervous because he knew he didn't have the ability or strength to keep his head above water for long.

In the rear of the boat, Runt continued winding the boat down the narrow, serpentine creek. He couldn't hear his captives talking over the motor's roar and the noisy rhythm the rain beat on the flat-bottom aluminum boat. He was watching the agent closely, though he'd seen the outline of her waist and back and knew she didn't have another pistol on her. He wasn't worried about John Allen—one push into the water and he'd be a goner. The man didn't have the strength or energy to swim.

◆ ◆ ◆

Hoss made the last turn on the road to the mound, right behind the FBI agents. They both had their flashing lights on and were driving fast, but he soon realized they were driving much faster than he was and floored his accelerator to keep up. His car only had the tribal police channels and was not encrypted like theirs to hear all the local law enforcement. He could tell by the way they were driving they were worried about something, presumably Agent Haden.

The FBI guys crossed the bridge next to the mound, and when Hoss made the turn, he could see brake lights. Then they quickly turned to the left on a gravel road he was familiar with. It didn't go anywhere, since the bridge was out.

Hoss grabbed his microphone and radioed that he was 10–23 at the Nanih Waiya Mound area. If the base responded, he didn't hear. After he turned, his headlights illuminated Agent Haden's car parked on the side of the gravel road. Two agents were searching it, while two others were running to the bridge. He slammed on his brakes and slid to a sideways stop behind her car.

With an urgency that was rare for him, he bailed out of the car. The agents at the car looked up at him, and he identified himself to them as he ran toward them. In another couple of minutes, Hoss and all the agents were gathered at the edge of the bridge. Hoss explained what he knew of the area. Garner explained what he knew from Agent Haden's call and texts.

"I'm going to try and call her," Agent Garner said as he pulled his phone out and dialed. "Maybe we can get the phone company to triangulate her location if the phone is still on."

Standing in the drizzling rain, each man was horrified to see a phone light up on the bridge. When one of the agents carefully balanced his way out to the phone, he also retrieved a Benelli shotgun he'd found lying along a rotting board in the middle of the bridge and handed it over to Agent Garner.

"Hasn't been fired, but she had one in the barrel!" Garner announced. They all knew that meant she'd felt threatened. The fact she'd left the gun behind was even more worrisome.

The men flooded the surrounding area with flashlights but couldn't see anything helpful.

Looking down, then back up the creek, Agent Garner had two obvious options. Maybe three, if he gave any credence to the thought that they'd left via a vehicle.

"She was going to the camp that's on the next road up," Hoss said.

"That's where she started, but she ended up here for sure," Agent Garner said. "After that I don't know."

Suddenly they could see blue flashing lights turning onto the gravel road behind them, but Hoss's car and Agent Haden's had the road blocked.

As the senior agent in the bunch, Agent Garner knew decisions needed to be made, so he began making them.

"Hoss, take the deputies and go check out the camp. They may have gone back up there. We'll go down to that next bridge, and maybe we'll get lucky. I'll tell one of the sheriff's units to seal off this road and stay here with their eyes peeled."

Everybody took off running, knowing seconds could count. Agent Garner screamed as he ran, "Stay in radio contact!"

Hoss stopped running, and everyone stopped with him.

"What?" Agent Garner asked.

"I don't have a radio!"

Garner pointed at an agent and said, "Go with him. Let's move!"

◆ ◆ ◆

The extra weight in the front of the boat made it a bit more difficult to steer with the bow pushing water, but it wasn't anything Runt couldn't handle. The boat was built for three people. They had traversed at least a mile away from the old bridge when they slowed as the motor began sputtering. He picked up the gas tank, and it had plenty of fuel. After he quickly unrolled a kink in the black-rubber fuel line, the motor roared back to life.

"You were right," John Allen said to Emma. "Winston murdered Jim Hudson just like you thought. Runt told me. And they killed the guy whose job I took. Said he was threatening to destroy their livelihood."

Emma took this in, then a thought hit her. "Where the hell is Winston?"

"I don't know for sure. The night they kidnapped me, I kicked his knee in a way a knee doesn't bend. Runt says he can't walk."

"Good for you. I sure wanted to arrest that son of a bitch. My guys couldn't find him at his house tonight, but they have a bulletin out on him. We'll find him."

"Do you have your phone?"

"It's on the bridge. I thought I was going swimming."

John Allen and Emma stared at each other while the boat navigated the black water. Neither could see the other's eyes, but they each felt an unspoken concern for the other.

The rain had turned to a steady drizzle, and Emma's cap gave her eyes relief from the moisture. She formulated her plan and knew that if she waited for the right moment when Runt was distracted, it would work. She just had to wait. She considered telling John Allen but decided against it.

Runt was watching her like a hawk. He was leaning on one knee so he could see both her and the creek. His right hand held her favorite pistol, and the laser revealed everywhere it pointed. It was the first time she'd been so close to the other end of a pistol.

After a few more minutes that seemed like hours, she saw Runt peering at something as they rounded a bend. Whatever he saw was up high. She strained to turn her head but couldn't turn it far enough.

Seeing her trying to look ahead, John Allen said, "There's another bridge. This one is more modern."

At that moment everyone heard a car engine, the sound of it rapidly building. It was obvious the vehicle was traveling at a high rate of speed. As they pulled to within about fifty yards of the bridge, blue lights suddenly reflected off the green leaves of the trees, then a police cruiser sped across the bridge.

Shaken, Runt stood to observe the vehicle.

Seeing him distracted, Emma pulled her left pants leg up and drew a small 0.380 Walther semiautomatic from her ankle holster. In one motion she worked the action and pointed the pistol at Runt's chest. Realizing she would have to shoot right over John Allen's head, she said, "Keep your head down," just loud enough for him to hear, and observed his head lower by an inch or two.

When Runt had watched the blue lights and vehicle pass over the bridge and pick up speed, he'd smiled, knowing they hadn't seen him.

But when he looked back down, the smile vanished in his shock at finding the FBI agent aiming something at him.

Emma tightened her grip. "It's over. Drop the pistol!"

For a split second Runt tried to assess the threat. He couldn't see clearly what was in her hands. It could be a stick. He made his decision and started raising the pistol in his hand, and before it was halfway up, the agent placed two bullets in his chest, center of mass, just like she'd been taught.

Runt reflex-fired once into the bottom of the boat, punching a neat hole next to John Allen's thigh, and fell back into the motor.

John Allen was momentarily deaf from the pistol report near his ears, as well as blinded by the flash.

Runt had fallen against the motor and managed to twist the handle to full throttle in his death spasm. Emma had just started to get up as the boat responded to the motor's thrust and pushed her into John Allen. She managed to turn her head in time to see a huge metal bridge piling shooting toward them, and before she could react, the boat crashed into it at full speed. She and John Allen were tossed like projectiles into the water. Runt crashed headfirst into the front of the boat.

Caved in like a beer can, the aluminum boat immediately started taking on water. The motor quit from the jolt of the impact, and silence fell on the creek.

When Emma surfaced twenty-five feet away, she realized she'd lost her pistol. She treaded water in the darkness.

"John Allen!" she cried, spitting water between breaths. Her body ached from the recent fall, and her muscles burned with the exertion it took to keep her head above water. "John Allen!"

Feeling herself begin to panic, she called his name over and over. Spreading her arms wide, she tried swimming in an arc, hoping her searching hands happened upon him.

"John Allen!" she screamed.

Chapter 37

The FBI agents were standing outside their vehicles, giving last-minute instructions to a pair of Winston County deputies, when they heard the pistol shots. The reports were more than a half mile away but could be heard plainly in the still, damp night.

Their vehicles' blue lights illuminated everyone's faces, and they all had the same surprised reactions. Every man pointed in the same direction, but there were various ideas as to where the shots had come from. Hoss estimated the shots to be near the Nanih Waiya Mound, while another deputy screamed and pointed to the bridge on the paved road.

With the courage that propels law-enforcement officers into the teeth of trouble, they all jumped into their vehicles and threw gravel as they tore off toward the gunfire.

◆ ◆ ◆

The FBI agents were the first to arrive at the bridge. There were two deputy vehicles right on their tails, and Hoss brought up the rear. Agent Garner didn't let the vehicle stop before he was out and crouched at the bridge's concrete edge. He didn't see anything at first, but as he grabbed his flashlight, he heard Agent Haden screaming for help.

"Get some lights down there!" Agent Garner yelled.

Within seconds every officer had his flashlight pointed toward the water, illuminating the immediate area as bright as daylight. Thirty-five feet beneath them, the black water of the creek was lazily flowing. On the far bank, Agent Garner saw a set of eyes glow fire-red, then disappear underwater. Alligator eyes.

Wrapped tightly against the bridge piling was an aluminum boat with its front half crushed. A body floated faceup at the rear of the motor.

"Help! I need help!"

Directing his beam straight down toward these cries, Agent Garner found Agent Haden treading water under the bridge. In an exhausted voice, she went back to hollering for John Allen.

"Emma, we're here!" Agent Garner yelled back. He gave serious consideration to jumping over the bridge but thought better of it. There were lots of logs, and he didn't know the depth. Two deputies had already started wading through the kudzu at the end of the bridge, and he turned to follow their lead.

Garner knew he had to make sense of who was whom. Shots had been fired, and the agents needed to know who, what, and where as fast as they could.

As he approached the bridge's concrete edge, he and Hoss watched the scene unfold beneath them. The drizzle was soaking them both. Garner could clearly hear the female agent's desperate cries for John Allen, and if he leaned out over the edge, he could see her thrashing about in the creek. As he stepped off the bridge to climb down, he saw Hoss run to the other side of the bridge and probe the dark water along that bank with his flashlight.

As he climbed down the bank, Agent Garner pointed to the dead guy behind the boat and instructed an agent to concentrate on that body.

As he hit the creek bank, he called to Emma. "Tell us what to do!"

"John Allen's in the water, and his hands are tied!"

Everybody's lights were already searching the water's surface, each man claiming a piece of territory without having to be told to do so. They saw nothing, not even a string of telltale bubbles.

Agent Garner tried to get Emma to swim to the bank, but she wasn't having it. She kept diving and swimming underwater with her arms spread wide, hoping to touch him. Two other agents shed their firearms and shoes and dove in to assist.

◆ ◆ ◆

The force of the crash had tossed John Allen well clear of the crumpled boat. His eyes were still blinded from the flash of the pistol, and his ears rang from the gunshot as he flew through the air and hit his head on an old cypress log. His body flowed into a giant snag of driftwood, and he was suspended in it for a few minutes, fortunately with his head above water. Unfortunately, he was in no condition to make sense of Emma's cries as she called out his name.

As the law-enforcement officers arrived, his body gently sank and drifted in the current created around the bridge pilings. His senses weren't functioning, and his arms were, of course, still securely tied behind his body, so it would've been useless even if he'd tried to use them.

Under the water his mind slowly woke from its dream state; then all at once John Allen was fully conscious and sucking in water as he tried to breathe. Panic flooded his brain as he tried to swim but couldn't. Not knowing which direction was up or down, his mind raced with thoughts of Sadie and the unborn child he'd never know, and of his parents hearing about his death and being devastated. Emma flashed through his mind, and he could see her strength and determination to find him. He could hear her screaming his name. A flash of green light bathed the water above him, and in what he thought were the final seconds of his life, John Allen was certain he saw an eagle flying above him against that backdrop—an eagle in the water.

As he wondered at this image of the eagle, his feet hit something soft. It was mud. He was touching the bottom of the creek. With all the strength he possessed, he used his legs to push himself straight up toward the light.

When John Allen surfaced, he was only a few feet from Emma. She'd been treading water almost directly over him, fanning her arms out as widely she could with every stroke, longing for contact with any part of him. Hearing the gasping sound he made trying to catch his breath, she wheeled and lunged for him.

High above, Hoss could see it all and started screaming at the two officers in the water, pointing beneath him at the pair. When they reached Emma and John Allen, she was holding his head above water and trying to pull him to the bank. Each of the agents grabbed one of them and pulled them twenty feet to the creek's edge, where other deputies had waded out waist-deep to help.

"Unit thirty-three to base," one deputy said into his shoulder-mounted microphone just before John Allen was close enough to be able to grab on to him. "Request an ambulance at the bridge before the Nanih Waiya Indian mounds immediately."

The officers pulled John Allen up onto a bare spot on the bank where fishermen had worn the vegetation to bare dirt. The zip ties were carefully cut, and he was laid out on his back. He coughed twice, rolled onto his side, and expelled creek water.

Agent Haden, in her soaked T-shirt and sweatpants and without her FBI cap, looked like a civilian to the deputies. She was on her knees trying to catch her breath, but her eyes were glued on John Allen in the glow of the flashlights.

Emma watched him struggle to breathe and saw the crimp marks around his wrists. His hands were almost black from lack of blood, and his feet weren't much better. *What has this man been through?*

Exhausted, she looked up at Agent Garner, and her eyes said thank you. She didn't have the strength to speak yet. Agent Garner identified her to everyone around them as a distinguished agent for the FBI.

The officers excitedly fired off appropriate questions: Who fired the shots? Who else was in the boat? Who was the body in the creek? Was the area now secure?

When Agent Haden had caught her breath, she said, "Let's get him to a hospital. This area's secure."

Chapter 38

Three hours later, at Neshoba County General Hospital, John Allen was being observed by a nurse and by Hoss, who sat in a chair beside his bed.

The young doctor on call in the ER hadn't looked old enough to be practicing medicine, but John Allen hadn't cared. Anyone was better than Runt, and anywhere was better than the skinning shed.

IV fluids drained into his left arm at a slow, steady drip. The events of the night were still very clear to him, but the sedative combined with the quiet, warm hospital bed left him wanting to close his eyes and forget.

A soft knock on the door brought Hoss to his feet as Agent Garner helped Agent Haden into his room. She had a slight limp and was obviously sore from her fall into the boat. The hospital had given her a set of pink scrubs to wear. John Allen blinked his eyes and was suddenly self-conscious about his appearance, especially the nappy hospital gown. Stepping back near Agent Garner at the door, Hoss observed John Allen's behavior and shook his head, smiling.

"Hey there," John Allen said as he tried to sit up. "Are you okay?"

She slowly completed her walk to the edge of the bed and placed her hand on his arm. "I'm sore, but I'll be okay. They gave me some really good painkillers."

Agent Garner looked relaxed and content, but he was still very businesslike as he told John Allen, "Tomorrow, when you're up to it, we'll need to get a statement from you."

John Allen nodded at him. "No problem. I have a lot to tell."

Emma's eyes opened wide, and she slammed her hand on the bed. "Oh, we picked up Winston Walker. He was eating wings at a Hooters in Alabama, and a trooper recognized his car tag. Long story short, he tased him, and Walker is being extradited back to Jackson."

John Allen smiled as much at Emma's happiness as anything else. "That's good. I wish I could have been the one who tased him."

"Me, too," she said and patted his arm. "But we got him. Thanks to you."

Hoss said, "It sounds like you've got more to charge him with than he can defend."

Emma beamed. "He's going to need two lawyers!"

"Yeah, you did good, John Allen. That was a tough situation," Agent Garner said. Then he waved and added, "I'll be outside, and I'm going to make sure they get your car back, Emma."

Emma thanked him, although she didn't plan on leaving the hospital anytime soon. She had so much to tell John Allen, but it could all wait. She was happy just to stay here with him, and John Allen didn't want her going anywhere.

Hoss started for the door, too, but John Allen asked him to wait.

"They killed Wyatt Hub. I think I know where his body is, but you're not gonna like it."

Hoss stared right at John Allen.

"They buried him in the Nanih Waiya Mound."

Hoss winced, knowing the complications this presented, but he was confident they could figure a way. His jaw muscles could be seen clenching. "Let's keep it quiet until we find him. We'll get him out."

"Right, and uh—I think my car may be at the bottom of a lake."

Hoss smiled again. "It was. It's out now."

"Do we have good insurance?"

"We'll soon find out," Hoss said with a laugh. "In the meantime, we have an El Camino you can drive. I'll see you tomorrow," Hoss added, laughing again as he eased out the door.

Emma smiled and straightened the blanket around John Allen. "Is there anybody I can call for you? Like your parents, or a girlfriend who might be worried about you?"

"No, I'll wait until tomorrow to call my parents so they don't worry all night."

Emma squeezed his arm, wanting the rest of her question answered.

John Allen smiled at her and closed his eyes. "This may come as a surprise to you, but I don't have a girlfriend."

She cocked her head. "A guy with a Porsche? I expected a harem."

"I live in a barn."

Emma smiled and sat down on the edge of the bed. "I was worried about you."

"You shot your pistol right over my head. My ears are still ringing."

"You know I had to. I worried about that, too."

"It feels good to have someone worry about you," John Allen said softly. "So how in the world did you figure out where I was?"

"I'm a trained professional."

"That's obvious."

"Well, when I hadn't heard from you, I went to your barn looking for you," she said. "I was ready to wring your neck. The door was unlocked, and I was suspicious and looked around. When I saw your wedding ring, then your cell phone, I knew something was up. I couldn't understand why the skull was there. I clearly heard you sell it to him on your recordings, so I figured maybe he brought it back and took you. From there, we got a lucky break when Hoss had Runt's girlfriend in custody, and she told me about the hunting camp." She heaved a sigh. "I'm afraid if I had been five minutes later getting to that old bridge, we probably wouldn't be sitting here right now."

"Damn, you're good, and I am so lucky," John Allen said, then exhaled when he thought about just how close he'd come to death. Emma's amazing determination had saved him.

Being in the skinning shed had given him time to think about the past and the many regrets he had. Also, it had given him time to think about the future he wished he could have. Now, sitting in the hospital bed, his future seemed clear to him. Maybe not the details, but Emma was clearly in it.

He smiled at her and squeezed her hand in his. "I've decided I don't need to wear that ring anymore. I'm ready to move on with my life."

Emma's heart melted. To hide a tear, she busied herself trying to straighten his tangled hair. She couldn't do anything about her ear-to-ear grin, though, so she gave up and leaned over to kiss him.

Epilogue

When the chief learned that Wyatt Hub's body was buried in a shallow grave on the most sacred of mounds, she spared no expense in hiring a company with ground-penetrating sonar to assist the FBI in locating the body. The technology allowed them to find the disturbed soil and his remains without damaging the rest of the mound. The high-tech search took only four hours. The Choctaw Nation paid to rebury him with his family near Louisville, and Wyatt Hub's family would continue to receive his paychecks.

◆ ◆ ◆

Winston Walker sits in a cell awaiting trial for multiple crimes. He's had two attorneys quit and was recently forced to use a court-appointed lawyer. Facing a mountain of charges, he appeared ready to talk early on, then suddenly fell silent when word got out that he'd sold an artifact from the Moundville heist to an agent of the Choctaw Nation. This occasioned an exercise-yard visit from two very intimidating skinheads, who explained in frightening detail the various accidents they'd been asked to inflict upon Winston should he ever breathe one word about how he'd come by the pot. To this day, Winston refuses to discuss any details and has changed the focus of his legal strategy to begging for protection inside the jail. These pleas are falling on deaf ears. The prosecuting attorney is counting down the days to trial.

◆ ◆ ◆

Hoss continues his exhausting job of providing security in a world that attracts those dedicated to foiling his team's best efforts. Among the large amount of incriminating evidence discovered in Winston's vehicle were thirty-eight $1,000 casino chips. The final missing chip was found in the ashtray of Runt's truck.

Hoss and John Allen have grown closer through their shared experience, and nobody is prouder of the artifacts that John Allen is returning than Hoss.

◆ ◆ ◆

Runt's girlfriend, Gina, was able to walk away from her charges of possession of stolen merchandise in exchange for her assistance in locating John Allen. She didn't mourn Runt's death but quickly moved to Jackson, Mississippi, where she's dating the manager of Chili's in Canton.

◆ ◆ ◆

Jill Hudson was relieved to have Winston Walker behind bars. She moved with her sons to Biloxi to be closer to her parents and to get on with her life. She and Agent Haden stay in touch through e-mails.

◆ ◆ ◆

Agent Garner has spent a great deal of time working with the FBI's Principal Legal Adviser to build the cases against Winston Walker. Each time they study the timeline, they're reminded of just how lucky Agent Haden and John Allen Harper were.

◆ ◆ ◆

Emma has fallen head over heels for John Allen, and even Billy Joel approves of him. She continues to be a top agent with the Bureau in Jackson where, at the senior agent's insistence, she now spends more time working cold cases. This workload allows her to enjoy a social life for the first time since her divorce. She still works out every day, goes to the pistol range, and finds time to go fishing with John Allen. They currently live two hours apart, but they're together every weekend and at least one night during the week. The rest of the nights, they Skype.

◆ ◆ ◆

The last few months have been some of the best of John Allen's life. He's enjoying his job, although he now operates with a lot more caution. He and Emma couldn't be any closer, and some nights he listens to her diagram her cases as she sips wine. He still misses Sadie and thinks often of her and their unborn child, but he knows he's doing what's best for him. Emma also understands that sometimes he has a fountain of memories that bubble up. She helps him deal with them.

John Allen often thinks about the owl in Meridian and about the eagle image that led him to the water's surface. These were both such strange and surreal experiences. In the early days, he wanted to tell Hoss or talk to someone else with the tribe who'd believe him, but he's never mentioned a word about either experience to anyone. It now seems like a personal thing that doesn't need to be dissected.

◆ ◆ ◆

Jamarius Reed, the Neshoba County detective, was able to match the phone number that called Rosco Jones with the cell number that Winston had used to call John Allen. Two weeks after that call, Rosco's wife found a handwritten note in her Bible that explained that if something happened to him, the police should look at Winston Walker. Jamarius hasn't been able to prove it but believes Rosco likely decided not to sell the artifacts to Winston after all and made the mistake of meeting him under that remote bridge to tell him face-to-face.

On a hunch, Jamarius asked Hoss to allow the soil-penetrating sonar company to look in Rosco's one-acre garden. Hidden between his bushy squash plants, a foot deep, they found the artifacts from the Choctaw storage facility, wrapped up in plastic Walmart bags. The chief was relieved to have the artifacts returned and didn't pursue any charges that would bring public attention to what Rosco Jones may have planned. Learning of his daughter's plans and talents, the chief also offered to fund the girl's college tuition at any Mississippi college if she would come back and work for the Choctaw Nation for four years. The young lady, still grieving her father's death, played the violin so beautifully she won the talent competition at the Miss Mississippi Pageant.

◆ ◆ ◆

The ancient seed pot that John Allen hid in his gun safe turned out to be from the thirty-year-old Moundville burglary. When the agents searched the storage building where the rest of the artifacts had once been stored, they found nothing. The 250 priceless cultural artifacts that were stolen more than thirty years ago are still missing, and floating about the underworld of artifact collecting.

AUTHOR'S NOTE

This story is a work of fiction, but it is sadly true that people dig up and steal Indian artifacts from sites in alarming numbers each year. The Moundville theft really happened, and it's my understanding that nothing has ever been recovered. There's a website dedicated to these missing artifacts. Our local law-enforcement agencies are almost all too busy to investigate these crimes, which may appear to be victimless. But that's not how I see it, and I hope this story shines a little light on what I believe to be a shameful occurrence.

ACKNOWLEDGMENTS

I do enjoy telling stories. It requires me to spend many nights and weekends staring at a computer screen or out a window, which means a lot of work in the yard gets overlooked, and the burden is placed on my dear wife, Melissa. She and my daughter, Jessi, are due a big thank-you for allowing me to slip away and write.

I also want to thank my Mossy Oak and AFC families who continue to support me, as do the people of West Point, Mississippi, and Montgomery, Alabama. I owe a big thanks to retired agent Bill Gibson, who answered countless late-night questions about the FBI during this project. Tim Brooks and Dr. Bill Billington also helped with artifact-related and medical questions. There were many others who helped, and I can't thank everyone enough.

A big thank-you goes to the staff at Thomas & Mercer and to David Downing for his editorial prowess.

And, of course, thanks to my readers, who allow my stories to be a part of their free time. I hope you enjoyed the book.

ABOUT THE AUTHOR

Photo © 2016 Jason Cleveland

Bobby Cole, a native of Montgomery, Alabama, is the author of five novels: *Silent Approach, The Dummy Line, Moon Underfoot, The Rented Mule,* and *Old Money.* The president of Mossy Oak BioLogic, Cole is also an avid wildlife manager and hunter and supporter of the Catch-A-Dream Foundation. He lives with his wife and daughter in West Point, Mississippi.